Praise for Suzette Hollingsworth's novels

"This is an excellent, gifted writer, with a true future ahead of her." – CHARLOTTE CARTER

"This is a very fascinating novel. All the characters are very vibrant and come to life while reading them." -- Coffee Time Romance & More

"The wonderful way she writes I felt engaged in the travels and emotions provided through a very talented writer!" – RenaK, Amazon reader

"Her humor is refreshing, I laughed out-loud on a few occasions, shed a few tears, and sat on the edge of my seat for most of it." -- AnaMaree, Amazon reader

Sherlock Holmes and the Sword Princess was a finalist in the 2014 Pages From the Heart Contest

Also by Suzette Hollingsworth

published by Bookstrand
THE PARADOX: The Soldier and the Mystic
THE SERENADE: The Prince and the Siren
THE CONSPIRACY: The Cartoonist and the Contessa

To be released in 2015:

Sherlock Holmes & The Spy Who Danced on Horses
Sherlock Holmes & The Chocolate Menace

Sherlock Holmes
and the Case of the Sword Princess

The Great Detective In Love #1

**Sherlock Holmes solves the most perplexing mystery of his life—
unlocking the human heart.**

Published by Icicle Ridge Graphics. For permission requests, write to the publisher,
addressed "Attention: Permissions Coordinator," at the following website address
http://suzettehollingsworth.com/

Printed in the United States of America
ISBN: 978-0-9909952-3-4

Cover design by Fiona Jayde Media
Interior illustrations by Clint Hollingsworth.

Acknowledgements

Naturally, first and foremost, I must acknowledge Arthur Conan Doyle, who created the captivating characters of Sherlock Holmes and Dr. John Watson, so real in our minds that many consider them as historical figures rather than as fictional characters. To Doyle's vision of Holmes and Watson I have attempted to remain true.

I sincerely thank the community of authors who offer workshops, judge in contests, and participate in writer's loops, especially the Beaumonde chapter of RWA for their incredible insight and research assistance. No one becomes an author overnight, and the assistance and inspiration these talented authors/marvelous people provide is invaluable and critical. In particular, Delilah Marvelle (too nice for words!), Delle Jacobs (also delightful!), Emma Wildes, Charlotte Carter, Jo Beverly, Susan Elizabeth Phillips, Amanda Quick, Leslie Carroll, Nancy Mayer, Allison Lane, Vicky Dreiling, and many others who have helped me over the years (knowingly or unknowingly!), giving generously of their time and encouragement.

I have had the assistance of some incredible editors as well, inspiring and encouraging me, and who thankfully told me the truth as well. Editors extraordinaire all: Tina Winograd, Callie Burdette, Caroline Tolley, and Karinya Funsett-Topping of The Editorial Department.

And to those persons who have believed in me when I had a great deal to learn (and even now when I still do!): my husband Clint Hollingsworth, my BFF Charlsie Sterry, dearest and truest friends and mentors Susan Bartroff (also a great editor!) Donna Weiss, Harvey Gover, Keli Lock, Amy Brazil, and Gloria Stookey; my mom Mary Denison; and readers and friends Rena K, Anamaree O, and Rex G.

And, of course, to all true friends everywhere who keep our dreams alive when they falter in our hearts. Thank you, Michelle Berry, for the angel that you gave me to watch over me and for the angel that you are.

Dreams are more real than reality itself, they're closer to the self.
--GAO XINGJIAN, Dialogue and Rebuttal

Dedication

To the Girls of SHS '75

Sword Princesses and Beach Babes all

Connie, Charlsie, Jill, Julie, Kem, Lisa,
Margaret MH, Margaret SW, Michelle, Pam, SueAnn,
Sheri, Sandra, and Valerie

221B Baker Street, Westminster
London
1881

Chapter One

"*Blast*! Mrs. Hudson, how can I get any work done with dirty lab jars?" blared Sherlock Holmes from the laboratory of his second-floor flat on Baker Street.

"I'm sure I don't know, and I'm sure it isn't anything to do with me!" Mrs. Hudson retorted to the prominent detective, smoothing the white apron on her finely tailored blue and white striped pleated dress. "I'm paid to fix your meals and to keep your clothes washed and pressed—which is naw a job fit for a lady and no easy feat considerin' the vermin you associate with!"

"Mrs. Hudson, may we return to the matter at hand if it would not trouble you too much?" Sherlock sighed without looking up, shuffling through stacks of papers on his desk next to the laboratory table. He balanced himself precariously on a stool with the muscular control of an amateur boxer, his feet not touching the ground even while his hands flew wildly in a frantic search.

"And what might that be? I won't be putting my hand in your chemicals, I'll 'ave you know—I 'ave no intention of losing an arm! I've already lost me mind or I wouldn't be livin' in the same building with you!"

"Look! Look!" Holmes exclaimed as he flapped a letter in front of her nose. "This is a commission from King Nicholas I of Montenegro as regards his daughter, Princess Elena Petrović-Njegoš! What if I had lost this—or worse, never knew of its existence? What would happen to the princess then, I ask you, Mrs. Hudson?" He threw the letter on a nearby pile of papers, which quickly swallowed the letter, even as he continued his vigorous search.

Mrs. Hudson pulled at her white apron as she battled with an obvious desire to assist. "Are you looking for yer commitment papers to the *London Asylum for the Insane*? Or *mine*?"

"No, I'm looking for . . . *Aha!*" Underneath the papers he retrieved a Persian slipper, filled with his favorite tobacco, which he proceeded to place into his pipe. He lit the pipe and languidly indulged in a long puff before returning his attention to his landlady. "You know how I hate to repeat myself, Mrs. Hudson; lost forever are the discoveries which might have been made when one is doing so."

"Me sympathies 're with ye, Mr. 'Olmes. I hate it meself when you repeat yerself," retorted Mrs. Hudson, tapping her shoe on the wooden floor.

"I beg you to keep your mind on the problem at hand, Mrs. Hudson."

"Aye, I'm lookin' straight at it, Mr. 'Olmes."

"The matter at hand, as you are fully aware," he raised his eyebrow at her, "is that of maintaining some cleanliness and order in my laboratory."

"Auch now, that's too bad, so it is. Well then, why don't you take care of it instead of wasting yer time talking to me, Mister Sherlock 'Olmes? Ye're an able-bodied man so far as I can see: your insanity should not interfere with yer ability to clean." Her eyes moved past the filthy bearskin rug to the letters stuck to the mantelpiece with a jackknife.

"I hope you have no qualms with the lives of murdered young women on your conscience, Mrs. Hudson, because that's precisely what you do have. If my train of thought is sufficiently broken—and it is, I might add—the case might go unsolved, leaving this mad killer on the loose."

"And that's me fault? Because your jars ain't washed?"

"Precisely." Seating himself on his stool, he blew a smoke ring from his pipe, glancing at one of the jars on his laboratory table which had tipped over, a substance with an unusually pungent stench oozing from the jar.

"Well, glory be. I ahnt no world famous detective—and even I see that's flim-flammery." Mrs. Hudson tapped her foot.

"And yet—it is the reality of things," Sherlock concluded smugly while puffing on his pipe. "If it describes reality, then it must *be* logical, mustn't it? Truth can be nothing else."

"That's rubbish, that is. You, Mr. 'Olmes, 'ave naw the slightest acquaintance with reality. And if you was ever to be introduced, she would run screamin' off a cliff." Her eyes momentarily rested on handcuffs shuffled amongst Sherlock's papers. Surveying the wall above his desk, she observed a photograph, hung with uncharacteristic care, of a Miss Irene Adler.

"I beg to differ, my dear Mrs. Hudson. The reality of the situation is that I must be allowed to work and I must have no distractions when my mind is in its place of genius—which is most of the time. And if the environment is not conducive, and only Inspector LeStrade is available to solve the mystery . . . well, there you see the problem."

"Here's a mystery for ye, Mister 'Olmes: You need help in the laboratory, I ain't going to do it, so it is. What are you going to do?"

He raised an eyebrow at her. "Direct my excellent landlady to find someone to assist me, of course."

Chapter Two

"Wait for me, Elena!" Prince Danilo rode beside her, galloping his horse and still having a great deal of difficulty keeping pace with the beautiful Arabian princess. They rode outside Cetinje, the capital of Montenegro bordering the Adriatic Sea, amongst a plain surrounded by limestone mountains. From their mounts they could see Mt. Lovćen, the Black Mountain, ever sinister and foreshadowing.

"I wait for no one, brother, when there is a prize," replied the princess of Montenegro. True to her word, she did not let up on the speed of her favorite stallion.

His sister might be reserved, even listless and bored in social functions, but give her a spirited horse, the hunting hounds, and a quarry, and her eyes were suddenly aglow.

Make no mistake: the blood of their hunting ancestors flowed through the veins of Princess Elena Petrović-Njegoš. Suddenly she jolted the horse to a stop, still somehow maintaining her saddle, aimed her rifle and fired.

BANG! Once the bullet reached the heart of her prey, she jumped off the stallion to claim her quarry, pulling her *Shamshir* sword from its holder strapped to her left leg. She held tightly to the weapon's rhino horn hilt, the blade engraved in silver cross bar overlaid with a scrolling vine of wild roses.

Prince Danilo was an accomplished huntsman himself, but he was exerting a great deal of effort and yet was unable to keep pace with Elena. He glanced back to see the servants, who would dress the animal for the evening tribal celebration outside the palace, at least a kilometer behind him.

Prince Danilo chuckled to himself as he rode towards Elena. No other European royal family would think to celebrate in the city square with their people eating a deer their princess had killed.

Naturally, as the heir to the throne, Prince Danilo had been educated in Europe and had seen the world, understanding now the difference in other royal children's homes and upbringing from his own.

And the difference in *himself.* Montenegro had gained much status since he was a boy, only having just won Her independence from the Ottoman Empire in a fierce war of survival. But the danger was far from over. Without strong allies, the small country bordering Serbia, Turkey, and Bosnia was fair game to anyone.

They had to be a fierce people—and his soft-spoken, beautiful sister was no exception.

"Let the servants do that, Elena." He glanced at his sister tying up the deer. She continued her work without looking up.

"I won!" Elena smiled at him.

"You did, Elena. But I will win next time."

"I do not think so!"

He smiled in anticipation of the evening's festivities, to which no European ball could compare. There would be dancing and drinking around a great bonfire with a spit for roasting the deer. There would be a pig as well. The chiefs would wear crimson kappas and shining scabbards, and the maidens would wear red caps to which coins had been sewn as they danced round the fire.

The maidens. Prince Danilo smiled. He might find his own beautiful maiden.

Despite his tribal origins, their father, King Nicholas I of Montenegro, was determined to marry his daughters to European royalty, thereby creating strong alliances—and subsequently the continued independence of Montenegro—and even shy Elena was not exempt from the king's plan. *Especially* shy, *beautiful* Princess Elena.

Prince Danilo frowned. He hoped when he was king, it would not be necessary to offer his daughters as sacrifices. He forced himself to interject as much joviality into his voice as he could muster. "I will win because you will be in London in a finishing school for the rich, spoiled brats of European royalty."

Her face fell, reclaiming the listless expression of unperturbed boredom for which she was famous in European circles, having oft been compared to Leonardo da Vinci's "Madonna".

"I don't understand how you can be so mundane in the parlor and so vicious on the field, Elena." He laughed at the strange and predictable transformation from sharpened huntress to subdued Madonna, jumping off his horse to join her.

"I am a woman," she replied with a shrug as she cocked her rifle, moving her eyes along the horizon as she aimed. "We are more versatile than the man."

"What are you doing now, Elena?"

"I shot a rabbit. We must have enough food for all the people at the celebration tonight. If you were not so lazy, I would not have to do all the work."

"Elena, look at me."

She lowered her rifle and stared into her brother's eyes with affection. "Yes, Danilo?"

"Why do you go if you don't wish to? You have already been to St. Petersburg." She had even trained under the Empress of Russia, which had not improved her social shyness. All it seemed she had acquired were excellent skills in watercolor painting and pen and ink drawing. Along with tennis. Naturally Elena excelled at all sports.

She lowered her head in shame, clearly embarrassed that she had shown little improvement in the desired areas.

"Elena, you are so lovely just as you are," Danilo murmured. "Tell father that you are not going. I will help you."

"I wish to go. And I *will* learn what I need to know," she replied, bestowing upon the crown prince of Montenegro a glowing smile which few people were ever privileged to see.

"Why, Elena?" he asked.

"I am in love," she replied, her black eyes resolute. "And like the hunt, I will do whatever it takes to get my prize."

Danilo watched as his wild sister rode toward the rabbit, her stallion straining beneath her. She might be highborn, but she was Diana, goddess of the hunt.

Then suddenly a nightmare encroached upon them. Danilo watched in horror as she rode near a thicket of trees. Four men appeared out of the brush, pulling short swords from their long coats and rushing Elena as she rode by.

But her horse was not a timid beast, and Elena rode right over one of the men who tried to get the animal to throw its rider.

"Zaštiti princeza!" *Protect the princess!* He yelled to the servants, but they were at least a mile away. There wasn't time for him to reach her either.

Danilo threw his own rifle to his shoulder and took aim even as one of the bandits drew a pistol and positioned it towards Elena.

Please, God, guide my aim. The Prince, guardedly breathing out so as not to disrupt the overly long shot, carefully squeezed the trigger.

KPOW! The man stood for a moment, seeming to lower his pistol slowly, and then fell over into the grass.

Two men left. Still enough to kill his beloved sister in an instant.

Dear God, don't make me too late. "Haw!" Danilo kicked his horse into a fast run, even as the remaining men descended upon Elena.

She was pulling her rifle from its scabbard when a third man, cursing in a foreign language Danilo couldn't quite make out, tried to grab her stirrup. She discouraged his advance with the butt of her rifle adjoined to his head. He fell backward, presumably blacked out.

Almost there.

As Danilo reached Elena, the last attacker lost his nerve and turned on his heels, making a mad dash for the woods. Elena raised the rifle she had re-loaded.

She fired. Only a side-step from her steed saved the man's life. Her bullet grazed his leg, causing him to stumble for a moment, but he caught himself and was on his own horse in a matter of seconds, escaping into the forest.

Elena pulled another cartridge from her pouch and ejected the spent shell. She hurried to reload, but the skittish horse slowed her and the remaining assailant had covered some territory before she slammed the bolt home. She started to pursue just as Danilo reached her.

"Elena!" he yelled. "Stay here! The servants and I will catch him." There might be more of them in the forest, and she was clearly the object of their murderous plan. They didn't care about him, the crown prince. *Perplexing.*

"They would have killed me, Danilo," she replied. "They were serious."

"The dogs!" he muttered, not letting up the speed of his horse as he pursued the remaining attacker.

As he expected, Elena was right beside him. She understood, as he did, that she was the victim, and yet she would not let him fight alone, even with the servants not far behind at this point.

She raised her rifle even as she rode, aiming for the man.

"Elena!" he cried. "Don't kill him! I want him alive! We need information—"

"BANG!" The report from her rifle followed his command. Clearly she had no respect for her future king.

Damn! The man fell off his horse. How would they get any answers now? "Elena, I told you not to kill him."

"I didn't." She smiled at her brother. "I missed his heart by at least a centimeter."

"*Bastardo! Mi hai sparato!*" the fallen man muttered as he lay on the ground.

Italian. The man spoke Italian. Why would an Italian wish the princess of Montenegro harm?

Unless he was hired by someone else.

"I told you he was alive." She pulled her sword from its sheath, smiling as she did so, but her eyes were fierce. "But how long he remains so is up to him."

The crown prince watched his sister approach her assailant, sword in hand—and he felt a twinge of pity for the bastard.

Danilo thought of the English finishing school his father was sending Elena to. Danilo was well acquainted with English manners and the fine parties of the season. Breakfast, shopping, and morning calls to close friends. Rides in Hyde Park. After dinner, soirees or the opera, followed by balls and dances.

There was a fierce, bloodthirsty expression in Princess Elena's beautiful dark eyes as she touched the tip of the sword to the man's throat, demanding answers.

London will never be the same.

Chapter Three

"Who are . . . ?" Sherlock Holmes asked, his pipe almost falling from his lips. "And what are your qualifications, Miss . . . Miss?"

The young lady quietly moving about his laboratory glanced up at him inquisitively.

She knew very well that the Great Detective was unaccustomed to being surprised—and that there were few who had been allowed the privilege of seeing him so. He glanced at the burning logs in the fireplace and at the glistening bottles drying on the racks with something approaching displeasure if not surpassing it.

She curtseyed, taking her simple cotton sheath dress in both hands. "My name is Miss Mirabella H—"

"—Not important," Sherlock interrupted. "What is important is that you were dismissed from your prior place of employment—and that you are a relative of Mrs. Hudson's, so I have no reason to think you were hired for your credentials. How can I trust you will follow my directions to the letter, which most certainly includes not using my laboratory for your personal experimentation?"

How would he have known about her last position? Aunt Martha would never have told him. Mirabella felt her jaw drop in shock, which did not bode well for her powers of communication.

And how did he know she was Mrs. Hudson's niece? Technically she was a relation by marriage and bore her aunt no resemblance. True, they were both Scottish, but that was quite common in London. And Martha Hudson was from the north of Scotland, while Mirabella was from Dumfries, in the south. A keen detective such as Sherlock Holmes would easily detect the difference in their speech, not to mention their upbringing. The former Mr. Hudson, a successful merchant seafaring man, was brother to Mirabella's father, a curate, who had taken far more interest in education than his adventuring brother. Mirabella's father had educated all his children at home, even the girls.

Suddenly her prospective employer threw himself into a full circle, narrowly avoiding knocking over jars of explosive chemicals. He then moved to grab something on the newly cleaned wooden laboratory desk, waving it wildly in front of her nose. "What is this?" he demanded.

Before she could stop herself, she clutched Sherlock Holmes' wrist to prevent him from knocking her glasses off her head. She hoped it didn't anger him, but she could ill afford to replace them—either her glasses or her head. "Why it's a . . . a . . . spatu . . ."

"What is wrong with you, girl, can't you speak?" He grew wilder and most certainly closer, and she tightened her hold despite his piercing stare which would have frightened Genghis Khan.

Despite his well-tailored clothing, everything about the great detective's appearance was disturbing. Arched angular eyebrows, dark overlong wavy hair flying everywhere, and a pronounced unshaven jaw line framed by a cut on his lip as if he had quite recently been in a bar brawl. Could there be any doubt that he was not entirely stable mentally?

Not to mention that when she walked into this flat she had been met with the disturbing odors of tobacco, strong chemicals, rotting food, mold, dog hair, dust, liquor, a strange floral scent, and an overall impression of decay.

"Grrrrr! ZZZ-Zzzz-ZZzzz SNORT!" And she had been faced with a sleeping bulldog which vacillated between snoring and growling. As if the attack to her nose had not been enough, she had lived in fear of the dog awakening and attacking her in the flesh. When the dog awoke from his slumber and opened his mouth to display his massive jaws, her worst fears realized, he was less frightening than the man now before her.

"It's a *P-p-platina spatula,*" she managed to utter. Only when she saw that he was instantly calmer did she release his wrist. Fighting terror, her eyes were glued to the charismatic, devilishly dark man before her. The esteemed Sherlock Holmes was a madman—and a *bully.*

And yet she would give anything in the world to work for this scientific genius.

She must be crazy too.

"How did you know so much about me, Mr. Holmes?" she whispered. "I know my aunt wouldn't have told you."

"I don't need to be told anything, my girl. I can deduce it for myself."

"Then . . . *how?*" she gulped, backing away from the man.

"You certainly put yourself forward a great deal for someone who is asking something of me," Sherlock glared, rubbing his left wrist and appearing to be in some degree of exalted pain—like one of those strange people who finds pleasure in pain. Well, she didn't mean to grab him so hard, but the man was *dangerous.*

"Sir, you only just chastised me for not speaking"—she mustered her courage—"but now you are chastising me for speaking?"

"*Impressive. She thinks,*" he murmured, his recently bloodied lip twitching as if he were fighting a smile. "I suppose I cannot fault you for wishing to know the magnificent workings of my mind." Suddenly he turned to move towards his study. As if on impulse, he beckoned her to follow him, and when she did so—anyone else would dare say she was crazy to think so—but she knew very well the great man reached out his foot and tripped her!

Flailing her arms about wildly, she perceived instantly that she was going to knock something over. To avoid such a mishap, she forced herself to fall to the ground, her palms spread out in front of her to block her fall.

Either way, standing or lying down, she had no hope of being given this job. *Possibly it was for the best.* Even so, she would be mortified to break even the smallest, most inconsequential knick-knack belonging to Sherlock Holmes, or more importantly, bones belonging to her (not inconsequential).

He glanced down at her with the furrow in his brow much reduced and a curious expression on his face—not a smile, precisely, but something which might become one in a century or so.

"Take my hand, if you please," he offered. She stared at the strong hand of the incomparable detective for a moment, wondering what he had in store for her next. Possibly to pull her half-way to her feet and then throw her out the window.

Mirabella glanced at the window. It was closed.

She gave him her hand.

"You're not a feather of a girl, are you?" he grunted, assisting her to her feet. "*Just as I thought.*"

"*Well, I never!*" There was no hope of obtaining this position anyway, so why should she allow him to talk to her that way? Outside of the fact that the sun rose and set on him as far as she was concerned. "Mr. Holmes, no girl growing up on a farm and accustomed to hard work is particularly light. But I do not have an ounce of fat on me! In fact, some consider me *too* thin!"

"Did I call you *fat*, miss?" the great detective asked her pointedly, rubbing his back momentarily. Suddenly he frowned, disapproval evident. "Most certainly I did not. I wished to learn if your deceptively feminine frame is as muscular as was indicated. And, as usual, *I was right*."

"But . . ." She was truly confused now.

"Furthermore . . . I will satisfy your curiosity, miss, regarding my prior knowledge of your familial and employment status since you are clearly incapable of deriving the pattern of my thought processes for yourself." He smoothed his ivory ascot tie into a silk vest, seating himself on the stool in front of his laboratory, one leg extended.

"Your clothing is neatly pressed," he continued, "but well worn and certainly not of the first fashion. You have had a job in a laboratory— there is a hole on the sleeve of your dress which has been patched—a chemical burn, not a kitchen burn by the looks of it. Further supporting this theory, you have recently lost a patch of hair: it has grown back lighter and of a different length than the rest of your hair—an explosion of some type is responsible, I believe. Was it your error? I must presume so or you would still be in that employ. No doubt you were mixing something you shouldn't have been?"

"I was mixing something, but whether I shouldn't have been is a different matter—it was in an attempt to serve my employer." She ran her hands over her simple white and green cotton dress, fitted to the waist, with embarrassment. She might not be rich, but her clothes were clean and ironed. She checked to see if her brown hair was still pulled back into a neat bun, and if the green ribbon remained symmetrical after the violent attack upon her person.

And they said this was the *good* part of London.

Who was the deranged man before her to criticize her appearance anyway? His ivory silk ascot tie was stained—with blood, no less! His clothing was mismatched, and though well tailored, wrinkled. His eyes were bloodshot, and he looked as if he had neither slept nor bathed in the prior week. Certainly he had not had a haircut in a month, and it might have been that long since he had combed his hair. His face was fighting a beard, which was not successful in camouflaging various scars which appeared to be of recent attainment.

Sherlock Holmes might be a genius, but he didn't have any business correcting anyone with a pulse on proper grooming. In point of fact, there were those among the only recently deceased presenting a better appearance than the man before her.

"Have you never had anything go wrong in your laboratory, Mr. Holmes?" she demanded, her indignation rising. "Before you answer, recall that my aunt has lived in the same building with you for some time."

"*Impertinence.*" Once again a smile seemed to be tugging at his lips, but again was quickly subdued, unable to win the battle. "What I have or haven't done is none of your business, young lady; it's my home and I can do as I please. And it goes without saying that if you are running experiments in someone else's laboratory, you shouldn't be. Do I make myself clear?"

"Yes, sir. B-but how did you know I am a relative of Mrs. Hudson's? Technically I am her late husband's niece and I bear her no resemblance."

"You smell the same."

"*I beg your pardon?!?*"

"Same laundry soap, I would imagine." He rose from the stool and began to circle the room, weaving in and out of the dining table in front of the fire, stepping on the bear skin hearth rug, and moving to glance out the bay window facing Baker Street.

"No doubt the same soap which is used to clean your clothing, Mr. Holmes."

"Let me assure you, Miss Hudson, you and I do *not* smell the same," he murmured before turning to face her. "Well, then. I have no objection to a thinking person—in fact I prefer it, but it must be tempered with discipline and obedience—until you have your own laboratory which you may destroy at will. As I am convinced you someday shall."

"So m-may . . . I have the position?" she asked hopefully. Sherlock Holmes was young to his field, he had solved a few very difficult cases which Scotland Yard couldn't solve—she knew from her Aunt Martha— and he had already invented a scientific test for hemoglobin in blood, enabling the police to determine categorically if a stain was, in fact, blood or an old stain resembling blood.

This man before her, as unlikable as he was, was destined for greatness. Mirabella knew this as surely as she knew she was a country girl from Scotland. She could learn so much from him while saving to go to university. "It is the greatest wish of my heart. I am a true student of science, you know, and you are positively brilliant, Mr. Holmes."

"Very true."

"To merely be in your presence . . ."

"But should I like to be in *your* presence?" He moved to stoke the fire, his eyes averted from her. "That is the relevant question my girl. What I should like is to forget you are here and to find my work completed. I am of the opinion that you cannot manage it."

"Oh, but I *can.* You shall never find a harder worker, Mr. Holmes."

"Can you fix a cup of tea, young lady? Or will you argue about what is and isn't your job as Mrs. Hudson is always prone to do? It is quite clear to me that you are far too curious and intelligent for your own good."

"Oh, *no.* I mean *yes,* I make a very nice cup of tea."

"Then to it."

Scurrying to the kitchen, Mirabella hurriedly moved to light the wood stove. Her panic began to overtake her, knowing she could not make a cup of tea in under twenty minutes. It would take that long to get the stove hot enough and the water to boiling.

I so wish Aunt Martha had allowed Mr. Holmes his say! At this moment she wished with all her heart that her Aunt Martha had permitted Mr. Holmes to install a gas stove, as she knew he had desired. The tea would have taken far less time to make. Aunt Martha had refused, saying that Sherlock *bloody* 'Olmes didn't need any help blowing up the building.

Mirabella had seen the gas apparatus in Mr. Holmes' laboratory; if her Aunt Martha didn't know what it was, a student of science certainly did. That was information best kept to herself for the preservation of the peace, Mirabella reflected.

Oh, my goodness, there is a gas ring in the kitchen! Her eyes alighted upon the device and hope re-entered her heart. No doubt it was for instances such as this when a pot of tea was quickly desired.

So many modern conveniences! A laboratory with a microscope, vials, Bunsen burner, Geisler Tubes, and Bouquet Tubes—and a gas ring in the kitchen!

This place is heaven in its advancement. My heart longs to obtain this position!

Frantically she rummaged in her reticule which was wrapped around her wrist, her heart pounding in her chest. *I have a schilling!* The matches were easily found. Quickly she searched for the teapot, which must be found before inserting her only schilling into the coin slot of the gas ring to release the gas.

The teapot is empty. Next she looked about for the water. *Please, holy Father, let there be water.* She didn't want to have to run down to the first floor flat where she and Aunt Martha lived, that would take even more time. Aunt Martha had installed indoor running water—but for the first floor only. Just as the only toilet in the building—which, by necessity required running water—was on the first floor and shared by all the building's tenants. And thankful they all were to have it! The rest of the middle-class neighborhood on Baker Street shared a privy, which was nothing more than a hole over the ground in a brick building, similar to what Mirabella had grown up with on the farm, shared by her family.

Thank the heavens, there is a bucket on the counter holding water. She filled the teapot and set it on the gas burner before inserting the schilling. The water must boil for at least three minutes and the tea steeped for almost as long.

Next, Mirabella rummaged the cabinet for the tea leaves, easily found in a canister. The tea set itself was difficult to miss: a beautifully elaborate and exotic oriental pattern in navy blue and orange poppy, Mason's Mandalay Blue Pattern.

"I hope I haven't kept you too long, Mr. Holmes," she murmured, returning to the sitting room with the tea set.

"Precisely five and a half minutes," he murmured. He seemed displeased, but no more displeased than she had left him.

He appeared to be fixated on something observable through the window. Mr. Holmes was seated next to the fireplace, giving her the opportunity to observe him more closely.

"You might have asked me for a schilling," he stated without looking up.

"I presumed that you would wish me to resolve the situation myself," she replied softly.

Upon closer inspection, she was more approving of his attire if not his cleanliness. His clothing was fine, though looking as if it had been worn for many days.

Despite his gentlemanly attire, Sherlock Holmes had the physique of a middle-weight boxer. His muscles were taut and well-formed and he was slim. He had dark, almost black, overlong wavy hair. But his strongest and most alarming feature—which she always returned to—was the intensity of his gaze. As if he could discern one's darkest secrets.

Which was proving true.

As his eyes moved to settle on her, there was a definitive sarcasm intertwined with his unrelenting stare, as if he considered everyone inferior but was making a concerted effort to be amused by it rather than annoyed.

With little success.

Tick tock! Tick tock! She waited anxiously for the verdict. Mr. Holmes took a sip of the tea and frowned. Slowly he lowered the saucer to the mahogany marble table beside his armchair.

"What is it? Is something wrong with the tea?" She had steeped the tea in boiling water for precisely three minutes, just as her Aunt Martha had shown her.

"Quiet, girl! If there were something wrong with the tea, I would tell you. Have no doubt on that score." He was seated comfortably in a wing-backed armchair in a rose satin damask fabric situated next to a velvet purple settee. He did not motion to her to sit beside him, leaving her standing beside the walnut fireplace mantle.

Gasp! Her eyes completely took in the purple couch for the first time, which was possibly a mistake, given that her pulse was racing without any assistance from the décor. On the other hand, certainly if her heart had stopped and she had proceeded to heaven, seeing this couch in her dreams might have frightened the vital organ into its former rhythm and returned her to this room.

Mr. Holmes added a touch of cream to his teacup and then stirred it meticulously. "It is an excellent cup of tea. You *cannot* work for me, young lady, if you continue to put words into my mouth: I shall derive my own, and you shall attend to them. Do I make myself clear?"

"Well then . . . why . . ." She backed up until she was almost leaning against the mantle, placing her hand momentarily on the maroon wallpaper of questionable taste in rose and dark brown with inclinations towards purple in the triangular design.

"I shall ask the questions. It is transparent to me why you lost your last position. Be advised, my girl, if you are to be in my employ, you must *never* interrupt my train of thought. Why should genius be disrupted for drivel?"

Everything about him had the feel of power, prophecy, and unpredictability. Her current apprehension must have been how King Henry VIII's select wives felt as they were sensing the end of their relationship with the king—and their heads.

All good things must come to an end.

"Yes, sir." *Drivel.* Was he quite serious? She was not a world-class anything, but she was not stupid . . .

"Are you capable of comprehending what you read, miss? Do you write legibly and do you have good penmanship?"

"Certainly I can read and write, sir! I am even saving to go to university—and it is so difficult for girls to gain entry, you know—and I read everything I can get my hands on. I simply *live* at the university library. Science is my one true love. The best thing in the world would be to utilize scientific knowledge to invent something useful to society, and do you know—"

"Your dreams are not my concern."

"Why, no, I suppose . . ." She swallowed.

"My wishes must become yours if you are to work for me."

"Indeed they are, I—"

"I need all of the jars washed and the chemicals labeled in my laboratory. My index system along with the results of my experiments need to be kept up on a *daily* basis. I will not tolerate even the slightest error."

"Naturally, you would not." She narrowed her eyes on the man before her, so exceedingly stern in his expression, as if he didn't believe anyone could measure up to his expectations.

I will prove him wrong. The great Sherlock Holmes will be wrong about this one thing.

"I have a decade-old collection of finger prints, " he glared at her, the furrow to his brow returning. "It could be utilized to identify criminals if anyone at Scotland Yard had the wit and quickness of movement God bestowed upon a desert tortoise—which they do not, I assure you. Good God! The first thesis describing fingerprint patterns was published in eighteen hundred twenty-three by Purkyne! How long must we live in the dark ages?"

"It is a t-travesty, sir," she agreed. "I r-read Purkyne's paper myself—I believe he was a Czech physiologist—and I have been intrigued with the idea for some time."

"I don't need intrigue!" His words were harsh but it seemed to her that his smoky grey eyes were softening. "I need someone to classify and label my collection according to the twelve basic fingerprint types and cross-reference all alphabetically. It is therefore necessary that you have an elementary understanding of science. Can you take shorthand, Mrs. Hudson's niece?"

"No, but I assure you that I can name every instrument and every chemical in this laboratory," she replied indignantly, tugging at her worn dress.

"You will see many things which are not for the weak of stomach."

"The pursuit of knowledge trumps all other considerations. May I ask, Mr. Holmes," she ventured, raising her chin. She stood stiffly by the fireplace gazing down at him comfortably situated in his armchair by the fire, "Why did you call me intelligent earlier if you didn't even know if I could read and write?"

"*May you ask*? I'm sure I can't stop you from chattering and questioning me incessantly though it has been the greatest longing of my heart for the past fifteen minutes—fifteen minutes I will never be able to reclaim." He set his teacup on the mahogany marble table beside his armchair. "But once again, I shall answer you, young lady, my superior nature often getting the better of me. Because you knew the instrument which I waved at you is a *platina spatula*."

"Well of course, I—"

He coughed with discomfort, placing his hand in front of his mouth in a gentlemanly fashion, his gentile manners in great contradiction to his stinging tongue. "Not a *spatula*. To Mrs. Hudson it would have been no different than a stew-cooking utensil."

"Mr. Holmes, am I to understand that you have evaluated my intelligence over a *spatula*?"

"Frankly, I would be astonished if you understood anything, Mrs. Hudson's niece." He raised his eyebrows reprovingly. "But I am advised that you clearly have the wish to be in my employ."

She looked up. "I do, sir."

"Only an intelligent person would desire such a thing."

Chapter Four

"It cannot be accomplished by a single individual, even a genius such as myself."

"Perhaps you require the aid of a mere mortal, Holmes?" his flat-mate asked, looking up momentarily from his newspaper.

"I do," Holmes nodded. The two men sat facing each other in front of the fire on an unseasonably cold fall day in Westminster, London, each enjoying their pipes.

"Count me in," Watson murmured distractedly without the slightest hesitation.

"I must warn you, my good doctor, that the time may come when, in the interest of apprehending the criminal, it may be necessary to break the law."

"Too many laws on the books, I should say." The tall, slim man stretched out his left leg and rubbed it, the old war wounds acting up. Injuries aside, he was in the prime of life, looking to be in his early twenties but in actuality just having turned nine and twenty. All in all, he was a far different sight than the aimless convalescing soldier he had been when they had met some nine months prior.

"We might . . . I shudder to think it . . ." Holmes took a puff on his pipe "even end up incarcerated."

"Hmm . . . not a pretty picture. I can't say I enjoyed my last visit to the galleys."

"Though I dare say being a prisoner of war is a far different experience than our civilized London jail systems." Holmes raised his eyebrow at his friend as he surveyed him.

"You have a point, Holmes. But neither is to be recommended." Dr. Watson picked up the *Pall Mall Gazette* and began skimming the front page. He murmured aloud as he read, "The Turks are strengthening their army—with the apparent hope of recapturing the lost lands of the Ottoman Empire. I have strong doubts Russia will come to the Balkans' aid again if there is another war."

"I must concur. And that brings me to the case. So are you in, Doctor?" Sherlock pressed.

"Hmmm?" Dr. Watson glanced over the top of the paper. "Without a doubt."

"Excellent. There is no one I would rather have by my side."

"Nor I." Dr. Watson returned to his newspaper. "But let us waste no more time sitting about bantering."

"I agree entirely, Doctor, there is evil afoot to apprehend."

"What is the case Holmes?"

"There is an assassination attempt against the Princess of Montenegro, an exceptionally mysterious and beautiful young woman."

"The blaggards! Who would wish to harm the princess of a tiny Slavic country?"

"As for the reason to wish her dead, Princess Elena Petrović-Njegoš has a bewitching power over men. She is tall with black hair and black eyes. She rarely speaks and yet she has a Madonna-like countenance which captivates."

"Bewitching?" Dr. Watson chuckled. "Seriously, Holmes, you don't expect me to believe—"

"A duel was fought over our enchantress following a ball in St. Petersburg where there was presumably a heated argument over which of her suitors was entitled to the next dance. She was swept away in the middle of the ball amidst the ruckus."

"Doesn't seem like the type of woman anyone would wish dead," Dr. Watson considered, laying down the *Gazette*.

"Ah, but don't you comprehend, Watson?" Sherlock leaned closer towards him.

"No." John Watson shook his head, with the expression of one who speculated that a woman who held men captive in a spellbound state was precisely what one would wish. "Not in the least."

"What do you suppose has happened with this great beauty now out of the schoolroom and set loose upon the male realm, Watson?" Sherlock sighed impatiently, taking a puff on his pipe. "You of all men are aware of the weaknesses of your gender."

"Princess Elena has dazzled someone of note, I should think," Dr. Watson remarked without hesitation. "Someone . . . *of great power*?"

"Precisely, Watson!" Sherlock slapped the arm of his chair. "Prince Victor Emmanuel III, the prince of Naples and the crown prince of Italy." Sherlock cleared his throat, adding, "Called 'Vittorio' by his family and close friends."

Watson gave a low whistle. "Impressive."

"Many do not think Princess Elena is worthy of the House of Savoy," Sherlock stated, tapping the arm of his chair. "She is . . . *unusual*. . ."

"You've already said that, Holmes. She casts a spell over men."

"I am quite sure I never repeat myself," Sherlock replied tersely. "Except for the slow of mind. May I continue, if you please?"

"By all means, Holmes."

"Very well. As I said, Princess Elena is unusual amidst royalty. Her family is somewhat tribal. The so-called palace of Montenegro where she grew up along with her seven siblings is a plain white wooden residence. Furthermore, Princess Elena is an excellent huntress and can ride a horse like a master. When our Slavic royal was unknown and beautiful, however unconventional, she was of little importance. But Elena has caught in her small net a very large prize indeed."

"Do we know who is trying to kill the young lady?" asked Dr. Watson.

"There are endless possibilities, I should think. Where there is wealth and power there are always high stakes," considered Sherlock, raising an eyebrow at his friend. "It is highly probable that Prince Victor Emmanuel's uncle Amadeo, who is next in line for the throne, is not toasting the union. And though it is most distasteful to consider, I would not expect the crown prince's parents to be pleased, as their expectations must surely have been higher for the future Queen of Italy."

"Surely you don't think . . ." Watson exclaimed, his eyes widening.

"I cannot rule out any possibility at this point. It is the King of Montenegro who is paying to protect his daughter at this point. I have no other first hand knowledge of interest in her safety."

"Such a beautiful girl. Thrown to the wolves." Watson shook his head, an expression of disgust crossing his features.

"Frankly, outside of the star-crossed couple and King Nicholas, I can't think of anyone who would be pleased with the match. The anarchist movement is strong in Italy, which, by definition despises the monarchy and everyone associated with it. There will be a racist element which does not wish the crown prince of Italy to marry someone of the Slavic nationality. Possibly the attack has its roots in someone associated with one of the competing princesses for Prince Victor Emmanuel III's hand."

"So you don't know who instigated the attack on Princess Elena's life, Holmes, is that what you are saying?" pressed John Watson, taking a puff on his pipe.

"I have narrowed it down to the groups I discussed," muttered Sherlock with indignation.

"That makes it rather difficult," Watson considered.

"Some might say impossible," Sherlock murmured. "And we have no help from Scotland Yard on this one. The case is not considered in their jurisdiction."

"And the Foreign Office?" Watson asked.

"Mycroft? He is offering what little assistance he can." Sherlock exclaimed in a sudden fury, "Which is bloody short-sighted of the queen's government!"

"Why is that, Holmes?"

"If we do not succeed and Princess Elena Petrović-Njegoš is murdered, there are forces at work, trouble brewing across the globe, which could potentially lead to war on a massive scale. Montenegro is a small Serbian country, but She has among her allies Mother Russia."

"God save us if we fail!" Dr. Watson muttered. Sherlock could tell from his friend's expression that the good doctor understood the importance immediately.

"Somehow we must protect her—and bring the culprits to justice."

"Right you are, Holmes!" John Watson nodded vehemently, his expression determined. His lips suddenly formed a mischievous smile. "Where will Princess Elena be that we might keep an eye on her?"

"You, my good doctor, shall not get within a city block of the beauty."

"How then shall I assist in protecting her?" Dr. Watson asked quite innocently.

"You and I will focus on discovering her assailants. Her protection will be left to her bodyguards." Sherlock frowned. Something about the plan didn't suit him. "Although I would very much like to have an inside man. But our very gender makes it difficult . . ."

"Whatever are you talking about, Holmes?"

"Princess Elena will be enrolled in an exclusive finishing school for young ladies of royalty and the peerage. Extremely difficult to gain entrance to . . . But, no! What a fool I have been!"

"What is it, Holmes?" Dr. Watson placed the newspaper on the pipe rack beside his chair.

"We shall require the aid of a female." Sherlock was now resolved.

"You are the master of disguise," Dr. Watson protested. "You have been a female on many occasions."

"A *pretty* female."

"That *is* a bit of a sticky wicket." Dr. Watson tipped his hat to his friend.

"Your tea and tea cakes." Mirabella Hudson entered with a full tea service, whereby Dr. Watson removed his brown wool bowler hat and placed it on top of the paper.

"Miss Mirabella," he nodded. Holmes was forced to admit to himself that the good doctor looked particularly dashing, and it was obvious that Miss Hudson agreed with his assessment. But then, Watson was always one to garner the ladies' approval.

"I hope I'm not disturbing you, but you did say you wished your tea precisely at two o'clock, Mr. Holmes," Mirabella continued, setting the tea service before them and pouring their tea. "And though it's truly *not* my job, I did promise when you hired me that I wouldn't mention that to you. *So I won't.*"

"I am savoring the silence." Holmes glanced out the bay window looking onto the street, reassuring himself there was nothing outside of the ordinary mayhem one would expect to find in a den of iniquity which was the bustling London street below.

His armchair was situated so he could see Baker Street, and it was impossible not to hear Westminster clock chiming, the ringing of a bell on a carriage, the beating of feet on gravel (from the shouts, he could tell one of the Baker Street irregulars had given chase), cabbies crying (at each other. Crying at customers would utilize a different vocal tonality), and paper boys blasting out the news.

Sherlock glanced at his stash of opium on his desk, while recalling the location of the morphine and laudanum.

Not needed today. There is sufficient stimulation to occupy my mind.

"The laboratory is clean and all its contents labeled—and your index cards are updated and organized alphabetically, Mr. Holmes," Mirabella continued.

"I should hope so, as you appear to be leaving," he murmured as he moved his glance to Miss Mirabella Hudson. It was unnecessary as he had memorized everything about her, but it was nonetheless a pleasant exercise. It also disturbed him slightly, the origin of which he had not yet been able to determine.

Which further disturbed him.

She wore no jewelry, and her chestnut brown hair was pulled neatly back and tied with a simple blue ribbon, her heart-shaped face exaggerated by large sensitive eyes framed by fluttery lashes. Her complexion was flushed with color and she had an energetic healthiness about her.

Miss Mirabella Hudson wore a simple sheath cotton dress in royal blue, faded from wash. The neckline was rounded and trimmed in white lace. A leather corset vest worn on the outside of her dress accentuated her hourglass figure.

I cannot like it. He had observed the leather corset to be a common style for middle-class working girls, but her apparel made her like a barmaid in his book, worn brown leather boots adding to the effect. The bottom line was that Miss Mirabella Hudson was far too shapely to be wearing . . . a leather . . . tied in such a manner . . . a vest . . . *utterly lacking in decorum.*

"Aunt Martha and I are off to Newgate to procure the materials to make Christmas decorations for your study. Now that I have thoroughly cleaned it, decorations will look very nice in here don't you think? There is so much red and green already. Mostly blood and gangrene, but one works with what one has."

"Does one?" asked Holmes, returning his pipe to his mouth as he studied her.

"Christmas is little more than three months away, you know, and we have grand plans."

Holmes raised his eyebrows in such a manner as generally had the effect of quieting even Chief Constables of the Yard.

"Much as I love science, one needs something festive to offset all the chemicals and jars of dead things," she continued gaily.

Ah, but no such effect on Miss Mirabella Hudson. He had yet to come upon the method which would quiet her.

She glanced at the skeleton head on the mantle, and though he generally took considerable pleasure in his comprehension of the unspoken thoughts of others, it frightened him that he knew beyond a shadow of a doubt she was mentally placing a Santa Claus hat on the skull.

"Miss Belle, I am gravely disappointed in you," Sherlock pronounced.

"I have no doubt of that," she smiled, moving into the laboratory. "Well, I must finish up my chores so I can be off to Newgate."

"*Miss Hudson*!" Sherlock exclaimed. "Return here immediately."

She turned to glance at him but did not move away from the door. "Yes, sir?"

"I will not tolerate your impertinence. Return here at once."

She did as she was told, but her expression was brimming with impatience.

I am the one entitled to that sentiment and not she.

"What is it, Mr. Holmes? Your jars are washed, your specimens labeled, your tea served, and your flat is spotless. There is no cause to use an unkind tone with me."

"I will decide when there is cause and when there is not, is that clear?"

"Yes, sir." She sighed heavily.

"Where is my bearskin rug?"

"Your? . . . why . . . oh." Her eyebrows knitted into a frown as she glanced at the exquisite Persian rug in maroon, grey, and cornflower blue underneath their two mahogany Wingback chairs facing each other in front of the fireplace, a bottle of brandy visible on the sideboard. The armchairs in an embossed rose satin had been out of place before the addition of the Persian rug, being the only nice pieces of furniture in the flat. She smiled. "Isn't it beautiful?"

"Quite elegant, I should say, Holmes," Dr. Watson considered, stretching his legs out before him. "Changes the look of the place."

"I did not wish for a change." The Great Detective cleared his throat followed by a cough. "Answer my question, Miss Hudson."

"It was quite hideous, you know. And *filthy*. I moved it into your bedroom."

"It was terribly dirty," Dr. Watson agreed.

"And it still is," nodded Mirabella in agreement. "But Mr. Holmes' bedroom is such a frightful place that the dirt is barely noticeable in there."

"*Miss Hudson* . . ." Sherlock picked up his violin and began plucking on the strings.

"Every time I looked at it, it gave me the shivers," Mirabella replied. "The poor creature's mouth open in anguish and ferocity, the last breath it took a futile attempt to save its own life. Naturally, one must kill to eat, but why on earth does one see something magnificent and the first thought is, 'I must kill it'? I cannot for the life of me understand that."

"I cannot for the life of me understand why you do not comprehend that I am the employer and you are the employee," countered Sherlock. "The fact that I give you monetary compensation and you take it should be your first clue, Miss Hudson."

Her face was suddenly flushed with color as she bit her lip, which he found strangely pretty, before she suddenly turned to smile innocently at him, all the while backing towards the door. "Is there anything else I can do for you before I depart, Mr. Holmes?"

"What did you say we needed, Holmes?" Dr. Watson asked, tapping his finger on his chin as he watched Miss Mirabella sway to the door.

"A pretty female," muttered Sherlock, considering the young lady before him shooting angry darts from her eyes.

"I thought that was what you said."

The two men's eyes locked on each other, slow smiles forming on their lips in unison.

Chapter Five

"What do you mean I must have new clothes? How can anyone afford new clothes on the salary you pay me?" demanded Mirabella, staring at Mr. Holmes, who had the nerve to insult her clothing in front of the oh-so-kind (and handsome!) Dr. John H. Watson. And it wasn't the first time the great man had humiliated her in front of the exquisitely eligible doctor.

Mirabella was scurrying about the flat doing everything she could to escape from her captors that she might begin decorating the flat with the items she and Aunt Martha had procured in Newgate the day before. Sherlock was detaining her with one of his hair-brained schemes—involving *her* no less!

Why does he care what I am wearing? And what is wrong with my dress?

Hmphh! She had never in her life encountered anyone as rude as Sherlock Holmes!

"You live with your aunt downstairs—how many laboratory assistants are given free room and board?" demanded Holmes, looking over his copy of the *Pall Mall Gazette* while enjoying his morning tea only just poured by the object of his consternation. "That should make your salary sufficient."

"May I remind you, Mr. Holmes, that the building belongs to my Aunt Martha," Mirabella replied while dusting.

"And your point is?" Holmes persisted.

"You, most certainly, have not given me free room and board, so it cannot be calculated as a deduction to the salary you pay me." She dusted Sherlock's library shelves with an extra flourish.

"Bravo, Miss Mirabella!" exclaimed Watson, without taking his eyes from his paper. He and Holmes were on such easy terms it was difficult to believe they had only known each other some nine months. It was as if they had become friends from the moment of their meeting.

Mirabella could well understand how anyone would befriend John Watson, but befriending Sherlock Holmes was taking one's life into one's hands.

Although Dr. John Watson had his demons and his sleepless nights as well when the nightmares from the war revisited him. On such days

John Watson was distracted and sad—but never arrogant and unkind as was Sherlock Holmes.

And *never* as intense.

"If you feel that is relevant to our discussion, Miss Belle, I suppose it must be admitted," Holmes muttered with a nonchalant note of indifference as he snapped his newspaper.

"Only if you have no objection to my interjecting reason into the conversation, sir."

"Reason? *Ha!*" Sherlock laughed, almost sputtering out his tea. "From you, Miss Belle?"

"I certainly appreciate your kindness in allowing me to live in the building owned by my Aunt." *And for all you know, Mr. Sherlock Holmes, I may be the owner of the building someday and able to throw you out on your ear.*

What a delightful thought, she giggled to herself.

Dr. Watson looked up from reading *The Financial Times* long enough to mutter, "How odd that you overlooked such a significant point, Holmes."

She smiled sweetly at Dr. Watson. *Sigh.* How difficult it was to tear one's gaze away from twinkling turquoise blue eyes and blonde-streaked brown hair.

But tear she did, forcibly fixing a glare on the handsome doctor's illustrious companion, who repaid her deeply felt sacrifice by looking away as if he had heard nothing which had transpired.

She would not be deprived of beauty in vain.

"May I be allowed to remind you, Mr. Holmes, that I come to work every day, on time, clean and pressed, I have almost single-handedly classified your fingerprint collection, and I do an excellent job in your laboratory." She brushed a lock of her chestnut brown hair out of her eyes, her long hair kept tied at the nape of her neck as Mr. Holmes did not like hairs in his experiments destroying the evidence.

"Yes, you do, that is not at issue. Nor is your cleanliness."

"There, there, Miss Mirabella," Dr. Watson offered, straightening the vest of his three-piece brown tweed suit, turquoise threads running through-out the material.

He is positively dreamy. Did anyone else of her acquaintance have such a turn for fashion? A gold watch chain dangled from his vest, and his brown leather gloves and bowler hat sat beside him on the table, allowing one the privilege of enjoying the good doctor's always neatly cut dark blonde hair. She best liked to view it in the sunlight or the firelight where the streaks of blonde shown to advantage.

"Sherlock is not criticizing your appearance," Dr. Watson continued. "It is precisely because you are so pretty that your clothing has come into interest."

"Me? *Pretty?*" She looked at Dr. Watson and almost melted. How could anyone be *so* handsome and yet so *nice?* Nice. Sherlock, though very handsome in his own dark, demented way and more likely to turn heads of the two, did not know the meaning of the word *nice.*

And she knew very well she was not at all pretty: she was the plainest of girls, with thick brown hair, even browner eyes—though her mother had said they were large and expressive and lush with lashes. Of course one could not trust one's mother on such matters.

She supposed that her skin and features were well enough, but she was not a thin, frail girl as was the style. Though Aunt Martha had pronounced her undernourished upon her arrival. (who had the time or blunt to eat?) She had certainly filled out under her Aunt Martha's care, requiring that she let out the seams on her blouses! Her legs were her best feature, long and shapely (which no one saw!). Her height was slightly above average, some would say too tall. And she wore thick black glasses—and thoroughly grateful to have them, she was!

All in all, she was the plainest, most background, most *average*, perhaps even gangly, girl imaginable. She was barely noticeable—and hardly worth noticing.

"Of course you are pretty, Miss Mirabella," Dr. Watson muttered shyly, clearing his throat. "Sherlock and I are both in agreement on that."

She glanced at each of them with apprehension. *What horrible manner of joke is this?* She had never known Dr. Watson to be cruel.

"That is very kind of you to say," she murmured, "but I certainly am not going to spend my *hard-earned* money on clothing." She threw a spiteful glance at Sherlock Holmes, crossing her arms in front of her. "I am saving it for university."

"Which university shall you be attending, Miss Mirabella?" Dr. Watson asked.

"Naturally it would be the University of London, as this would be the only university which currently offers a degree to women," Sherlock stated with indifference. "Certainly Oxford and Cambridge do not."

Mirabella could barely contain her excitement. "Yes, you are correct, Mr. Holmes!"

"Of course I am," Sherlock murmured.

"Last year four women received a Bachelor of Arts degree from the University of London," Mirabella continued. "The first women ever to do so!"

"Ah, my alma mater, from which I obtained my degree in medicine," Dr. Watson pronounced proudly." And what shall your degree be in, Miss Hudson?"

"Chemistry. Or Biology."

"I shouldn't think so," Sherlock stated. "Women are almost universally excluded from studying medicine. And no woman has ever been granted a Bachelor of Science degree."

"Things are changing quickly, Mr. Holmes," she replied indignantly. "You wouldn't have thought ten years ago a woman would be allowed to earn a Bachelor of Arts degree." Having arrived at Sherlock's desk, Mirabella picked up the handcuffs, wondering, not for the first time if they had been used—and when?

"Don't touch those," grumbled Sherlock.

"Do forgive me." She returned the handcuffs to their shrine amongst his papers and below his photographs hung on the wall. *I didn't know they had a personal meaning.*

How she would love to lounge about and sip tea while reading. Mirabella picked up the duster and moved to apply it to the fireplace mantle, paying particular attention to the bust of Sherlock with the bullet hole through the head.

"It's all for the best." Sherlock remarked, taking a sip of his tea as he turned to Dr. Watson.

"What's all for the best?" she turned on Sherlock.

"We couldn't trust Miss Hudson to keep her tongue in her head anyway," Holmes replied, his gaze remaining on Watson. "Which is critical to the case."

"Trust me? What is this about? Are you . . ." She gulped, moving towards them as she flung her duster about, releasing dust into the air. "Mr. Holmes, are you going to allow me to go on one of your cases? Are you serious? What do I need to do? When do we start?"

"It is dangerous work, Miss Mirabella," Dr. Watson cautioned. "It was an ill-conceived notion. Upon further reflection, I seriously don't think . . ."

"Dangerous for whom?" laughed Sherlock. "Miss Hudson or the criminal? Personally, my pity goes out to the criminal."

"Oh, I have dreamed of this ever since first hearing my aunt speak of your detective and forensic work," Mirabella twirled in the middle of the room, her duster clutched to her chest. "I am very good at taking and preserving the integrity of specimens. And, as you know, the sight of blood—even cadavers—doesn't bother me at all. Well, maybe a little, I'm not without a heart *like some people.*"

"Ah, and how does your solitary heart cope with the vile and wicked things we see, Miss Hudson?" Sherlock asked with interest.

"The horrible things we see only fuels the desire to see justice done," she replied without hesitation, lunging her duster into the air. "At that point what can one do except avenge the innocent and protect others?"

"It is a lofty sentiment, but Miss Hudson has not been *trained* for this type of work," Watson insisted, his expression more concerned than ever. "I'm quite serious, Holmes."

"As am I," replied Holmes, pulling his pipe from his pocket. "And she will be. *Thoroughly* trained."

"Never fear on that subject, Dr. Watson," she nodded adamantly. "I can shoot a gun—and even wield a punch on occasion! My brothers were the best boxers in the county."

"Take my word for it, Watson," Sherlock nodded, "Miss Hudson is surprisingly strong." He rubbed his wrist absently.

"I might not know an awful lot about ladies' things, but Aunt Martha can sew. She has long offered to make a new wardrobe for me—but of course I can't afford the material as I must save every penny for university. Although it's not *that* expensive if you know where to shop. And I *do.* Why . . ."

Why indeed? Why on earth would she need elegant clothing to work on a case, anyway? The whole idea was peculiar. Probably another of Sherlock's misguided ideas. She had to keep an eye on him or he was likely to blow up the London flat or possibly kill himself with the chemicals and drugs he kept hanging about. The man was far too removed from the world at times. But if it meant she would be included on the mission, she would wear a burlap bag if Sherlock commanded it!

Her heart was pounding as she clutched the duster. Mirabella had no idea she wished to be on a criminal case so much.

I must be out of my mind.

Holmes tapped his index finger on his unshaven cheek. "In the first place, Miss Hudson, you have to focus on playing your part and keep your mouth closed. *It can't be done.* And you would have to make a visit with my optometrist and get those new glass lenses to put in the eye."

"Do you think so, Holmes?" asked Dr. Watson. "I like her glasses. They give her a very intellectual, sort of *modern* look."

"Now wait just a moment, Mr. Holmes, I am *not* sticking a piece of glass in my eye!" The burlap bag, yes. Glass in the eye, no. She intended to use these eyes for a while. "If you think I'll do that, you've got another thing coming!"

"No, the glasses would have to go." Sherlock's gaze was on Dr. Watson, ignoring her, even as all his remarks were clearly intended for her. "They don't fit the role. We can't take any chances. But it is of no moment; she can't keep her mouth closed, so it won't work. "

"I most certainly can!" She cleared her throat. "And I'm not the *only* person guilty of that transgression."

"Do you see what I mean, Watson? She's insubordinate, rude, *unfeminine*, and completely incapable of disciplining her tongue." He bestowed his warmest smile upon her. "But she's very good at washing jars and keeping the floors clean. Now run along, Miss Hudson. Attend to your parlor decorations and leave us to solving the real problems of the world."

Chapter Six

The real problems. She'd give him a real problem. Or two.

But the truth was that *Sherlock Holmes* was the real problem: he was utterly incorrigible. Cantankerous, rude, unpleasant, more than a little disturbed.

And the most brilliant man she had ever met.

A few hours later Mirabella was absorbed in sweeping the floors of the laboratory—for what seemed like the tenth time that day—when suddenly a horrible stench caught her nose, whiskey and heaven knows what else.

"Lor' luv a duck!" A dirty, smelly man stumbled into her. "Where is da nearest pub, miss?"

"How did *you* get in here? This is a private residence!" She gasped, startled and frightened at finding an intruder inside the building, inching backwards towards the fire poker while eyeing the location of Dr. Watson's pistol.

And then she recognized the intelligent silvery grey eyes looking back at her. His normally dark hair was almost black with soot—and he reeked. Of sardines, tobacco, *and whiskey.* "*Mr. Holmes,* is that you? And have you been *drinking?*"

"Blimey, I never drink when I'm workin'," he replied, chewing on the cigar hanging from his mouth and popping the suspenders which held up his too-large beige corduroy pants. He tipped his bowler hat to her. "And when I'm not workin' there are uvver bad 'abits mawer ter me taste, *Miss Belle.*" He winked at her.

"Oh, you *stink*, sir. If you'll pardon me for saying so."

"Spiffing. That's what I was goin' fer. Believabili'y is everythin' in dis business. Speakin 'ov which . . ." he took some crumpled bills out of his pocket and held them out to her. "Go an' buy yaaahrself some pret'y dresses. I've decided what yew are da best bird fer da job I 'ave in mind."

"Truly? Oh, Mr. Holmes, thank you! Oh, I promise you won't be disappointed . . ."

"I'm awready dissy-pointed."

She rushed forward to curtsey before him as hugging him would have been completely . . . frightful.

"Are those perfectly *safe?*" She stopped dead in her tracks as she stared at the crumpled bills he held out to her—and then at him. "I presume that you have read Robert Koch's recent publication on germ theory. Most notably his studies of the bacterium *Bacillus anthracis.*"

"Lawd above! There ain't no anthrax on deese pound notes, little missy. . . . . Thuff some gloves might be in order."

"Without a doubt," she frowned, making no movement towards the bills which appeared, at first glance, to be more money than she had seen in a lifetime. "If you would kindly place the bills on the chair—*your* chair, not Dr. Watson's—I will fumigate them and proceed to the *Ladies' Emporium.* Never fear, Mr. Holmes, my Aunt Martha is an excellent seamstress, and we shall make good use of your funds. What precisely do I need for the assignment?"

"Ye just deck yaaahrself aaaht fancy like a proper lady—ye'll need several ever-day gowns an' an evenin' gown wiv all da proper acoutremun's: crocheted gloves an' silk gloves, a lace parasol, a ladies' fan, a satin reticule, boots an' shoes, shiny bobbles, even feminine scent. An' a silk nightgown as a high-born gul' wud haf, fergive me fer bringin' up the unmentionables but they must be mentioned. And while yer at i' make yaaahrself a proper lab coat an' a dress fer greetin' me visitors." He handed her a card. "Me optometrist. Get some 'o those new glass lenses to replace the arful *black* glasses."

She stared at him. "Why did you change your mind Mr. Holmes? *About me,* that is?"

"I didn't, Miss Belle. I've only been known to change me mind *once.*" He straightened his posture and took out his pipe and lit it. He was suddenly out of character, extremely rare for him once he was in disguise.

"I see."

"I doubt that, Miss Belle," he replied, taking a long puff on his pipe. "Now run along before we embark upon the second instance."

Chapter Seven

"You know, of course, that we can only accept girls who are members of the peerage." Miss de Beauvais eyed Sherlock's stylish attire. "No matter how successful her connections." The proprietress was a brunette with her hair arranged in an ornate fashion, so stiff that it conceivably was meant to serve as a military helmet in the event of war.

A wise precaution in Sherlock's estimation. He approved of a sensible woman. He also approved of any person without a high degree of emotion or sentiment, a criteria which the lady before him likewise met.

"Naturally." Sherlock glanced about the elaborate office, the style much in keeping with the large parlor he had observed upon entering *Miss de Beauvais' Finishing School for Distinguished Young Ladies*. The wallpaper was of a green and gold triangular pattern with a border more orange than red. The ceiling was maroon and ivory while the carpet was maroon and green. Oil paintings of flowers of every variety decorated the walls, the colors so vivid that one expected to see bees flying from one picture to the next.

Glancing at the décor, one certainly felt their sting. In contrast, the Queen Anne chairs were starkly lacking in color, cushioned in cream and brown, as if there were no point in making the attempt.

"And what are the young lady's connections?" she pressed. "*Precisely?*"

Though *Miss de Beauvais'* was situated in the stylish part of town at 76 Regent Street, somehow it seemed appropriate that the exclusive finishing school was likewise nearby to *Piccadilly Circus*. That *Miss de Beauvais'* was also within walking distance of *Café Royal*, a favorite haunt of his and Watson's, was mere coincidence—and most convenient as a location to compare notes.

"My niece is the granddaughter of a distant land baron on her poor deceased mother's side." Sherlock mentally resolved to have Mycroft produce some piece of paper authenticated by someone of importance justified by national security issues. Mycroft had considerable clout, regardless of the Foreign Office's interest.

"I see. Perfectly suitable." She nodded agreeably, but her expressed commitment lacked conviction. Miss de Beauvais' lips were generally pursed, as if her primary motivation were containing her thoughts. Her face was elongated; there was nothing particularly unappealing—or appealing—about her features to which a make-up meant to look like the absence of make-up was applied. No doubt the fear of looking like a stage actress caused her to err on the colorless side, which she more than made up for in her choice of clothing and home décor. Glancing at her hands, Sherlock saw that her nails were short and buffed but unpainted. Miss de Beauvais had attended to every detail, even if her intent was neutrality, and perhaps not with the best results.

It struck Sherlock that this woman might be his female equivalent in temperament, outlook, and emotional detachment. It was amusing to contemplate making love to such a woman, one's twin as it were. Much like kissing a Venus flytrap.

"An impoverished land baron, but a baron nonetheless. I am too busy making money to concern myself with such things." Sherlock placed a heavy wad of bills on the desk between them. "All the cash holdings come from my branch of the family."

"Oh, I'm quite certain we will completely adore your lovely niece, Mr. . ." Her facial expression changed in an instant to a saintly sweetness, her good will towards him much improved, and he observed her eyeing with considerable sentimentality the wad of bills he had placed on her desk.

"Carnegie," Sherlock replied, tipping his silk top hat before removing it. "Lochlan Carnegie."

"*Carnegie?* By chance, are you a relation of Andrew Carnegie, the American tycoon, sir? I believe he has Scottish roots?" Her breathing became more rapid.

Sherlock took care to neither answer nor refute her assumption. He pulled out his gold pocket watch and looked at it. He then straightened his white silk tie, smoothing his false beard and well-oiled walrus moustache, before replying. "My niece does some type of volunteer work, at an orphanage, I believe it is. Only a few hours a week. And we must be allowed to visit her—my associate, Hamish, and I. She is most dear to us—an orphan herself you know, with only her two sinfully rich bachelor uncles to look to." He smiled his most winning smile, which by all accounts was not particularly winning. It was hoped that a belief in his massive wealth enhanced his charm. *"Miss* de Beauvais, is it?"

"Oh, I *am* sorry, that is out of the question, Mr. Carnegie." Her lips quivered but remained tightly held together. "Once the girls enter it is a *closed-door* policy. The girls are all required to stay here for the duration of their ten week term with little contact from the outside except that which we provide—under strict chaperonage, of course. It is a very intensive class and is completed just in time for the Christmas holiday—at which time they may return home for a few weeks. The final semester commences upon their return and ends in their coming out for the season as elegant, sophisticated young ladies, just in time for their presentation to Queen Victoria and all the accompanying balls and dinner parties."

"And by elegant and sophisticated, I presume you mean *marriageable*?" Sherlock asked, emphasizing the word as he leaned closer toward her. He could tell that she was attracted to either him or his money; he meant to discover which and to use that information to his advantage.

"Naturally." She nodded agreement. "This is my pledge to you." The young female entrepreneur wore a gown of orange silk which somehow blended in this frighteningly busy room of green, maroon, and orange. One was of the impression that Miss de Beauvais could not enter a room unless she were a perfect compliment to the décor—and that she must control everyone and everything in her environment.

Sherlock locked eyes across the desk with the business owner staring back at him whom he guessed had an unyielding will to rival his own. Two confirmed bachelors as it were.

So much alike, they should have been a match. Except for the fact that he detested her, which was perhaps a commentary on why he disliked to be alone in his own company unless he was focused on a case.

There was a significant difference in the expression of his and Miss de Beauvais' similar characteristics, however: her existence was completely devoted to the superficial aspects of life—and to herself. His dealt with the harsh realities—and to the service of society.

Sherlock asked himself, as he often had, if it would not be more profitable to be the criminal than to side with the law.

Naturally. No one can beat me. Sherlock knew very well that he could succeed as a criminal. Far stupider people had.

But it was never about the money for him: it was the occupation. *And I love my country.* He might not love his fellow man, but he would be on the side of right. Otherwise he could easily foresee the downfall of civilization.

Sherlock took another wad of bills and placed it on the table. "Will I be allowed to visit my niece—or shall I take these substantially heavy piles of currency with me and place her elsewhere?"

"Such a fine establishment as this is very expensive to run," she murmured, eyeing the bills caressingly while shaking her head.

He opened his leather bag and placed both stacks of bills within. "Do pardon me, Miss de Beauvais, but this is too much money to place in my wallet. It simply *won't fit.* In much the same way I fear my niece will not fit in here. Though I must say it was a pleasure to meet you." He winked at her, rising and reaching for his hat.

"We can make a slight exception in the case of your dear niece. Mirabella . . . *Carnegie*, is it? Surely your brief familial visits can be arranged so that they don't disturb the other girls." She cleared her throat. "And certainly charity work is to be commended."

Assessing the woman before him, Sherlock was convinced she had no notion of the jewel he was placing in her care—nor cared, outside of the benefit to herself. *If a single hair from Miss Belle's head is 'disturbed' as you put it, you shall regret the day we met, Miss de Beauvais.*

In point of fact, Miss Hudson was the key to his future, his ticket to solving the case. His ticket to . . . *everything.*

Miss Mirabella Hudson had done the one thing anyone rarely did— she had *surprised* him. Sherlock had no notion of the girl's usefulness when he hired her, but the fact was that he couldn't possibly solve this without the hoyden. She might be rude and boisterous—but she was also *essential.* Miss Belle was a spitfire—and an intelligent one at that—a girl who was willing to work beside him and take all the risks he was willing to take.

And this assignment was his first international case.

My key to fame.

Not that he cared about money or fame, but Sherlock cared desperately, frantically about work. *I must have employment.* To be without mental stimulation was anathema to him. He was a young detective, considered an eccentric, disliked by most, and though he could personally care less about whether or not anyone liked him, he knew very well that his reputation was fragile. He was on the brink of being termed brilliant—or insane.

The laughing stock of London.

Not succeeding could destroy my career. Above all, he must have an exceptional reputation to have occupation, particularly given his social standing. Because this was such a high profile assignment, it had the power to make him—or to ruin him.

Sherlock nodded tersely, and returned the money to the table. "I'm gratified you can see fit to accommodate us, Miss de Beauvais."

"I see no reason why we cannot have a mutually profitable relationship," she murmured with a smile.

Without a doubt there was an element of danger inherent to the case—particularly to Miss Hudson. But his young ward knew of the danger and had chosen to proceed. Naturally Sherlock hoped she would emerge unscathed—outside the fact that he wished her no harm, he would have to find a new place to live and a new assistant were any harm to come to her. But most of all, he wished her to *succeed.*

"I cannot think of one, Miss de Beauvais."

Chapter Eight

"Good morning, Officer." Mirabella nodded to a policeman wandering the halls, his silver buttons catching the light which drifted through the floor-to-ceiling Gothic arched windows.

Mirabella took a deep breath, working up all her nerve. She dreaded coming here. For her, it was the saddest place on earth: 18 Charing Cross Road.

She glanced up at the sign *"Lady Graham's Orphan Asylum for the Female Children of Deceased Officers of the Police, est. 1865, 18 Charing Cross Road."*

"Miss." He tipped his hat to her. There was always a bobby in *Lady Graham's*—visiting the child of a murdered partner or just paying his respects. With the building's medieval stone arches, one expected to see a knight of old rather than a bobby, but both lent a false sense of protection.

She turned to glance out the arched windows. Within view was the *Bank of England*, the home of Dr. Watson's bank notes as it were, the *Charing Cross Hotel*, and across the street the telegram office utilized by Sherlock Holmes and Dr. Watson.

What a different world it was, only steps away. Having had a delightful childhood growing up on a farm outside Dumfries, it was difficult for her to imagine growing up at *Lady Graham's*.

Whatever her upbringing might have lacked, she never lacked for dreams. Having a strong bent for science and especially a love of chemistry, her dream had always been to go to university. A dream which seemed impossible as often as not, but whatever anyone took from her, she still had her greatest asset: *herself.*

When one lost one's belief in oneself one had lost *everything.*

These walls were filled with those who had lost everything.

Whenever Mirabella felt particularly sad, she offered up the thing she felt was missing in her own life to someone else. Her mother had taught her that. Once a week, whatever her personal disappointments, she taught science to young female orphans at *Lady Graham's*.

Bang! Crash! Entering the Great Hall, where dozens of children would meet for each meal, she wondered why it was always so noisy. Shouldn't all these children meandering about aimlessly be *somewhere*? Doing *something*?

Initially there had been a benefactress, Lady Graham, then city funds and donations had been added upon her death along with a trustee. As long as there was money involved, the children had value.

At *Lady Graham's* the children were fed and clothed—even minimally schooled, though no one was required to attend Mirabella's science class. She had been volunteering for some six weeks, and certain questions began to occur to her.

"Good afternoon, Miss Bickers." She nodded to the headmistress, whose expression never wavered from a stern frown and who only engaged in conversation with reluctance.

"Miss Hudson," Miss Bickers nodded disapprovingly. "Yer class is a-waitin'." The sturdy woman in her early thirties with angular features and stringy, brown greying hair tied in a bun glared at her. Miss Bickers wore a brown tailored suit consisting of a full skirt and a long jacket ornamented with a voluminous brown velvet bow at the bosom which would be less unexpected on a child's frivolous outfit than on the gown of a hardened matron. But the fabric was of a fine quality.

"That is a beautiful ring," Mirabella exclaimed, not being one to hide her thoughts. On Miss Bickers' finger she wore a sparkling ruby ring.

Miss Bickers replied defensively, "It's a family heirloom."

Certainly Mirabella would have thought a ring such as that to be an impossible purchase on a headmistress' salary, but she hadn't intended any insult, only to admire the ring.

"It is stunning," she murmured, attempting to change the subject. "I believe that you teach math class, Miss Bickers?"

"Math and art. I am a painter." Miss Bickers held her head high. "What's it 'ave to do wif' you, miss?"

"I am only interested in the girls' education, beg pardon." Mirabella curtseyed, bowing her head momentarily, wondering what on earth there was to take offense in with such an ordinary question. She glanced about the Great Hall, noticing that the walls were noticeably devoid of any art work—either by children or adults. She murmured, "I would love to see your paintings."

"They'se not fer public viewing."

The headmistress' reaction only made Mirabella more determined, as most efforts to subdue her did. "Do you teach English as well, Miss Bickers?"

"Nah. It ain't me strong suit."

Well that is a shocking bit of news.

"Officer McLaughlin volunteers," Miss Bickers added.

"Is he a good teacher?"

"I reckon' as not." Miss Bickers shrugged indifferently, her stiff brown shift dress taking a few seconds to return to its original position once her shoulders reclined. Though tall and slim, the headmistress was well-fed and somewhat muscular. Her features were good and she might have been pretty had she worn her hair in a less severe manner and smiled on occasion, although that could be nothing more than speculation as it had never been observed.

"Miss Bickers, here is the receipt for my supplies," she took it out of her bag. "And my hansom cab ride—I would prefer to walk, but it is a distance and I have a great deal to carry. You had said at the outset that, though my services are unpaid, the orphanage would reimburse me for my expenses?"

"O'course," replied Miss Bickers, pursing her lips and tapping her foot on the stone floor. "I don't takes to extravagant spending, but we don' deny the girls anythin' either."

"And how does the girls' education progress?" She had learned from the Great Detective to be direct in her questions. Falling back only tended to invite others to trample.

"Well enough," Miss Bickers looked at the younger woman over her glasses.

"The children, can they all read and do their figures?" Mirabella asked.

"Those what wants to can," Miss Bickers sniffed with indifference.

"What is the plan for their future?" Mirabella pressed on, mustering her courage. "That is to say, what are they being trained for? I only ask so I may be of any assistance I can."

"They'se gettin' math, art, and reading, what more is there? We don't have no call for French and music here." Miss Bickers sneered, nonplussed. She smoothed her hair back, but there was no need as it appeared to be lacquered to her head. "I do teach 'em watercolor, which is a fine sight better than the other orphanages. We've run a very tight ship 'ere these five years, 'an the Board 'o Trustees is very pleased wif' our work. We are always on budget."

"I'm sure you're doing an excellent job, Miss Bickers," reassured Mirabella. "My only concern is for the girls. I do wish that you would require more of the girls to take my science class. Don't you agree that a very little math, art, and English is hardly sufficient for a governess position? By your own admission, some of the girls can't even read and do basic arithmetic."

"A governess position?" repeated Miss Bickers, looking at Mirabella as if she had lost her mind.

Mirabella felt some guilt, knowing that she had just been assigned the most marvelous of positions—to assist on a case with the brilliant Sherlock Holmes! Such good fortune she never could have imagined. She had no idea what the assignment involved—other than the fact that she was required to have fine apparel, so it was clear that she was to have a visible part—if only for an instant and however insignificant.

"I agree that being a governess is unlikely to be the secret wish of any girl's heart—being low paying and demanding—but it is a respectable position and is the highest attainment your most intelligent girls could strive for," Mirabella replied. "And yet the curriculum at *Lady Graham's* does not prepare even your top students for such a post. Neither is such a limited subject base sufficient for any girl to hope to marry well."

"Marry well?" Miss Bickers laughed. Mirabella was encouraged, at least, that her companion's indignation had been turned to merriment. "A poor girl can't 'ope to marry well! Unless she is the most beautiful of gulls."

Miss Bickers moved her eyes along Mirabella, indicating that she had no great opinion of the younger woman's beauty.

Mirabella sighed self-consciously. She had heretofore believed herself to look presentable if not becoming in a white lace blouse, a black velvet choker with a pale blue cameo, a blue linen skirt, and a straw hat with peonies on it.

She bit her lip. Her own beauty, or more likely the lack therein, had absolutely nothing to do with the subject at hand, and well Miss Bickers knew it. The point was, as much as Mirabella felt that the poor deserved the same opportunities as the rich, even she would prefer to see the girls trained to work in servitude to the middle and upper classes—like herself—than to have no training in anything at all.

That was a recipe for disaster.

"Is that what you want, miss? To marry well?" Miss Bickers inquired in an acerbic politeness.

"Oh, no! I want to enter university and study science. I'm saving all my money to do so." Again, she felt a twinge of guilt. She was supposed to be focused on chemistry and biology—and, for some reason, the thought of detective work had her giddy with excitement.

Perhaps Sherlock Holmes' madness is contagious.

"I sees. You have a job and you want to enter university. And what would happen after that?"

"Well, I would be a scientist. I have ideas, you know." *And I certainly will not feel guilty for having dreams!*

"Ah." Miss Bickers replied. "I have ideas too, but the money don't fall out of the sky."

Having delivered her commentary along with undisguised regalement, Miss Bickers left the room and returned with a tin box. The older woman scrutinized Mirabella's receipts, pulling several crisp, new pound notes out from the tin box which contained a great deal of cash to Mirabella's way of thinking.

Miss Bickers made very neat entries into a ledger, adding the numbers accurately in her head, and handed the notes to Mirabella. It appeared that the headmistress was qualified to teach elementary mathematics at least.

"I hope you do not take offence at my interest in the curriculum, Miss Bickers," Mirabella murmured contritely. "I only think of the girls' futures."

"Their future, you say?" Miss Bickers' eyes scrutinized her with both disdain and ridicule. "Let me tell you about my *past*."

"Well, certainly, Miss Bickers, if you think—"

"First of all, many of these childrens here was abandoned."

"Yes, I expect so." Mirabella did know that child abandonment was rampant. London was a young town, with one-third of the population youth, many of them on the street.

"Did you know, miss, that in some places such as this, the nurses administer Godfrey's Cordial to the young-uns, for the colic in babies?"

"A cordial? What do you mean, Miss Bickers?"

"A mix of opium and treacle," Miss Bickers replied.

Gasp! Mirabella threw her hand over her mouth.

"What do you know about the workhouses, missy?" Miss Bickers persisted.

"Well . . . I . . . only what I read . . ." Mirabella replied, somewhat startled at the intensity of Miss Bickers' gaze.

"You don't know *nuthin'*, miss," snapped Miss Bickers, scowling. "Just as I thought. *What you read.* You and your book learnin' makes you think you know everthin'."

"And were you . . . did you live . . . ?" asked Mirabella, suddenly concerned.

"I'll tell you somethin', Miss Hoighty Toighty. These girls are as lucky as can be. They have food and they only works a few hours a day. Most of 'em ain't sick—and when they is, we have a *real doctor*. I rarely discipline the little knee biters and I lets them do as they please. Do you know how's orphans on the streets get their next meal?"

"Oh, yes, I keep my eyes open, Miss Bickers," she replied confidently, nodding her head. "I've seen children employed as chimney sweeps, errand boys, shoe blacks, and selling matches and flowers."

And reporting on criminal activity. Sherlock Holmes' street urchins, a most industrious group of boys termed the *Baker Street Irregulars*, made up to a shilling a day—and sometimes up to a guinea if they produced some piece of truly important information. "And I suspect that charity steps in to help."

"Charity? Ha! Ha! They ain't no charity in London," she spat. "Leastways very little. No, the youngin's live meal to meal by begging, crime, working in factories, mines, and sweatshops. And by selling themselves to *prostitution*, that's how."

"Oh, my!" Mirabella reddened.

"Does the suffering of others embarrass ye, miss?" asked Miss Bickers. "Prepare to be embarrassed. You well-to-dos don't know nuthin' of what the poor endure."

"Well-to do? I am not rich! I am a working girl. Why, I work night and day for my employer, as needed, and when I'm not working, I am studying. I also help my aunt with her chores."

Miss Bickers rolled her eyes at her. "Work? You don't know nuthin' about work, miss. Me pa he worked in the glue factory and me ma made soap. They never stopped workin' and we almost starved. We lived in a tenement house with a dirt floor and a tin roof until me pa died of cholera and me ma died of typhus, as did most of the younguns. When me ma and pa died, I went into a workhouse at the age of twelve. Most of those who entered wif' me is now dead." She sniffed. "My family was real people to me what I loved—they was not insects!"

"Oh, Miss Bickers," whispered Mirabella, wiping her eyes. "I am so sorry." She admonished herself for her insensitivity. It was not that long ago that two thousand open sewers drained into the Thames, the river being the source of London's drinking water. Cholera and typhus, along with other water-borne diseases, were, not surprisingly, rampant. No effort was made to solve the problem until the odor of the Thames offended Parliament itself, huge noses peeking out from under white wigs in dismay.

Mirabella did the math in her head; Miss Bickers would have been about ten years old at the time of "The Great Stink," in the summer of eighteen hundred fifty eight.

"What with the Poor Law which divided the poor into the deserving and the undeserving," Miss Bickers replied with a sneer. "Guess which one we was?"

"But the Poor Law established aid for the poor!" exclaimed Mirabella, astonished.

"See what your book learnin' did for ye?" Miss Bickers chuckled though she did not appear amused. "The Poor Law done away with all forms of aid. Except fer the workhouses which are no more than prisons!"

"Prisons for the poor . . ." murmured Mirabella.

"They's no visitors allowed inside and *no passes out*." Miss Bickers lowered her voice and moved closer to her. "What's more, do you know that families are separated when they enters the workhouses? They even separated mothers from their babies. I know of one woman who wanted to nurse her infant who was sick, and the guard took away the woman's clothes and beat her for crying fer her child."

Mirabella gasped, stepping back and involuntarily running her hands along her pale blue linen skirt. The sound of her brown boot hitting the stone floor was the only sound to reach her ears.

"You see, miss," Miss Bickers shrugged, the misplaced brown velvet bow on her chest somehow intimidating. "There ain't no English and science classes in the workhouses. The fourteen-hour work days don't allow much time for that."

Mirabella felt ashamed of her earlier internal commentary on Miss Bickers' English skills and wondered how the older woman managed to learn anything—and to live. "How did you survive, Miss Bickers?"

"By using this." Miss Bickers tapped her index finger on her forehead. "Here we lives in the richest country in the world. But the rich likes to blame the poor for their own misfortune. The Whigs made the workhouses because they want to punish the poor for bein' poor. They likes to say as how the poor 'as learned to work the system. But if you asks me," Miss Bickers continued, "the rich is the ones who 'ave figured out how to work the system."

"And yet, every now and again, someone slips through the cracks and advances, like yourself, Miss Bickers."

"We will all finish in the station we was born into," Miss Bickers slammed the tin box shut.

Not if I have anything to say about it.

"Good day, Miss Bickers. My class awaits." Mirabella curtseyed and thanked Miss Bickers.

"I'm not accustomed to bein' idle meself. Go study your science." Miss Bickers turned on her heel and walked away, the 'click, click' of her brown leather shoes hitting the stone floor with some force.

As Mirabella walked to her classroom, it struck her as odd that a person with such a background as Miss Bickers would have an expensive ruby as a family heirloom. Wouldn't the parents have sold it for food and medical care? Unless it had enormous sentimental value, which was difficult to envision.

"Good morning, class." Mirabella entered the meager room with grey stone floors and worn wooden walls and once again wished they had a *real* science laboratory. She could not help but think of the fine laboratory—though small—in Sherlock Holmes' flat with gleaming glassware, nicely labeled jars, and state-of-the art equipment.

The laboratory I have been forbidden to use.

"Good morning, Miss Hudson," her class of three—no *four*— beamed at her. She was honestly surprised when anyone but Amity came back even though there were some seventy girls in the orphanage. Most of the girls in the hallway had a vacuous expression, unlike these four, as bright as rays of sunshine.

"Amity. Susan. Gloria. And who do we have here?" Mirabella nodded to a red-headed cherub.

"My name is Candice," the little girl replied, smiling, adding proudly. "My father was a police constable."

"How very impressive!" exclaimed Mirabella. "And do you have an interest in science, Candice?"

Candice shook her head. "No, but I do like these other girls. And I heard there was food."

A hand shot up.

"Yes, Amity?"

"Did you get a new position, Miss Hudson?" the little girl whose parents had died in a fire asked. Somehow Amity and her younger sister, Susan, had escaped the fire. "After you lost your other job?"

"Why, yes, Amity, how did you know?"

"I listened," the always alert and watchful child with short honey-toned hair and large golden brown eyes shrugged.

"Who told you, Amity?" Mirabella asked.

"A beautiful, tall girl with *black* eyes riding a horse and carrying a sword."

"How interesting, Amity," Mirabella replied. It was not unusual for children who had lost everything to have overactive imaginations—although Amity had had her eleventh birthday now and was a bit old for such wild tales.

Still, Mirabella could not bring herself to correct Amity; she was glad for any comfort the children could find. Ironically, Amity—who rarely emerged from her fantasy world—was the only one of her students who appeared to have a natural ability in math and science. The child had a way of knowing.

"But the sword is very sharp," Amity shuddered.

"First," Mirabella reached into her bag, pulling out four beautiful red apples—one for her and one for each of . . . oh, no, five total today. She felt her stomach growl. Oh, she couldn't bear to ask anyone to share, they always looked so hungry, and how their eyes lit up to see those apples.

Ignoring her own hunger, Mirabella murmured, "Nourishment is important for the brain to work at its best."

"That's right!" the girls nodded in vehement agreement.

"May I ask you, class, why you always seem so *hungry?* Aren't you fed here?"

Everyone moaned in unison.

"What is it class?"

"Mr. McVittie is *horrible,*" Susan remarked, evincing a contorted facial expression.

"Who is Mr. McVittie?" she asked softly.

"The cook," explained Amity.

"He doesn't know how to cook," added Gloria, giggling as she set down her needlepoint, her notebook unopened.

"We had a very nice ham on Sunday," corrected Candice, her carrot-red hair bobbing, offsetting her copper-colored eyes beautifully. Candice looked to be the healthiest of the girls. "I'm nine years old you know!"

"Oh, that ham was *so good!*" added blonde Susan, tiny for an eight-year-old. "Even the rolls tasted like bread instead of sawdust," Gloria added. Gloria was the prettiest child Mirabella had ever seen, with brunette hair, dark eyes, dimples, and a smile that would warm the sun.

"That's because Candy made them," stated Susan matter-of-factly.

"Is it true?" asked Mirabella of the girls. "Did Candice make the rolls?"

Amity nodded. "The only way we ever have anything good is when Candice helps in the kitchen."

"But I have to have special permission," Candice explained. "Miss Bickers says there is lots of big equipment in the kitchen and she has to be sure it is safe before I can help."

Mirabella raised her eyebrows. Miss Bickers didn't strike her as the over-protective type. "Hmmm . . . and what else do you know about Miss Bickers, Candice?"

Candice blushed, as if she knew a great secret. "Her first name is Minerva."

"How did you know that, Candice?"

"I overheard Mr. McVittie calling her by her first name." Candice giggled, joined in by all the little girls.

How strange. It would be very odd for a fellow employee to call the headmistress by her first name.

"Today, class, we are going to study finger printing." Mirabella cleared her throat. Now that the apples had been eaten, Mirabella began the class, placing a brown wooden box on the desk and opening it. "The authorities dismiss finger printing, treating it as an art form. But I foresee that there will be enormous implications for the identification of criminals."

Susan began waving her hand wildly. Despite resembling a Dresden doll, she was obviously athletic, and in addition, Mirabella knew for a fact that the little girl had a lovely singing voice.

"Yes Susan?"

"What is a criminal?"

"That's the *bad guy,* Sukey,*"* answered Gloria, rolling her eyes.

"Quite right," agreed Mirabella. "Please come to the table and bring your notebooks."

Gloria reluctantly set down her needlepoint and joined the other girls.

First the young girls went over their arithmetic. "You are doing very well class. Miss Bickers is doing a good job."

"And now for a very special treat. Everyone has a unique fingerprint," Mirabella continued. "No two are alike, even among identical twins. There are twelve distinct classifications. Your assignment will be to fingerprint your friends, label them, and classify them, until we have each of the twelve categories represented."

Mirabella removed from the wooden box the ink, a blotter, a roller, a rag, a small bottle of turpentine, a piece of wood, and a record book. She rolled a thin layer of ink on the wood piece and blotted it, wiping her hands on the rag. "I am now blotting the ink, class, to insure that there is not so much ink as to saturate the skin. A very small amount of ink is needed. If we smudge the ink, we won't be able to see the detail in the fingerprint."

"Hold the other person's thumb, *you* must apply the pressure, don't allow your subject to do it." She then took Susan's little thumb firmly in her hand, rolling the thumb slowly on the black ink. "Go slowly but with no pauses to insure an even print."

"Roll towards Susan for the thumbprint, starting with the point of most resistance." Susan's thumb was then placed on the record book, rolling towards Susan from the point of most to least resistance.

"Sukey's looks like little loops!" Amity exclaimed, looking at Susan's thumbprint.

"No, it's whirly-whirls!" Susan stated.

"It's both," replied Mirabella. "You see these curves? Do you see where the ridge ends?"

"But this one splits into other ridges," Susan considered.

"Excellent observation!" Mirabella approved. "These are two of the important distinctions which make each fingerprint unique: where the ridges end—and where they split into other ridges."

"Like a road," Candice stated.

"Or a tree with branches!" Susan interjected. "With little swirly birds singing on them."

"Oh, no! A smudge!" Gloria exclaimed, her eye attuned to every deviation.

"The utmost detail must be seen. Move at a steady pace with an even amount of pressure to get the least amount of smudges. Now, Amity, you take Candice's thumbprint."

"I'll mess it up!" exclaimed Amity.

"Then we'll do it again," replied Mirabella. "This is just for practice. It's the only way to learn. I'll tell you a secret: most of the policemen at Scotland Yard don't know how to do this."

"No!" the girls all replied in unison and astonishment.

"It is true," replied Mirabella. "You will know something Scotland Yard does not know."

"We know more than the coppers?" Gloria demanded.

"We should tell them," Amity suggested. "So then they will know."

"Someone far pushier than you has that well in hand," Mirabella murmured.

Amity took Candice's thumbprint with great care, and it was a passably good representation in Mirabella's mind.

"Mine looks like an arch—like over the train tunnels," Candice stated when her fingerprint had been taken.

"Excellent, Candice!" Mirabella stated. "Only a very small percentage of the population has fingerprints with that shape."

"It's an elaborate pattern," Gloria considered, tapping her dimpled cheek. "Much like a knitting pattern."

"I don't want to use a blanket with that pattern," giggled Susan. "I might get lost in the bed."

"It is too hard! How will we get someone to do that for us?"

Candice asked almost breathlessly, her copper brown eyes disturbed.

"Ah, that is where the detective work comes in. I will leave my box with you, and you must guard it and treat it like a magical box. Surely you can lure someone in here with one of Amity's fairy stories," Mirabella smiled, holding her finger to her lips. "Shhh! It's all *very* secret."

"Do we have to sneak out from our beds at night and go into the streets?" Candice asked with a shudder.

"Amity and me lived in the streets for a while—until they found us after the fire—and I never want to go back there," Susan exclaimed in a lilting, though strained, musical voice, waving her arms and looking almost ferocious in spite of her blonde hair and blue eyes.

"Most assuredly, you must not, under *any circumstances* venture out at night—or without an adult chaperone!" admonished Mirabella. "And anyone who would tell you to do so is *not* to be trusted!"

"It was very scary," agreed Amity, nodding wildly, suddenly looking to be the oldest and wisest in the room. "Even I knew they would find me and Sukey and I was still frightened. You can't sleep out in the light where people can see you—and it is *so cold*. And sometimes you are wet. And *always* you are hungry."

"I'll bet that's where Sukey learned to run so fast!" considered Gloria, covering her mouth with her hands.

"*No one* can run as fast as Sukey," Amity agreed proudly.

"I remember being hungry," Candice nodded sadly, her expression suddenly distant. "When I feel scared of being hungry now, I cook or plant."

"I do not like *any* place outside *Lady Graham's*," agreed Sukey, her expressive eyes frightened.

"I never want to leave," Candice chimed in. "They used to work us *very* hard at the other place, the work is easy *here*, and there is never anyone who would hurt you."

"Before they found out how important Candice's father was and went and got her," confided Susan. "At *the workhouse*."

"Oh, *no!*" exclaimed Mirabella, clutching her chest staring at the beautiful little girl before her. "You can't mean it!" Everyone shuddered, Mirabella most of all. At least *Lady Graham's* was an orphanage rather than a workhouse, which, from Miss Bickers' description was nothing more than a prison where children were worked until they died.

Utterly inexcusable.

Mirabella heard the bells of Westminster Abbey ringing in the background. *Whatsoever you do to the least of them, you do unto me.*

"My papa was a *police constable,"* repeated Candice, her rosy lips forming an awed whisper, obviously very proud of her parentage which had saved her life.

"They don't care what we do here," explained tiny Susan in a whisper, her large blue-grey eyes appearing even larger against her pale white skin. "No one cares—except Miss Bella."

"It *is* very boring here," confided Gloria, sighing, fingering her beautifully embroidered apron. All of the girls wore simple brown shift cotton dresses with white aprons and white caps with the exception of Gloria whose apron was outlined in lovely flowers. "I wish there was more to do. We get the smallest allotment of knitting yarn and almost no embroidery thread. If I had more, I would decorate *everyone's* apron." She kicked her serviceable brown boots against the table, revealing white knee socks.

"But your classes must take up a great deal of time," considered Mirabella. "And don't you have homework?"

The girls laughed.

"I don't like homework," chimed in Candice, her carrot-red hair bobbing. "I like to work in the garden and the kitchen. I only come here for the apple. I want to plant the seeds in the garden." Gingerly she unfolded her handkerchief containing all the apple seeds, displaying them proudly before refolding the cloth.

"Oh, your tomatoes were so good last year!" Amity exclaimed rubbing her stomach, even as Candice beamed.

"Is your library sufficient?" pressed Mirabella, attempting to return the subject to their scholastics.

"What's a . . . *library?*" asked Susan, glancing up.

"What's *sufficient?*" asked Candice.

"A library is a room with books," answered Mirabella. All the girls looked at her blankly.

Oh, this was *very* bad. She swallowed hard. "And sheet music. A library would have sheet music also."

Susan's jaw dropped. *"Music?* I want to go to the library! Where is it?"

"Oh, dear," murmured Mirabella. "Tell me, girls, how long do

your classes last every day?"

"From eight o'clock to ten o'clock," replied Amity. "And then we have homework. We all do ours, but lots of girls don't because Miss Bickers doesn't grade it anyway."

"I don't think she knows the answers herself," Gloria giggled, kicking her legs back and forth in the chair which was too high off the ground for her.

"Then what do you do?" asked Mirabella.

"Well, we have to wash and press our clothes and clean our rooms," answered Amity.

"And then it's time for lunch!" exclaimed Susan happily.

"In the afternoon, we clean the big rooms, and if we finish we get to sew or garden or play games, whatever we like to do," explained Candice.

"You girls do all the cleaning here?" Mirabella asked, startled.

"Yes," they all nodded in unison.

Perhaps they were being trained for domestic help after all. Cooking. Cleaning. Sewing. They weren't being overworked, she supposed, but these girls were far too bright to ignore their education.

"Is it difficult?" asked Mirabella.

"No, I run down the halls while I'm doing it, and I mop really fast, so I do that," replied Susan.

"And she sings while she mops," Amity added with a giggle.

"I mostly do the sewing. And all of the girls here have to help with the sewing and mopping and cleaning, so it's not so bad. Although I am the best seamstress," answered Gloria proudly. "And Candice helps with the cooking when they let her in the kitchen."

"And the gardening," added Candice.

"Where is Miss Bickers while you are doing the cleaning, cooking, sewing, and gardening?" asked Mirabella.

The girls all looked at each other, as if they knew, but didn't care to say.

"*All* of us know what it is like outside *Lady Graham's*, and we are all good girls," stated Amity, as if to divert the conversation.

"Do you have any music or dance classes?" asked Mirabella, although she already knew the answer.

The girls shook their heads.

No music, very little science, no French or German, and nothing for the exceptional students. They weren't even *required* to read and do their figures! The only requirement was their domestic chores.

"I wish we had singing class *all day*," interjected Susan.

"What about art classes?"

"Oh, *yes*," exclaimed Amity. "That is my *favorite* class! I like to paint trees and birds and—well, *everything*—even bugs!"

"Bugs! *Yuck*!" exclaimed Gloria.

"Is Miss Bickers a good teacher?" asked Mirabella.

"Oh, *yes*!" replied Amity. "Miss Bickers is a *very* good artist. She can draw *anything*. And paint, too! Most days after dinner we have an art class—and then we all clean up and wash ourselves at the wash basin before we go to bed."

"And on Saturday evening we even have tea and cookies in the parlor before bed!" added Gloria. "Mr. McVittie is off on Saturday night so they are pretty good!"

"Candice helps makes the cookies!" exclaimed Susan. "Yum!"

"Sometimes one of the policeman friends will come in and sing or otherwise play games with us," added Gloria, her dimples showing as she smiled. "It is *very* fun."

Amity whispered something in the younger girl's ear, to which Susan nodded emphatically.

"And does Miss Bickers paint a great deal?" asked Mirabella.

"That's all she does!" Amity laughed. "And except for the class we aren't allowed to go into her studio. She even keeps the door locked."

"Does Miss Bickers ever take you on field excursions?" asked Mirabella, frowning. "When she's not painting that is?"

"Oh, yes," Amity emphasized. "On Sunday we all go to church. We have a big ham for lunch—and then we do whatever we wish the rest of the day."

"We can even play badminton!" exclaimed Susan, clapping her hands together.

"I see. On Sunday you go to church. That wasn't precisely what I mean as a field excursion," managed Mirabella, placing her pencil beside her tablet. "Do you go to the parks—Hyde Park or Kensington Gardens for example?"

"Do you mean the gardens where the birds are?" asked Susan, her face lit up.

"Yes," Mirabella answered after some moments.

"No," replied the girls in unison.

"Ah-ha. And the London zoo. Has anyone ever taken you there?"

"Do you mean the cages where the birds are?" asked Susan. "The bigger birds like the pink flamingo?"

"Yes, I believe they have flamingos and the zoo," Mirabella state. "No."

"The Tower of London, St. Paul's Cathedral, Madame Tussauds wax museum, or Wyld's Monster Globe in Leicester Square, has anyone ever taken you there?"

"I heard Madame Tussauds has monsters. I've seen monsters and I did not like them," replied Susan, perplexed. "Why would I want anyone to take me to see monsters?"

Mirabella cleared her throat. "You certainly should not, Miss Susan. But these are not *real* monsters."

"I've seen the underground railway!" exclaimed Candice, clearly aware of her worldly status. "I hid there once."

"It sounds to me as if you girls have entirely too much time on your hands," considered Mirabella. "I definitely need to give you more homework and assignments—and to take you on more field trips."

Seeing that their faces lit up at the suggestion, she saw that her assumption had not been far off.

"I'll do the homework, but I don't want to leave *Lady Graham's*." Candice shook her head.

"I'll go if there's birds. Or singing. I love to hear singing," considered Susan, turning to Candice. "What if there are seeds? I'll bet you'd go if there were seeds, Candy."

"I'll go if it's away from here," Gloria agreed without hesitation, smirking at the other girls. "Miss Bella only means for a day, she doesn't mean *forever*."

"There you are," smiled Mirabella. "Gloria is not afraid to go outside these walls and to see the world."

"Are you sure it's safe, Miss Bella?" asked Amity. "I don't think it's safe."

"It isn't entirely safe," agreed Mirabella. "But it is glorious! I am just a farm girl and I was never so happy as when I came to London. Or, rather . . ." she paused, realizing the truth for the first time, "when I got my new position."

"Your new job?" Amity asked.

"Yes." Mirabella nodded, unable to stop herself from giggling. "However much my employer vexes me—and he does, terribly, almost beyond endurance!—it is the most fascinating existence imaginable to be in the presence of the Great Detective."

They are stared at her blankly.

"You like to be vexed?" Gloria asked.

"Oh, no!" Mirabella replied vehemently, rolling her eyes. "When you find the profession you were meant to do, whether it be motherhood, or sweeping the floors, or, like Candice, baking cookies, you will know."

Not for the first time, Mirabella thanked her lucky stars she had found a position with Sherlock Holmes. As she pictured Sherlock sitting in his armchair, smoking a pipe and reflecting on the case, she smiled. The odd thing was that, although he expected so much from her, she always seemed to be able to meet his expectations, even surprising herself.

I feel that somehow, in some way, I am becoming more myself when I am with him.

Perhaps Sherlock understood her better than she thought.

Miss Bickers was right, in these times it was very rare indeed for anyone to advance beyond the station he or she—and particularly she—was born into. For everyone except the very rich, life was hard, inflexible, and powerless.

She looked about her at the beautiful, beaming faces looking up at her. That was what she wanted for these girls: that they might realize their gifts and talents.

"All right ladies, let's analyze our fingerprints and categorize them," Mirabella announced confidently, but she felt discouraged. Unless their education was stepped up, how on earth were any of them going to function outside the orphanage when they reached adulthood?

In her heart she didn't believe that any of them outside of Amity had even the slightest interest in science. But here they all were, giving their best. For an apple.

After the class was complete, with four of the twelve categories represented, and the girls very lively at realizing they had something which was uniquely theirs and quite special, Mirabella began to pack up her supplies.

"Oh! Oh!" exclaimed Gloria, waving her hand frantically.

"Yes, Gloria?"

"Miss Mirabella! I know it's not science, but can we make Christmas gifts for each other this year? Last year some of the girls didn't receive any gifts."

"I don't think Father Christmas can find us," suggested Susan.

"That's because there is no—" explained Gloria, shaking her head.

"—YES, we will," interjected Mirabella. "And I will write a letter to Father Christmas giving him explicit directions to the orphanage—he might have thought you were somewhere else and couldn't find you. It is a very difficult building to see from the sky. But never fear: it's more than three months away so we have ample time for my letter to reach the North Pole. What would you like to make this year? Stockings with your names? Or wool scarves and mittens?"

"Or . . . what about lace hankies?" asked Gloria, the wheels in her mind clearly turning. "With flowers embroidered on them in *every* color."

"I could make cookies," suggested Candice, a suggestion which gained everyone's approval.

"If only I had enough yarn, I would knit blankets for *everyone,*" Gloria stated. "It's *cold* in the winter."

"Dolls! I wish you would make dolls, Gloria!" exclaimed Candice excitedly. "I want a doll with little black buttons for eyes and a red checkered dress."

"I want a notebook for drawing. Not for numbers," considered Susan, her finger to her white cheek. "And . . . and . . . a *pencil!* Is that too much to ask? If it is, maybe just the *pencil.* And one piece of paper. I wish to write a *song!*"

Mirabella felt her eyes watering even as she rummaged through her bag until she found a small tablet and a pencil—which she handed to Susan, giving her a hug. The little Dresden Doll appeared as if she might cry.

"I want a kitten," added Gloria. "When I had a Mommy and Daddy—we had a kitten. If I make blankets or dolls for everyone—may I have a kitten?"

"I'm sorry, I don't have one of those in my bag," giggled Mirabella. "But we'll write a letter to Father Christmas. And please . . . let's not mention the kitten to Miss Bickers."

All the girls shook their heads in immediate agreement, understanding evident in their expressions.

Proof that they are more savvy than other children of the same age, mused Mirabella. She would not wish this life on any of them, but it was evident that the orphan girls had not gone through their trials and learned nothing.

". . . And you, Susan, what would you like from Father Christmas?" pressed Mirabella. "Besides your pencil?"

"A new badminton racket?" suggested Amity. "Sukey is quite the best player!"

"She is," Candice agreed. "She beats *everyone*!"

"No," considered Susan, her blonde hair waving back and forth as she shook her head. "I'd like a dress of my own to wear on Saturday night and to Sunday church—not a uniform. A blue *velvet* dress. With *ribbons.*"

"I could make it if I had some material," Gloria stomped her brown serviceable boot on the floor.

Watching little Susan sway under the heavy brown material, Mirabella concluded that a less flattering outfit could not have been chosen. She determined to ask Miss Bickers if she might make a work dress in a different color: blue or green or pink.

But she already knew the answer: if she couldn't make a dress for *everyone* it wasn't likely to happen.

Dresses for Sunday church and special occasions were a different matter, however.

"I forgot the most important thing. I'd like my daddy back," sighed Candice, rubbing her eyes with her fist.

"We all would," whispered Amity, putting her arm around Candice.

Glancing at four pairs of sorrowful eyes which revealed the heartbreak in each of their lives—for a single moment not hiding the devastating grief—Mirabella perceived the girls' wisdom and depth of character for the first time. It wasn't an intelligence of math and science—*yet*—but it was a staggering luminosity nonetheless.

Such resilience. Mirabella took out her handkerchief and dabbed her own eyes. They all carried the pain with them; it had not diminished. Like Miss Bickers, they had lost their families, but somehow these children were all still open to happiness and brewing with love for life.

This was a brilliance of the soul—and the intellect—which surpassed all others.

"And what would you like for Christmas, Amity?" murmured Mirabella, swallowing hard. Now that she had a real job and her Aunt Martha provided her with room and board, she could spare a little to make nice presents for everyone—and her aunt was an excellent seamstress and would be happy to help her, she was sure.

And soon I will be on a real case with the amazing Sherlock Holmes! Mirabella was beside herself with excitement, even having no idea what the mission was as yet. It was just like Sherlock to tell her in his own time.

I am thrilled beyond measure! When she would have expected to feel dread and fear—no doubt there would be some small danger involved—all she felt instead was excitement! She had always thought she wanted to be in a laboratory experimenting, but she found that she longed for the thrill of the chase and the solving of the mystery.

"Hmmm . . ." considered Amity. "I know! A crystal ball!"

The other girls laughed in unison. "You don't need one Amy," giggled Susan. "You already *know.*"

"Maybe a notepad and a paint set, then, to put my drawings and stories in," giggled Amity. "I so love art. It's like the *best* dessert!"

Susan gingerly tore one of the pages from her new treasure and handed it to Amity. "Just *don't* draw any *bugs* on it!"

"Oh! I almost forgot!" Mirabella rummaged in her bag. And then she found the most unexpected luxury: a box of chocolates.

The "oohs" and "ahs" were very loud indeed.

"*Where* did you get *that*, Miss Bella?" Amity, her most curious student, asked, leaning over the desk.

"This," she held up the box, "is a gift from the renowned detective, *Sherlock Holmes*, to you, girls! When I told him how smart you are, and how you are all young scientists, he *could not resist*!"

Mirabella reminded herself that she had spoken the truth. The Great Detective was, in fact, not given the opportunity to resist his charitable impulses: his donation to London's poor was unbeknownst to him and was deducted from her unnecessarily extravagant clothing allowance for her first case (not yet commenced or even disclosed).

She felt only the slightest guilt over the chocolates which Sherlock had paid for; it was wrong to take so much for oneself without giving to those who were less fortunate.

"You did an excellent job today, girls, I am very proud of you." Mirabella held out the open box to her girls, even as she plopped a creamy dark chocolate orange soufflé into her mouth, savoring the divine confection. "Never forget that we are every bit as smart as the boys."

Mirabella said it though she didn't believe it in her heart. For the first time, apprehension encroached upon her excitement.

She hoped that Sherlock and John would not be sorry that they had trusted in her. She didn't even know the details of her assignment, and yet an uneasiness that it would be well beyond her abilities suddenly reared its ugly head.

The obvious fact that she would be required to present herself as a lady did not bode well. She was about as sophisticated as a barnyard chicken. And the only dancing she knew was country dancing.

For goodness' sake, calm down, Mirabella Hudson! Even though she felt fear and apprehension over bumbling the case, she would no doubt have a very small and inconsequential part. Perhaps she would be asked to dress up and deliver a note or something in that vein. It would be utterly ridiculous for Sherlock to trust her with more than that.

Of course he would not! She almost laughed at the absurdity of her fears.

"Now, line up and come select your piece of chocolate as reward for your superior performance."

Chapter Nine

"A *finishing* school?" Mirabella fell into the basket chair next to Holmes' fireside chair, never more astonished in her life. "My assignment is to attend a *finishing school* for ten weeks?"

"It is," Sherlock murmured, not looking up from his book, John Clerk Maxwell's "Molecules," a book which she herself had thoroughly enjoyed, but it annoyed her to no end that he was ignoring her after pronouncing her terrible fate—a fate which he intended to instigate.

"Have you gone quite mad, Mr. Holmes? When European royalty wish their daughters to become sophisticated—they send them to *Miss de Beauvais'*."

"So I have heard," replied Sherlock disinterestedly, putting his book on the end table beside him and picking up his violin. His white cotton Byronesque blouse was open at the chest as he plucked on the violin, revealing the impressive results of a life of athletic pursuits.

"Of all the places I *do not belong* a finishing school is at the top of the list." Having been raised on a country farm, she could milk a cow, make butter, grind wheat, shoot and skin a pheasant, and given a little dirt, grow her own vegetables.

"Sadly, I must agree."

She rolled her eyes at him, but what could she say as he was only agreeing with her?

I am as far from refined as can be! If the truth be known, she could even make whiskey. A country girl did not come of age without learning the truly important skills. She could brew the whiskey, pass it around at the barn dance along with her apple pie, and dance an Irish jig after serving up the dinner.

And this country girl was being enrolled in not just any finishing school but the premier finishing school in London: *Miss de Beauvais' Finishing School for Distinguished Young Ladies.*

The horror of her fate took complete hold of her in an instant.

"Then w-w-hy would you—Mr. Holmes, I c-c-annot conceive . . ." she wailed. "I will be the laughing stock of all of London inside of an hour!"

"Indeed?" Sherlock glanced up at her in the most annoyingly condescending manner. "And how will all of London, as you put it, discover your location, Miss Hudson? And why should the good citizens of Great Britain care? I believe you overestimate the general population's interest in your comings and goings, Miss Hudson."

"I can never be one of them!" exclaimed Mirabella, throwing her head into her hands. "They will spot me as an imposter within seconds!"

"Certainly they would in those clothes," Sherlock murmured without argument. "Why haven't you procured more appropriate attire?"

"Aunt Martha is working on my wardrobe. And this dress is new." Indignantly Mirabella sat straight up in the basket chair, smoothing her new pink gown framed in white lace which she had only just sewn. "Though my dress might be simple, it is not faded and I think it looks very well."

"The neckline is lower cut than is common for day wear," Sherlock muttered.

She raised her eyebrows. "The square neckline is trimmed in lace and still within the bounds of decorum." She was not a fine lady who could look forward to wearing a wickedly revealing ball gown during her London season and this was the concession she made to herself.

"In the meantime, discard forever the leather corset and procure a new pair of leather boots," he added.

She stood and tugged at the leather corset vest wrapped around her waist which accentuated her hourglass shape. Her waistline might not be twenty inches, but at least she had one.

Leave it to Sherlock Holmes to make her feel she was inadequate at the very moment she was feeling pleased with herself.

Involuntarily Mirabella pushed her bangs out of her eyes. She had taken great pains to pin her hair atop her head in a simple but becoming style, accented with a pink velvet ribbon, a treasured gift from her aunt. Truly the only part of her outfit to find fault with were her worn brown boots which she had once thought so stylish and which still served her well.

"So you are a fashion expert, Mr. Holmes?" She placed her hands on her waist, standing in front of the Great Detective.

"I am not. Consult with your aunt; her language leaves much to be desired, unlike your own which is passable—there is just too much of it—but Mrs. Hudson *is* a fashionable woman. If that fails, there is no greater expert on women than our good doctor."

"I am, in fact, well versed on ladies' fashions," Dr. Watson stated, only just entering the parlor from his rooms. "And I would be happy to assist, Miss Mirabella." She spun around to look at him, which always raised her spirits to behold the handsome doctor.

"Yes, yes, Watson is the man for the job," Sherlock reiterated. "Take a look at his fine raiment molded perfectly to his form. Any other professional man not in the upper classes would consider a tailor-made suit made to his measurements well beyond his income."

"And what would you have me do, Holmes? Shop at *E. Moses & Son*? And wear a mass-produced suit?" John Watson formed the words "mass-produced" with disdain, as if they were poison on his lips.

"That, or shop at Petticoat Lane," Sherlock replied, nonplussed, placing tobacco into his pipe.

"Second-hand clothing? Are you quite mad, Holmes?" Watson exclaimed, placing his hand to his forehead as if he were preparing to faint.

"There is an excellent quality of clothing available at Petticoat Lane," rebuffed Sherlock. "Much of the clothing was cast off by the upper crust."

"Several seasons ago," Watson rebuffed disdainfully.

"Almost every item in my wardrobe is from that source."

"That is most evident," muttered Dr. Watson, "including your women's corsets and bonnets, Holmes."

"I have to procure my women's clothing somewhere, and I certainly won't pay top dollar." Sherlock shrugged. "The assortment at Petticoat Lane is exceptional, and the quality not far behind." He turned to Mirabella. "But I will admit that Watson has the right of it where you are concerned, Miss Belle. Clothing made specifically to your proportions will immediately set you apart as a high-born miss. Pre-fabricated clothing will reveal you to be of the middle-class. That will never do. It must be believed that you are of the upper class."

Sherlock took a puff on his pipe before adding, "You must pretend you are wealthy—just as Watson does."

"Really, Holmes! Just because I wish to dress with distinction," Dr. Watson protested.

"And what do you think of my outfit, Dr. Watson?" Mirabella interjected, turning towards him as he moved to be seated in his armchair next to the fire. She curtsied before him.

John Watson took a moment to answer as he was visibly shaken from Sherlock's suggestion that he could save money by dismissing his tailor.

"Although the leather corset is most becoming and I know it to be the style in some circles," John Watson smiled appreciatively at her, "an upper class young lady would not wear it. It does define your station in life, Miss Mirabella."

"I guarantee if I take off the corset, no one will be fooled as to my station in life!" she exclaimed, almost in tears as she covered her mouth with her hands.

"Very likely," agreed Sherlock, looking about for a piece of sheet music, adding distractedly, "A lady does not flaunt her goods. She knows her worth."

"A bit more coarsely than I would have put it, old man," Watson reprimanded, leaning back in his seat. He cleared his throat. "I'm not saying that you shouldn't wear a corset, Miss Mirabella, but it should be worn under the clothing."

"Well naturally a corset must be worn on the inside of the clothing," Mirabella muttered, picking up the duster to keep her hands busy as she glanced at him through her eyelashes. It was a most embarrassing topic, which ordinarily she would never discuss with a gentleman, but he was a doctor after all. "A young lady can't go without one."

"Of course. There are a great deal of health benefits to corseting," Dr. Watson stated in his professional tone of voice. "A corset supports the back—and holds women's organs in place."

Sherlock raised his eyebrow at his mate, placing the sheet of music on the table before him, studying it while he conversed. "You believe that women have a greater need to hold their organs in place than men do?"

"It is not my belief, but a medical fact," Dr. Watson replied in his professional capacity. "It is well known in medical circles. The male is the stronger sex and in less need of support. The corset is also needed due to the childbearing functions of women."

"Ah. I marvel that the women in Jane Austen's era were able to bear children at all—as did my mother and your mother, being as they were without the aid of corsets."

"M-men are much more active in their everyday lives," Dr. Watson protested.

"And yet our organs follow us about quite nicely." Sherlock chuckled, glancing up momentarily. "I would question that supposition, Watson. Consider that the corset is nothing more than a whim of fashion. And, as such, Miss Belle must wear one—and on the correct side of her clothing."

"You, unlike me, are not well versed in medicine, Holmes," Dr. Watson retorted.

"Back to the matter at hand." Sherlock turned his gaze to Mirabella, now dusting the fireplace mantle. "More than clothing or speech, a woman's attitude defines her station in life. I can assure you that if the Duchess of Devonshire were dressed in a barmaid's clothing, you would know she wasn't a barmaid."

"So it is hopeless," she concluded, turning to face him. Sherlock's words were the final nail in the coffin, having the effect of convincing her that she was incapable of performing this assignment. "No matter what I wear, I will be unable to fool anyone. Is this what you are telling me, Mr. Holmes?"

"To the contrary," Sherlock replied. "I am saying that you must also work on the manner in which you present yourself to others, Miss Belle—in addition to improving your wardrobe."

"How can I be anyone other than who I am? Oh *no!*" She gasped, suddenly realizing her situation, as she dropped the duster where she stood and covered her face with her hands. "I've already spent half of your money on apparel, Mr. Holmes! Even with all the frugalities it was a huge sum!"

"Precisely."

"I'll have to pay it back," she gulped. "I can't go *there.*"

"Can't go *where?*" Sherlock looked up momentarily from plucking his violin. His complexion was clear, healed of all wounds, and he was unusually well-groomed, his hair over-long but his face shaven. He was of a calmer bent than she had seen him in recent days.

Unlike herself, whom he had only just ignited a fire under.

"I can't go a finishing school."

"Why not, pray tell? From your complete lack of knowledge on how to be a proper young lady, you would seem to be the perfect candidate."

Dr. Watson cleared his throat, sitting across from them. "Now, Holmes, if she doesn't want to . . ." He tipped his brown derby hat at Holmes, running his hands along his leather suspenders, the muscles in his arms accentuated as he leaned forward in his chair.

Mirabella shook her head vehemently. "Because I would be found out even before I opened my mouth, your cover would be disclosed, and it would be impossible to place someone who might be *successful* at that point in *Miss de Beauvais'*."

"*Before* you open your mouth, Miss Hudson? In the first place, it is not possible to measure the unit of time before you open your mouth— that moment of silence is not be detectable to the human ear," Sherlock considered. His tone was strangely consoling. "But I shouldn't regard it, my dear. Fortunately we are not so foolish as to place our hopes for success on the rare instances when you are not making noise."

"What Holmes means to say is that all will be well," Watson choked in his attempt to stifle his laughter, forming a fist in front of his lips. "Clearly there is a plan in place masterminded by our friend here."

"If I am so stupid and have nothing to contribute to this conversation, I wonder that you should wish me to be part of your ingenious plan, Mr. Holmes," Mirabella retorted, attempting to appear sophisticated and aloof although her heart was sinking. Sherlock's rudeness had, at least, taken her mind off her devastation as she narrowed her eyes in anger at him. "And besides, you only prove my point: we are all in agreement that I am not sophisticated enough to enter *Miss de Beauvais'*."

"I beg you do not concern yourself, my girl," Sherlock replied consolingly. "There will be many awkward, gangling females without polish in the institution—hence their presence alongside you. The only difference between them and you is that they are awkward, gangling females *with money.*"

"Thank you, Mr. Holmes, my confidence has risen to new heights with your encouraging words. I am much consoled." Her eyes moved along the mantelpiece where a wax replica of Holmes' head proudly sat—a hole carved through the wax by a gun shot. At this moment she could well understand the sentiment which caused the shooter to put it there.

"Excellent. I am glad to be of service." Sherlock pronounced.

"*Neigh!*" As the sounds from the activity outside their London flat drifted through the window, Sherlock picked up his magnifying glass and began studying his violin strings through the device. Almost as if in the room with them, the whinny of a horse being walked in the street and the shouts of a hansom cab driver joined the conversation.

"And now may we discuss how *you* might be of service, Miss Hudson," murmured Sherlock, not moving his eyes from his violin. "Then may we proceed to the outline of your assignment?"

"No! I cannot do it! Have you not been listening? I am a total and utter failure at . . . at . . . being a *girl*," she gasped, standing to move to the bay window and glance at the passers-by on Baker Street, her back to the gentlemen. "And what's more, I don't *want* to be one!"

"At that, you have failed miserably." Dr. Watson cleared his throat, making a point to look away, selecting a teacake from the table between them while eyeing the blueberries and cream next to the tea service.

"At *everything* I have failed miserably!" She spun around to face Sherlock. "I want to be a scientist. I have no need whatsoever to go to *finishing school.*"

Dr. Watson straightened his fashionable silk tie and set his hat on the table between them, brushing his hand through his blonde-streaked hair. "It might reduce the escalating turmoil, Holmes, if you were to explain to Miss Mirabella that the finishing school is not for the purpose of finishing *her* but of finishing someone else."

"It might." Sherlock returned to playing his violin in a most annoying manner as they spoke. "However, I do not know why I must explain everything to Miss Belle as if *I* were working *for her* before it behooves her to behave in a professional capacity, or failing professionalism, *like a lady*. Perhaps there would be a benefit in her attendance at the finishing school after all."

"What is the purpose of the finishing school if not to finish me?" repeated Mirabella, suddenly interested.

"We don't know," offered Watson. "A government plot, anarchists, criminals. To be quite honest, we don't yet know."

"Please *please* Mr. Holmes, send someone else." It was clear that this particular role was wholly unsuited to her abilities. Doomed to failure. "Not me! I'll pay you back for the clothes! I never wanted them anyway!"

"There aren't enough dirty jars in all of London for you to pay me back, Miss Hudson. And if there were, you might have enough money to enter university, oh . . . you're seventeen years of age now . . . when you are thirty-five years old."

"Egad!" She gulped hard, taking the handkerchief Dr. Watson handed her to dab her eyes. She was utterly shocked at the idea of being so ancient. *"Even older than you,* Mr. Holmes!"

"Yes, a regular fossil," he frowned, popping a blueberry in his mouth as he glanced at the clock on the mantelpiece. "It is unlikely you shall live that long."

"Tell her, Holmes. I've had quite enough of this," admonished Dr. Watson, leaning forward in his leather chair as he turned towards her. "There is a certain danger, Miss Mirabella."

"Well, naturally, Dr. Watson. It is a case of some type—there must be a criminal element," exclaimed Mirabella. "Of course there is a danger! That doesn't frighten me in the least. But a finishing school? The very idea is utterly *terrifying*!"

"But don't you see, Miss Belle?" Sherlock began.

"Don't I see what?"

She thought she saw something approaching a smile on his lips as set down his violin—*finally! Praise the heavens!*—picking up his teacup and taking a sip of tea. "The finishing school is not the important part of the assignment. It is something to be endured. The case requires a particular type of girl, whom I believe you to be. This is precisely why I have chosen you for this position."

"Whatever do you mean?"

"I tested you on the first day of our meeting—did you not observe it?"

"I observed that you almost blinded me with your spatula!"

"My *platina* spatula."

"Very well, I . . ."

"I was testing your reflexes and your strength. Frankly, I was astonished."

"Holmes is rarely astonished," remarked Dr. Watson, stirring a lump of sugar into his cup of tea.

"I don't see how blinding me with your spatula should astonish you," shrugged Mirabella, returning from the window framed by sheer white curtains to sit beside them in the wicker chair.

"Don't slouch," Sherlock commanded. "And it taught me something of your fighting potential."

"I don't know how to fight! Granted, I had a regular tussle with my brothers, but not a real—"

"You will learn to fight by the time we are finished with you. I'm something of a boxer myself, you know. The raw material is there— that's all we need."

"Sherlock Holmes!" she exclaimed, suddenly indignant as she jumped from her chair to a standing position. "You purposely tripped me! I *knew* it!"

"Of course I did. I do everything with purpose." He sniffed defensively. "I'm not wandering about willy nilly not having any idea what I am doing."

"For shame, Mr. Holmes!" She passed her finger back and forth. "Don't you feel ashamed of yourself for attacking an unsuspecting woman?"

"Naturally I don't. I meant no harm to your person: it was a scientific experiment only."

Dr. Watson broke into laughter, unable to contain himself any longer. "And what was the purpose of this *experiment*?"

"I wanted to see how Miss Hudson regarded her surroundings—and if she could fall. I wanted to observe her instinct for survival."

"Mr. Holmes, if I had any instinct for survival whatsoever, I would have run screaming from this place long ago." A picture of the Great Detective's bedroom came immediately to mind, the walls of which were lined with pictures of celebrated criminals. She avoided the room as much as possible, which was macabre to say the least, but it was necessary to dust on occasion.

It must be a very strange person indeed who would consider pictures of one's enemies on one's bedroom walls to be conducive to a good night's sleep. Dr. Watson's bedroom, on the other hand . . . she blushed, realizing she should not be thinking about such things.

Sherlock glanced up at her without comment, and it disconcerted her that she knew the meaning of his expression: their discussion would not be of a much longer duration. As all of Scotland Yard knew as well, once a conversation was no longer of interest to Sherlock Holmes, he disengaged himself without apology or aplomb and regardless of whom it might offend.

She made one last attempt at reasoning with the unreasonable. "But that is neither here nor there. What is to the point is that survival in the midst of a mad scientist waving a spatula about is a far different thing from fighting criminals!"

"Watson and I will teach you every manner of self-defense, Miss Belle." He dismissed her with a wave of his hand. "Then—and only then—shall you enter *Miss de Beauvais' Finishing School for Distinguished Young Ladies.*"

Chapter Ten

"Now I am completely baffled!" Mirabella pursued the conversation anew in a final attempt to gain more information about the proposed mission. It was beginning to look as if her secondary plan, that of jumping from the London Tower had more merit under the present circumstances.

"*Sit down*, Miss Hudson!" commanded Holmes. "If you should ever cease chattering for even three seconds—I am quite certain I would explain it all to you. Why is it that the less you know about a subject, the more you speak about it?"

"Oh, I'm so very sorry. Please do forgive my thoughtlessness in interrupting your plans for my torture." She swallowed hard, moving past the brass accoutrements on the fireplace mantle to sit in the basket chair situated next to Dr. Watson. "I always talk when I am frightened out of my mind. Yes, please do tell me everything."

Sherlock raised his eyebrows disapprovingly at her. "You understand that this is in the strictest confidence—and can go no further than this. You cannot even tell Mrs. Hudson."

"Not even Aunt Martha?" Mirabella covered her mouth in dismay.

"Absolutely not. Do you wish to put her life in danger?"

"No, of course not."

"Then you will promise me that everything I say to you is in the strictest confidence—upon threat of dismissal."

"I promise," she gulped, running her hands along the pink velvet ribbon in her hair as she sat back, attempting to disappear into her chair.

"There is a young lady—a *princess* of a small Slavic country."

"A Slavic princess?" she asked, suddenly mesmerized. She could not help herself, the romance of it all swept her away. She sighed. "Like an Arabian princess?"

"A Serbian princess, to be precise." Holmes sighed heavily as he placed his teacup on the table. "Pray, may I continue Miss Belle?"

She nodded, wrapping her hands around her cheeks. "Of which country?"

"Montenegro." Holmes closed his eyes momentarily, as if he were listening to music. He often did this even as he was speaking, tapping his fingers on the arm of his chair or picking up his violin and going through the motions of the notes. At this time he picked up his violin.

"Oh," she sighed. "The Black Mountains . . ."

Sherlock opened his eyes and momentarily separated the violin from his chin. "Princess Elena has caught the eye of Prince Victor Emmanuel III of Italy."

"The crown prince. Oh, *my*," she sighed. "Like a fairytale."

"Some do not consider it so," Watson mused with raised eyebrows, his expression foreboding.

Sherlock nodded indifferently, continuing with his piece in his mind. "Princess Elena Petrović-Njegoš of Montenegro is not favored— many do not think she is worthy of the House of Savoy. But the Prince of Naples was smitten—he saw her at a ball in St. Petersburg."

"He *saw* her?" Mirabella repeated disbelieving, her eyes moving from Holmes to Watson. "All this because he saw her? She can be no more than a stranger to him."

"Prince Victor Emmanuel had only just introduced himself to her when a fight ensued over Elena and she was swept away from the ball under guard," Watson explained, nodding his chin towards her.

"A *fight*? In a formal ball?" Mirabella asked, disbelieving.

"Princess Elena's popularity on the dance floor and the lack of openings on her dance card inspired a heated argument which led to a duel between Prince Arsen of Serbia and Baron Carl Gustav von Mannerheim of Finland," Dr. Watson explained matter-of-factly as if it were an every day occurrence.

"I understand that the Baron was wounded in the duel," Sherlock added.

"I never heard of such a thing in civilized society!" Mirabella exclaimed.

"The Princess of Montenegro must be quite beautiful to have inspired such emotions," Dr. Watson murmured.

Sherlock shrugged, placing the violin beside his chair. "They say there is a Madonna-like quality to her countenance: serene and contained. She is tall, slim, with very dark hair and eyes."

"And she is somewhat tribal," added Watson, watching the proceedings with obvious interest.

"*Tribal?*" Mirabella repeated in a disbelieving manner. "Do you mean she paints her face and performs voodoo?"

"Unlikely," Holmes reflected, turning his calabash pipe round in his hands in a circular motion, deep in thought. "But this is not information we are privy to. What we do know is that Princess Elena is an excellent huntress—hence she knows how to use weapons—and can ride a horse like a master."

"So, what is the problem?" Mirabella asked, fast losing interest. "Why must she enter a finishing school? Wouldn't it be safer to hide her somewhere until her marriage to Prince Victor Emmanuel?"

"In the first place, the marriage is not settled," Sherlock replied with more criticism in his expression towards her than Mirabella felt was necessary. "The two have never spoken outside of the brief introduction at the St. Petersburg ball. And, in the second place, Princess Elena requires a finishing school."

"Why? It sounds as if she doesn't require any assistance in procuring admirers. In fact, her primary problem is that she has too many," Mirabella persisted, feeling a sense of inadequacy as she murmured the words. "She appears to be all that is elegance."

"The princess of Montenegro does not speak," Sherlock muttered with indifference, as if he were growing bored with the conversation.

"Whatever do you mean, Mr. Holmes? Of course she speaks." Mirabella rolled her eyes.

"Not in social situations." Holmes cleared his throat. "She becomes positively tongue-tied: she does not engage in polite conversation. Unlike you, Miss Belle, who never stops talking, she cannot find her tongue. Would that you could lose yours and she would find it."

"Princess Elena is not the only individual with difficulty making *polite* conversation," murmured Mirabella.

"Fortunately my continued survival does not depend upon it."

That remains to be seen. "But if the princess is so inept in society, how is it that a duel was fought over her attentions?" she asked incredulously.

"Even I can answer that," smiled Watson with an expression of first-hand knowledge which she could not like, his turquoise eyes particularly entrancing. "The very beautiful can manage a lack of speech more than the very ugly. The plain girl must compensate with personality—not so with beauty."

"She merely stands about and smiles—or dances—which is mistaken for solemnity and fashionable boredom," added Holmes.

"Still—I don't think she needs our help," shrugged Mirabella, wrapping her arms around her waist.

"Ah, well, fortunately for our pocketbooks and my reputation, Miss Hudson, what you think and what the royal family of Montenegro thinks are two different things. The king strongly desires this alliance with Italy—it would be an excellent connection for their little country."

"But what does *she* desire? The princess I mean."

"That is not your concern. She is not paying you—the royal family is."

"And that is not all," added Dr. Watson, moving to lean against the walnut fireplace mantel, facing her, his large muscular frame never more apparent. "Princess Elena is not the first royal daughter in need of training in the ways of society. It should be a straightforward matter to simply place her in a finishing school. But there is a threat on her life."

"How deplorable! It can't be true!" Mirabella exclaimed, momentarily covering her mouth with her hand in dismay. "Why would anyone wish her dead? Just because she cannot make good conversation—"

"Miss Belle, *think*," demanded Sherlock, his brow suddenly knitted into a frown.

"Well, because . . . you said . . . some do not wish the union, I suppose. And yet—"

"Correct." Sherlock pronounced, his expression not favorable but slightly less agitated.

"But why should anyone possibly care if the princess of Montenegro marries the crown prince of Italy? Does Prince Victor Emmanuel's family oppose the match?"

"It is a logical deduction." Sherlock nodded approvingly. "We would not expect King Umberto I and Princess Margherita of Savoy, the Queen consort of Italy, to favor the match, but we have no way of knowing since we are in the employ of Montenegro and not on a first name basis with the royal family of Italy."

"And, even if they did not favor the match, would they stoop to murdering their son's intended?" asked Watson. "It does not seem likely."

"Stranger things have happened." Sherlock shrugged. He added, "Another interesting fact is that Princess Elena's mother, Queen consort Milena Vukotić, does *not* favor the match, in opposition to her husband."

"Why is that?" Mirabella asked, her countenance falling in heartfelt sympathy for the princess. "Oh, my. This is far worse than Romeo and Juliet! Everything is stacked against them—and this is making less and less sense."

"If you would only *think*, Miss Hudson, and apply what you know, the mystery unfolding before us would not be so confusing," Sherlock countered. "Lives depend upon your utilizing your brain, Miss Hudson. *Perhaps your own life.*"

"I give up." Mirabella sighed heavily. "Why does the queen of Montenegro not favor the match?"

"Elena would necessarily have to become Catholic to marry Prince Victor Emmanuel," Sherlock replied mechanically, tapping his forefinger on his cheek. "Italy is a Catholic country."

"And you believe the queen objects to her religion?" Mirabella asked.

"I can see no other reason," Sherlock considered. "Queen Milena has married off other daughters to international royals without any obvious objections."

"For a small Slavic country, the king and queen of Montenegro have done very well in their daughters' alliances," Dr. Watson mused. "One daughter will wed a Battenberg prince, another the cousin of Alexander I. Anastasija will marry the duke of Leuchtenberg.

"What religion is Princess Elena?" Mirabella asked.

"Serbian Orthodox," Sherlock replied.

"It *is* a Christian religion," Mirabella mused.

"Historically, the Catholics do not consider the Protestants to be Christian and vice-versa. There is often disagreement among the various sects. That they all follow Christ appears to be less important than who is superior to whom." Sherlock smiled.

"To some, religious belief is important in marriage," Mirabella replied indignantly, placing her hands on her hips. "Apparently their religion is of greater concern to the queen consort than to the king. And Queen Milena's wishes are of no moment, which tells me how women are viewed and how the daughter was raised."

"Unless it is the daughter's wishes which are the motivating factor," Dr. Watson mused. "Perhaps King Nicholas respects his daughter *that much.*"

"I seriously doubt if that is the case," Mirabella pronounced.

"Miss Hudson, we may speculate, but we do not draw conclusions until we have the facts at hand," he admonished a bit more severely than was the norm, even for him. "Otherwise, we are engaging in nothing but malicious gossip. Moreover, *lives are at stake.* Perhaps the lives of entire countries. We must be utterly devoted to the facts and nothing more."

"At any rate, I fail to see what I can do," murmured Mirabella.

"I am so pleased that we finally come to how you might be of assistance, Miss Belle," remarked Sherlock cordially. "Do I dare to hope that is an interest of yours? To be perfectly honest, my dear girl, I had fully anticipated having to beg my employee to do that which is useful to me. And, yet, in a record time of only forty-five minutes, you have alluded to the subject. Granted it is a mere hint on your part, but it fills my heart with anticipation."

"You might have told me at any time, Mr. Holmes, I am sure," muttered Mirabella. Rolling her eyes, she caught sight of the stacks of papers on Sherlock's desk, held in place with a microscope. No matter how fast she dusted and organized, he was always just ahead of her in creating disaster. She shuddered to think about the mess which would be waiting for her upon her return from the finishing school.

I had best not go. There is too much to do here.

"I was waiting until you had given me permission to explain the circumstances in the hope that you might look favorably upon my humble request." Sherlock took a puff on his pipe.

She glared at him in a manner which she hoped was quite unfavorable.

"You, Miss Belle, will be in the school to protect Princess Elena. And to acquaint yourself with others who attempt to worm their way into her affections. To *watch, learn, report*—and protect."

"Oh, yes, I see," Mirabella murmured, understanding at once. "To try to learn who might wish her harm."

"An insider, as it were," Dr. Watson repeated.

Mirabella gulped, sitting straight up in alarm, and exclaiming, "But what if she does not . . . *like* me?"

"Not an issue. Princess Elena has been instructed to stay close to you at all times by the king and queen of Montenegro."

"And where will you and Dr. Watson be?" Mirabella gulped.

"We will be nearby, watching and investigating. We will have a trusted man posted on the inside at all times. Princess Elena herself has two large Serbian bodyguards." He added softly, "I am taking every precaution to insure that no harm comes to you, Miss Belle."

John Watson turned abruptly towards Sherlock, worry written across his face. "How much danger is there, Holmes? If you think these men capable of murder, should Miss Mirabella truly be involved?"

"There is a danger," Sherlock agreed, his expression severe. "But if Miss Hudson pays attention and does as she is told, she will emerge unscathed."

"Oh, I don't think, Holmes—" Watson shook his head.

"Any lack of safety is entirely at her door. *I will not fail her*," Sherlock insisted.

"I'm not afraid of the villains!" Mirabella protested. "Only of the finishing school!"

John Watson could not help chuckling despite the concern in his eyes. "Miss Mirabella, I beg you to consider refusing the case."

"It is not an option," Sherlock stated abruptly. "Let me remind you that this case is the source of all our incomes, upon which depends my reputation. If my reputation is ruined, none of us will eat, and you, Miss Hudson, will never go to university."

"I could support us with my medical practice," Dr. Watson protested.

Sherlock tapped his pipe on his armchair, his eyebrows raised. "You, Dr. Watson, have ten to fifteen medical clients per week."

"I have enough," Watson retorted, looking every bit the professional man as he raised his chin and narrowed his eyes.

"Although the number is an improvement over having no patients, as you had when you returned from the war and you in fact were the patient, and I think it the ideal practice for you at this time, it is not enough to support either you or us."

"I would not put Miss Mirabella in harm's way—"

"My good man, you do not produce enough income to support your clothing and gambling, much less to house and feed us all. And as for my professional career, it is a new endeavor for me as well. I am young, I am disliked, and my reputation could be destroyed with one failed case," Sherlock argued, somber again, turning towards Mirabella. "Without this case, Miss Hudson, you do not have a position. *None of us do.*"

"But how . . . how will I communicate with you while in the school?" she asked, swallowing hard. Sherlock's words had cinched the deal: she was unlikely to find another position, steady employment was not her strong suit, and she would not be a charge on her aunt with no funds of her own.

Mirabella was quite determined. *I will go to university.*

"The telegraph office is some blocks away," Sherlock stated.

"Which is by no means an immediate communication," Mirabella protested.

"You can get a message to us through our man," Sherlock added. "The princess has two bodyguards and a trusted representative who will also know how to reach us. And we will visit you like clockwork. You will determine with Princess Elena when she attends to her toilette or some such thing and set a regular time for us to visit." He sighed with indifference. "Do not worry, Miss Hudson, by the time we have finished your training you will be perfectly capable of protecting both yourself and the princess, should the need arise which I do not anticipate."

Her heart lifted somewhat at the idea of training in the fighting arts. Now *that* was a useful subject.

She had longed to be on one of Sherlock's cases. And after all, her part was rather insignificant. The princess had bodyguards. Sherlock and Dr. Watson would be investigating who the attacker was.

"What is it now, Miss Mirabella?" asked John Watson affectionately, his ordinarily crisp manner somewhat softened. He ran his fingers along his moustache while his elbow rested on the mantelpiece.

"Oh, nothing." She sighed. It was only John Watson who ever noticed that something was amiss—or asked her how she felt. "It only just crossed my mind that no doubt for the price of this most exclusive finishing school for only ten weeks, I might have attended the university for one year."

"Yes, but *I* am not paying your tuition," advised Sherlock. "King Nicholas I of Montenegro is. And why do you need to go to the university when you have the finest science teacher in the world not only in your vicinity—but *paying* you to be in his vicinity?"

"And to wash his jars, clean his floors, label his chemicals, and index his experiments—leaving him free to do the *science*," interjected Dr. Watson, moving towards the gasogene, where the ginger, sugar, and water were already in the lower compartment. He placed a cup beneath the spout, adding tartaric acid and sodium bicarbonate to the upper compartment. The experiment begun, and the carbon dioxide forming which would produce a gas to push the liquid in the lower compartment through the spout in the form of a carbonated ginger beverage, he returned to his seat.

"As I recall, Miss Hudson said it was her greatest wish to be in my presence," considered Sherlock. "Which, I might add, was a very sensible remark, one of the few I have heard her utter."

"Please don't misunderstand, Mr. Holmes. I am ever so grateful to have this position. But perhaps I would someday wish to be a scientist rather than a dishwasher and a maid," replied Mirabella, rising to take the ginger beer to Dr. Watson. "For example, that article on molecules you were reading by Maxwell, do you not find it fascinating?"

"In what way, Miss Belle?" Sherlock asked, raising his eyebrows in apparent interest.

"Maxwell cites the eventual diffusion of all gases, which he declares is proof of the motion of molecules," she replied.

"I find it far more interesting and applicable—remember that all science is relevant only in its application to our work—that the diffusion of liquids might require a day whereas the equivalent in gases requires one second," Sherlock considered.

"And even more interesting is that certain liquids can diffuse through colloid solids such as jelly and gum," Mirabella added.

"Speaking of jelly and gum, what shall we be having for dinner, Miss Belle?" Sherlock asked.

She glared at him. She was attempting to show Sherlock Holmes she was worthy of academic advancement, and in one fell swoop, he had relegated her to the role of domestic servant without the slightest nod to her scientific understanding. Apparently he considered her to be incapable of intelligent conversation.

Dr. Watson picked up his newspaper and began scanning it while sipping his ginger ale, oblivious to her aggravation—and obviously bored with the conversation.

"Won't it be time to make our dinner?" Sherlock commanded. It was not a question.

"So you'll be dining in, Mr. Holmes?" she asked. Mrs. Hudson provided the breakfast, while Mirabella prepared the afternoon tea and the dinner if the gentlemen were not dining out, often utilizing food from her aunt's larder. The meat had to be purchased almost daily, the vegetables and fruits every few days, the breads made at home or sometimes bought.

"As I said," he replied curtly.

Mentally Mirabella scanned the contents of Aunt Martha's wooden, porcelain-lined box in which she kept the fresh food purchased daily from the market. Ice was delivered three times per week which went into the box.

The icebox is empty. The results of her mental scan returned the verdict. Very often Mirabella did not do the shopping, as she had enough to do just keeping the flat clean, tending to the laboratory, and preparing meals as needed. *Sigh. But today I shall be going shopping.*

Naturally Mirabella had every intention of preparing the dinner—it was her job—but she might wish to be treated with the regard given to an apprentice rather than as a domestic.

"To be sure, you will have your dinner, Mr. Holmes," she replied. "Ordinarily you do not express such an interest in it, so I am encouraged to see that your appetite is improving."

"All of our appetites are improving," Sherlock murmured in a low voice, glancing at Watson and then at her. She must be mistaken, it seemed there was a flash of anger in his eyes to match her own.

What reason could Sherlock possibly have for anger? She did precisely everything he told her to do—and more.

Dr. Watson looked up from his paper momentarily. "I have certainly filled out since eating Miss Mirabella's excellent cooking."

"Yes, you have, Watson," Sherlock stated in monotone. "We have all noticed."

What to make for dinner tonight? Sherlock had a partiality for roast beef and Yorkshire pudding, while John favored fish, cream of asparagus soup made with ale, and apple tarts for dessert.

"You are making progress in your understanding of the sciences, Miss Belle," Sherlock's face once again expressionless. "Don't you see that you will be a scientist—if you stay with me. But if you wish to simply receive the endorsement of the world—and forego the greatest opportunity you ever had, that of actually *learning* something, *becoming* someone—by all means, go to university."

"Not endorsement but *enlightenment* is the purpose of the university, Mr. Holmes," she corrected him, nonplussed.

"That has been my singular endeavor these many months—to no avail," Sherlock stated.

Oh, that is outside of enough!

Fish and soup it is.

Mirabella felt the heat rise in her cheeks. "It is interesting to me, Mr. Holmes, how someone so utterly unpretentious and genuine can be such a fine actor. One minute you are a gentleman of the first water, gallant and accommodating, able to impress the most high born of ladies, and the next you are honest to the point of cruelty. Which tells me that you clearly comprehend polite behavior and understand how to execute it—you simply don't *choose* to exhibit courtesy towards *me*."

"It is the greatest form of flattery that I should be myself with you, Miss Belle."

"Indeed, Mr. Holmes. I would be most gratified if you could find it in your heart to flatter me *less*."

She turned on her heel, grabbed her purse as she moved past the kitchen, and left the room before even the Great Detective could fashion a reply.

Chapter Eleven

"Oh, Aunt Martha," Mirabella exclaimed, gazing at the jewels in the velvet case. "They are too beautiful! You can't possibly wish for me to wear them."

Mirabella watched her aunt turn the diamond and amethyst necklace round in her hand, the matching bracelet and earrings secured in the case.

I don't dare touch them! Mirabella watched in wonderment as her aunt held the sparkling necklace out to her. Still in her undergarments, Mirabella had only just finished bathing at her wash basin when Aunt Martha had knocked on the door.

With only the tiniest voice whispering in her ear that her life was about to change, Mirabella had proceeded as she did every morning before breakfast: she had filled her blue and white porcelain wash basin with warm water (so different from the broken clay pot used at home in Dumfries!), a flannel rag and the soap already laid out. The slop pail was on the floor below her dresser. Mirabella had dipped the flannel into the warm water, rubbed the flannel along the soap, then applied the flannel to her body. The flannel rag was then rinsed, wrung out, and used to rinse the soaped area on her body, going under the loose sleeping clothing which was worn for warmth. When the water became dirty, it was poured into the slop pail. This process was repeated until every inch of her body was clean.

Mirabella knew very well that she was fortunate to be living in such luxury; at home the bar of soap was closely guarded, bought in exchange for a choice piece of meat.

And here she had her own room and her own wash basin! She glanced at the tin of Yardley of London talcum powder, a gift from her aunt, which she powdered herself with after her wash. She was the most fortunate girl in the world to have been taken under her aunt Martha's wing.

Looking at the sparkling jewels being held out before her, Mirabella reflected that she had previously considered her own wash basin and bar of soap to be the supreme indulgence.

"Diamonds?" she murmured, not realizing she was speaking out loud. "This is too much!"

"I do naw have much use for them, my bonnie lassie. I ne're wear such finery." Martha Hudson insisted, "You must take them, dear Mirabella. It is only a loan, so it is."

"Oh, my!" Mirabella exclaimed, her eyes fixated on the sparkling stones, but still unable to take the expensive jewels into her hands.

With her toe, Mirabella pushed the slop pail filled with the dirty water until the metal pail was hidden underneath her dresser, somehow offensive with such beautiful ornaments as these in the same room!

This day had started so normally—well, as normal as any day could be when one lived in the same building with Sherlock Holmes, who had commanded her to present herself in her new wardrobe the first thing this morning for his approval (for her *first detective assignment*!) Between Aunt Martha and herself frantically sewing every evening, along with some of the garments being farmed out, her outfits were almost completed to their satisfaction.

Whether or not Mr. Sherlock Holmes would be satisfied was another matter altogether, however. She had been training in the fighting arts for several weeks, and he was, characteristically, not pleased with her progress. Sherlock and John would continue in her training even after she was in *Miss de Beauvais'* on Sundays—her only "day of rest".

"Take them, my dear," the elder woman insisted.

Mirabella was afraid her legs would buckle underneath her as her eyes fixated on the glistening jewels. "Oh, I couldn't, Aunt Martha! What if anything should happen to them? I should have to jump off the London Bridge in shame!"

She started to feel dizzy. In truth, the last few weeks had been such a whirlwind. All her bones and muscles ached from the strenuous exercise. Even her brain ached. She was too tired to feel even the slightest nervousness over what was to come.

"You're alright, my gurl," Aunt Martha smiled, placing the jewels on the dresser in the velvet case and ran her hands along Mirabella's hips, smoothing down the young woman's drawers with an approving eye. "Turned out very nicely didn't they, m'dear? A very fine cotton. I likes the lace below the knees. Even the most elegant young lady in that school you're going to havne go' anythin' nicer."

"Oh, I'm quite sure of that!" Mirabella exclaimed, adding with a giggle. "I never thought to have lace on my drawers!"

After bathing, of course, Mirabella had put on her cotton chemise and her drawers. Thereafter her corset had gone over her chemise, pushing up her bosom and straightening her posture. She resisted the impulse to tie the stays more tightly than usual to appear even slimmer in the outfit she would be showing Sherlock. What difference would an inch make? And regardless of Sherlock's opinion of her wardrobe, her beautiful outfit wouldn't stop Sherlock from assigning her hard labor! She would naturally change into another dress but wouldn't have time to adjust her corset.

In general, Mirabella didn't tie the stays too tightly as she would be working all day—some days even scrubbing floors and transporting coal and wood. Reducing the waistline with an overtight corset was for the idle wealthy, not for the working classes. But no self-respecting girl would be without one under her garments.

Attached to her corset were her garters: Mirabella had learned after an unfortunate—and humiliating!—mishap to be certain her garters were secure and could hold up her stockings.

And what beautiful stockings they were. This was her greatest pleasure of all the items she had been required to obtain.

"But where—where did you get this beautiful jewelry, Aunt Martha?" Mirabella looked up into her aunt's twinkling green eyes as she hesitantly took the precious jewels into her hands, making every effort to keep from dropping them with her shaking hands.

"A gift from me husband after one of his naval successes. They apprehended a pirate vessel, so it is. The jewels—they're o' the first water, if I do say so meself."

"Do you think . . . do you think they are stolen?" Mirabella asked, gasping.

"Aye, I hope so! What a fine story." Martha smiled, her green eyes twinkling.

Oh, heavens! That's all I need is to be in that fancy finishing school and for someone there to recognize the family jewels.

"You know, lassie," Aunt Martha continued, clearly unconcerned that her jewelry might belong to someone else. Her husband gave them to her, therefore they were hers. "It is almost unheard of for a common born man like your uncle Robert to become an officer in the navy—which is reserved for the younger sons of earls and dukes and the like, there it be—he has to be someone special, as was me Robert." She paused, her lip quivering as her eyes softened. "There was Captain James Cook 'afore him, rose up through the ranks as well. And then, when me Robert retired, he became a seafarin' merchant, and a success he was at that as well, so it is."

"This building—in Baker Street—is that how you came by it?" Mirabella asked with some hesitation as it was truly none of her business. But it was so unusual that anyone of the working classes would have any property, particularly a property in such a prestigious part of town. And how strange to think that they might be living off the spoils of pirates!

"Oh, no!" Aunt Martha laughed in her lilting way. "It is mine fair and square, so it is. Until such a day as Sherlock 'Olmes blows it up."

"But how . . . a woman . . ."

"I actually kept house for a Mr. and Mrs. Haversham for many years, who died without heirs." She smiled. "Mr. Haversham left it to me."

"Oh, my!" Mirabella gasped in surprise. "A woman with her own property!"

"I took prestigious good care of them for many years. And as to that," Aunt Martha put her arm around her niece, "Never let anyone tell you what you can't do, lassie. You shall go to university if that's what you wish." There was a determined twinkle in her eye. "You're the smartest gurl I ever met. I know this is true, so I do."

"Thank you, Aunt Martha," Mirabella hugged her aunt back.

"Anyways, the jewels, they was won in a fair fight. The spoils of war and the regulations of the Queen's navy, there it be. And here—" Aunt Martha moved to her jewelry chest. "You must take this wee trinket too." She held out a pearl necklace with matching earrings, bracelet, and broach.

"What a lovely luster the pearls have," Mirabella murmured.

"The diamonds o' course you should wear to evening events, lassie. The sparklers will work for even the opera."

"I should say so!" Mirabella set the amethysts and diamonds back into the velvet case. She fingered her gold cross, swallowing hard. "I still say my own jewelry shall suffice."

"Oh, the lovely gold cross will do very well for day wear. It shows a humility and devotion which is very becoming in a gur-rl." Mrs. Hudson rolled her 'r' with the Scottish brogue that was so becoming to the ear and must have enchanted Robert Hudson so many years ago, along with her then red hair and green eyes. She added definitively, "But the pearls for evening dinners, and the diamonds for balls and the opera, so it is."

"Oh, my goodness, I've never even been to the opera." Mirabella giggled. "Do you really think I shall be going, Aunt Martha? To an actual ball? I've only ever been to a barn dance."

Martha nodded with approval, before her expression grew stern. "I do naw know what that 'Olmes is up to, but the fact is that you'll be goin' into a place for debutantes, and I shan't be havin' anyone lookin' down on me dear niece."

"But I don't have to put on airs for anyone, Aunt Martha."

"Auch, but I think you do, lassie." Aunt Martha winked at her. "That's precisely what all this is for, isn't it?"

Chapter Twelve

I'm between the Devil and the deep blue sea . . . Sherlock Holmes was in a rare state: he was utterly astounded. Involuntarily he stood from his wing-backed rose damask armchair, his long cherry-wood pipe dangling from his lips.

On the previous evening he had instructed Miss Belle to show him, ultimately for his acceptance or refusal, the wardrobe for her new assignment.

She had kept him waiting this morning for an unacceptably lengthy amount of time—so long, in fact, that Watson had actually grown impatient and left to do their grocery shopping.

Finally, Miss Belle arrived from her downstairs room wearing one of her new gowns. If one could call the arrangement of silk and gauze held together with thread a "gown". It might better be described as a *costume*.

"What in God's name is this abomination to fashion . . . ?" He caught his cherry-wood pipe with his right hand in the split second before it fell out of his mouth.

If he hadn't been feeling agitated before Miss Belle's arrival, he certainly did now.

Perched on the tip of Miss Belle's nose were little round *purple-tinted* glasses ornamented with wrought-iron curlicues! She peered over the glasses, teasing him with those gorgeous brown eyes framed by lush lashes.

Not that he cared about the feminine wiles—he had sworn off women prior to and after Irene Adler—it was simply a point of scientific interest that Miss Hudson had developed them overnight.

Nothing more.

But he felt himself to be quite unhinged. Why should he be anything but utterly confident in the ultimate success of his plan? It was time for Miss Belle to enter *Miss de Beauvais' School for Distinguished Young Ladies*. They had completed Miss Belle's training in the fighting arts, which was surely sufficient for her purposes.

What if she isn't ready? He hadn't expected to be this worried about her safety. *He* had trained her after all.

"Do you refer to my glasses, Mr. Holmes?" She pouted, showing her pink lips to advantage while she tapped the rim of the strange metal configurement perched on her nose.

Miss Belle never wore make-up! He observed that her lips and cheeks were rose-toned, which was also her scent.

"So you have bathed, Miss Hudson, I see . . ." he muttered, moving to lean against the fireplace rather than returning to his chair, as he wished to take in the full effect. "No wonder it took so long for you to arrive this morning. I shall expect you to be more prompt when you are on my time in future."

She frowned at him, putting one hand on her hip, which only served to exaggerate her curviness, something which needed no accentuation. He glanced out the window onto Baker Street momentarily.

"Do you have no reply, Miss Hudson?" He loosened the tie around his neck as he beheld her.

Mirabella rolled her eyes at him. *The audacity!* Lifting her chin in a manner which was actually quite . . . *enticing* . . . she stated, "I do not, Mr. Holmes."

"I expect to be answered when I address you, Miss Hudson," he commanded.

Instead of answering him, she turned around ninety degrees and looked over her shoulder at him, winking her eye! "There is your answer, Mr. Holmes. But the question is—does the Great Detective know how to interpret it?"

Where has all this come from? As he had initially suspected, this indecorous outfit was the work of the Devil.

His eyes scanned the ensemble in question with aggravation. She wore laced black leather boots with just enough heel to be stylish but not ridiculous. Her muted dusty purple skirt in a crinkled India weave (more grey than purple) had a large flounce at the bottom – but the skirt was short – barely covering her ankles! *Most alluring.* Of course, the boots covered her ankles, but the shape of her leg was clearly alluded to . . .

"Completely unacceptable!" Sherlock proclaimed. "This . . . this . . . frock would make my dear mother blush with dismay." The chit's blouse was far too ruffled, which did not hide her shapeliness, overflowing underneath a purple jacket which had the appearance of a leather finish. Purple leather. Whoever heard of such a thing? And this ridiculous outfit he had paid for!

Well, to be perfectly honest, King Nicholas I of Montenegro had paid for it, but the money had flowed through his own hands in a sort of implied endorsement.

Altogether untrue.

"Oh, Mr. Holmes?" she asked demurely. "Will your dear mother be in the finishing school?"

She is teasing me! Sherlock almost dropped his jaw realizing how a little bit of finery—if one could call it that—could change a perfectly appropriate servant girl into a . . . well, he didn't know what she was but he could not like it!

"It is not considered lady-like for a high-born girl to add color to the face," he managed. "One is supposed to have a natural beauty."

"I understand. Change the anatomy with the corset. Natural. Do not apply color to the face. Unnatural."

"At least your hair is appropriate," he muttered.

Her lustrous chestnut-brown hair was curled and stylishly arranged atop her head. A cute little satin lavender box hat with a velvet rose bow—well, there was no other word for it besides *cute*—was placed strategically atop her head.

The rest of her was anything but cute: adorable maybe, if he ever used such a word, which he never would.

"Oh, do you like the style?" she asked, patting her sweeping hairdo.

"I didn't say that I 'like it,' I said that it is appropriate. The eighties are definitely setting out to be the decade of the grandiose, voluminous hairstyles. Many ladies require hair pieces, but you have more than enough to spare, Miss Hudson."

"Thank you . . . I think . . ." she murmured, pulling on her ear which brought attention to the exquisite jewelry she was wearing. It was remarkable that he hadn't noticed the jewels before, sparkling as they were in the morning light. In the evening they would be stunning.

Her earrings were drop diamonds and amethysts as was a ring on her finger—certainly he had told her that she needed jewelry—but this was far too glamorous. Surely he hadn't given her enough funds to pay for that!

What the devil . . .

Martha Hudson, of course. Sherlock admonished himself for his slowness of wit. He must be addle-headed! *What is wrong with me today that I can't think straight?*

He had never imagined that such a transformation was possible. Why, even Irene Adler on her best day . . .

All-in-all Miss Mirabella Hudson looked to be nothing like the current style—and yet utterly more stylish than all other ladies. There could be no doubt in anyone's mind that she was wearing the next trend. She would turn heads wherever she went.

"This is certainly not what I had in mind, Miss Hudson, that is the relevant point," he stated, looking away so as to regain his composure.

She was not stick thin, she did not have the artificially created, unnatural waist which one had learned to associate with high fashion—and she looked utterly sensual.

Whereas the ladies of the remarkable era of Queen Victoria were subdued, feminine, delicate, and helpless, Miss Belle was confident, brazen, independent, intellectual.

And utterly desirable.

"Of course it is not what you had in mind, Mr. Holmes," she demurred, non-plussed as she moved to the fireplace, swaying her hips as she moved. She turned to peer at him again over her shoulder. "Your mind does not travel in that direction."

I wish she wouldn't do that.

"And what direction is that, Miss Hudson?" he challenged.

"Fashion, of course," she murmured, but there was a wicked smile on her lips. That he most certainly did like.

Sherlock couldn't think of anything more disgusting than being a lecherous old man. Why, Miss Belle was not yet eighteen years of age, and he was seven and twenty, ten years her senior. "What is this outfit you are wearing, Miss Hudson?" he demanded. "Do you call this fashion?"

Why was he doing the math in his head? An utter waste of brain cells which had best been applied elsewhere. This was what became of anything to do with the emotions—nothing but a waste of time and a misdirection of one's gifts.

She raised her chin, her eyes shooting anger at him in a manner which he found bewitching. "This is my day dress."

Eighteen is a very marriageable age. And of course, it was a very common thing for a girl to marry a man ten years her senior—in fact it was the norm since all but the wealthiest of men had to establish themselves in society before taking a bride.

"In a conservative young ladies school – where one blends in by always playing it safe and fitting in—you will not belong, Miss Hudson," he stated tersely.

"Surely you must allow for individual taste. You are positively primeval, Mr. Holmes. These are very modern times we live in."

His eyes rested on her fitted bodice a tad longer than was necessary for impartial assessment. He was feeling even more discomfited by her familiarity of address than usual. He took out his handkerchief and dotted his brow, falling into his chair and revisiting the only thing which came to his mind. *"Purple glasses.* I've never seen such a thing."

"They look exactly like your glasses, Mr. Holmes: small and round."

"Exactly like mine. Except they are different in every way. I told you to procure glass lenses for the eye as I recall, Miss Hudson."

"And I informed you that I would not stick glass in my eyes. Is old age affecting the memory of the great Sherlock Holmes?"

"Old? I would hardly call seven and twenty years old." Now he was truly angry. And why was he wasting time with pointless banter? What did he care for his employee's opinions on the subject?

Much too old for me her expression seemed to say. For some reason, he felt a stab of pain.

Ridiculous.

He stared at her. He found that he could do nothing else.

"How old is Dr. John Watson?" she asked casually, parting those luscious lips.

"He's nine and twenty years of age." *So if I am too old for you, Watson is ancient.* "If it is any of your business, Miss Belle, which it isn't. And don't think you have fooled me: I have seen you flirt with Watson, Miss Hudson."

"John is even older than you, Sherlock?" she gasped.

"Yes, Miss Belle, even older than the old man."

"He looks so young . . . And so fashionable . . . " she murmured wistfully. She turned to stare at him. "You seem much older, Mr. Holmes."

"This is not a game, Miss Hudson; there are criminals at large."

Although he had never expected nor intended for her to come into harm's way. Instead, his objective was that she should be on the inside of the finishing school, watching and communicating that which she observed—she was a very bright girl, and this task was imminently suited to her abilities. Even so, it was necessary to take every precaution: hence the fencing and boxing lessons.

Then why am I suddenly so apprehensive about her safety?

In truth, he didn't like the idea of Miss Belle being on a case, at the same time her versatility and adaptability continuously impressed him—and he was a very difficult person to impress. Finding another young woman as capable as Miss Hudson was an impossibility.

Her choices are her own responsibility and not mine. Although Miss Belle might complain, she was so good at everything he gave her that he had to think she wished to do it. One did not put so much into an endeavor one did not enjoy.

Or at least that was what he told himself. *The truth is that the girl has no idea what she is getting into.*

But he had never before felt guilty over someone else's acquiescing to his plans. Even he did not worry over the Baker Street Irregulars, who were children. Better that they should at least be on the side of the law if they were determined to throw themselves into dangerous situations. And the generous payments he gave them kept them fed and clothed.

"Very well, if you would prefer that game to this one," she shrugged, looking over her glasses, looking something like a cross between a librarian and a stage dancer.

"I would. These clothes do not suit you in more ways than one, Miss Hudson," he replied sternly. She was acting as if the outfit became her, which was far from the case. They might become a lady of the first fashion, but *not* Miss Belle. "Do you have an evening gown?"

"Oh, yes, it is much more in the normal way of things."

"Ah. Normal for whom? And I hope that you have several other . . . *day* dresses. Current fashion requires that daywear be higher to the neck. Above all, Miss Hudson, you must adhere to current fashions—"

"Mr. Holmes! Calm yourself. I can't imagine what has gotten into you. Aunt Martha is working as quickly as she can—and is almost finished. If you were not so much work to manage. . ."

"*No one* manages me, Miss Hudson." Inadvertently he straightened the navy blue silk scarf around his neck, pushing his too-long hair out of the way.

"Who has time? You're so busy managing everyone else."

He was hard on her. *Very hard on her.* To insure that she stayed alive. She was still young and careless—as evidenced by her behavior.

"One does what one must. Now, about your other day dresses. Are they in the same . . . same . . . *style* as this abomination to fashion?" He waved his hand fervently.

"They are all different, but not the same as this," she replied without hesitation.

"Oh, good. Now you are making riddles about your style of dress, Miss Hudson. My life is complete." His eyes travelled to her well-turned ankle—peeking underneath her too-short skirt.

"And jewelry? I suppose that you have an entire jewelry case full of jewels now on my funds." He knew very well that the blunt he had given her wouldn't buy the jewels she now wore, they must be Mrs. Hudson's. No one else of Miss Belle's acquaintance would be in possession of such precious stones—or trust her with them.

And glad that she had them, he was. The finery made her station in life much more convincing, and he couldn't have possibly furnished the ostentatious ornaments.

"Naturally I do not." She rolled her eyes at him, as if she were reading his thoughts—something no one had ever successfully managed before. "I have a pearl set, and of course my gold cross for day wear."

"You will need something for evening wear."

"I need no more jewelry than this; it is quite versatile. And . . ." she sighed. "It is finer than anything I had ever hoped to wear."

He raised his eyebrows, adding brusquely, "It will probably do."

"I do have one question, however, Mr. Holmes."

"Only one?"

"I wondered if . . . *may I* . . ."

"Yes?"

"Well, I must have something to do in the evenings, you know, something which keeps me with the other young ladies, and you know that I volunteer at the orphanage? Well, I thought that we might make Christmas presents for the girls in my class. And I was so careful and frugal with your money, I thought that possibly . . ."

"That was your clothing allowance and your pin money—and your payment for the next ten weeks. Whatever is left over you may keep. With one provision: *you must play your role convincingly*. And in order to do so you must not scrimp on your wardrobe." His tone and his countenance were stern. He picked up the newspaper beside his chair and pretended to read it. "Eccentric is acceptable, though it would not have been my design choice. But you must not appear to want for anything."

"I understand," she nodded somberly even as she paced the room, as if the idea of pampering herself was painful to her.

"And you may keep all the apparel as well." He glanced up at her.

"Oh, *no, I couldn't!*" She turned abruptly to face him. Suddenly her face lit up like Scottish the night sky, as if he had promised her the moon.

"The gowns are yours to *keep*. There will be other cases. I will not be able to pay to outfit you again in this type of finery, naturally. The success of a case depends on believability, and someone could die if we fail. *And that someone could be you, young lady*." He had the ridiculous compulsion to impress upon her the need to be cautious.

"But if I were to leave your employ . . ."

"I know what you are thinking, Miss Hudson," he replied sternly. "That you will sell these garments and attend university. Outside of the jewelry, you wouldn't get much."

"I won't be selling the jewelry!" she gasped. "That would be thievery!"

Just as I thought. The jewels belonged to someone else.

"No one else would want those clothes, I assure you, certainly not for the price it cost you to acquire them. A wealthy young lady would never wear hand-me-downs—and a servant girl has no need for such clothing." He moved to the window looking out over Baker Street and pretended to be interested in the organ grinder below, relieved to have his back to her. "There might be a blind young woman who would not mind wearing this outfit—but it would be cruel to thrust your apparel on her." He turned to face her again. "At any rate, I am forbidding you to sell it—or any of your gowns."

"So . . . you have no objection if the ladies at *Miss de Beauvais'* make Christmas gifts for the girls in the orphanage?" she pressed, this appearing to be even more important to her than the hope of increasing her savings account.

"You have not yet met the debutantes, Miss Belle." He turned to face her. "What makes you think that you can convince them to do so?"

"I'm sure they are *quite nice*." She smiled wistfully. "They are all rich and have everything they need. Why shouldn't they be?"

"Don't be so sure," he muttered, moving his pipe to his lips as he returned to his wing-backed armchair, his eyebrows raised. "Have you travelled in high society before, Miss Belle?"

"Naturally I have not." She shook her head. "But even if they all disliked me—that would put even more time at my disposal!" Her expression was suddenly quite determined. "If I don't persuade them, I will make the gifts myself. I cannot *bear* to be idle for ten weeks!"

"Don't expect to have any freedom where you are going, Miss Hudson. Miss de Beauvais made it very clear that you will be under lock and key," he warned, taking a puff on his pipe. There were some things better left unsaid to Miss Hudson. She was the type to take a mile if given an inch.

"I thought you said you had already obtained permission for me to leave as needed, Mr. Holmes?" she asked coquettishly.

"Miss de Beauvais gave it quite reluctantly," he muttered. "And it was for a few hours a week only—which we will need for your fencing practice. Your skills are still not where I would like." He added somberly, "I would not push that one as you do me, young lady."

"Why not?"

"Because she is a barracuda," he replied simply.

"She can't be worse than Miss Bickers," Mirabella murmured.

Interesting. Sherlock considered Miss Belle's fallen expression.

"Miss de Beauvais could hardly object to a young lady showing charity to those less fortunate, could she?" Mirabella asked, her eyes returning to their natural glow.

"Clearly you haven't met her." Sherlock sighed heavily before adding, "What a terrible thing it would be to deny charity to those in need."

"Indeed it would!" Miss Belle exclaimed, placing her hands on her waist.

Studying her foot tapping the wooden floorboards incessantly, he longed for some peace and quiet that he might complete his scientific reading and experimentation for the afternoon. He glanced at the latest issues of *Hue and Cry* and *The London Police Gazette* on the mahogany table beside him. He could see no harm in Miss Belle volunteering at an orphanage.

Wait. It is Miss Mirabella Hudson we are talking about. If there is a way to turn a harmless activity into a dangerous threat, she will find it. Miss Belle was nothing if not an accident waiting to happen.

"Do I have your word that you will not jeopardize our mission, Miss Hudson? Above all else, you must play your part."

"Of course, Mr. Holmes. What could be more fitting than a wealthy young lady looking for charitable outlets?"

"Then I will leave it to your better judgment, Miss Belle."

There was no doubt in his mind that he would regret those words for the rest of his life.

Chapter Thirteen

"You're not very good with a needle, are you, Miss Carnegie?" Alexandra giggled, leaning over her own expertly executed embroidery to observe Mirabella's failed attempt, having much in common with the appearance of chicken seed scattered in a barnyard. "I would think a country girl such as yourself would at least be able to sew."

"I have no accomplishments at all, Lady Alexandra, is that what you wish to hear?" Mirabella replied to the Duke and Duchess of Glazebury's daughter, surprised at how the title failed to impress her after only two weeks in *Miss de Beauvais'*.

But even less impressed than she was with Lady Alexandra was the rest of the group with her, Mirabella knew. It had not taken long to peg her as the country bumpkin. She either didn't curtsy low enough or high enough, her skin was lightly tanned (Heaven forbid! Only the lower classes were out in the elements working), her nails were shorter than those of the other girls, and her hands rougher.

Working with chemicals in a laboratory did nothing to soften the skin. Apparently sulfuric acid was not the best skin softener.

My first scientific discovery! That should be an entry for her upcoming autobiography, "The Annals of an Insignificant Nobody", subtitled, "Unaccomplished at Everything and Disagreeable to All."

As if her appearance weren't evidence enough of her lack of breeding, Mirabella was actually nice to the staff (a grievous *faux pas*!), more outspoken, and a bit more boisterous than the others.

Mirabella was such a sore thumb amongst these high class ladies that she was perfectly miserable.

There was nothing in this luxurious existence to console her. Even the private toilette room—with a toilet and even a bathtub with hot running water!—did not compensate her for being perfectly abhorred.

Hmmm. Mirabella reconsidered. A hot bath in the evening—drawn by someone else, no less!—was a bit of heaven on earth, if the truth be told.

Her mother would never believe the depravity she had sunk to. She didn't believe it herself.

Dejection and desolation could make one do odd things—even bathe. To be sure, Martha Hudson's lodgings at 221 Baker Street had on the premises a large copper tub which the landlady placed in her kitchen every Sunday morning before church. Aunt Martha then heated the hot water which allowed for a bath for herself each week.

But Mirabella was too shy for that—even with her aunt in attendance—and preferred using her wash basin in the privacy of her own room, a decided luxury compared to the cracked clay bowl she and her older sisters had shared. At home on the farm, Mirabella's father and the children bathed in the kitchen once a week with her mother in attendance.

Her mother and the older girls never did so. Modesty forbade it.

My worst fears are being realized. Living under the influence of Sherlock Holmes was obviously turning her into a disreputable young lady. Aunt Martha had said that Sherlock Holmes—who had communicated in every way possible that he was *not* shy nor modest!—often frequented the Turkish baths, a public bathing house.

And here she was, Mirabella Hudson, in a finishing school for the idle wealthy, bathing in a bathtub! What next? Would her soul be cast into the depths of Hades?

"I don't know *why* we are helping you make Christmas gifts for the orphanage—when your own offering is not very good," Alexandra added.

"That would be an excellent reason for us to assist," murmured Princess Elena.

"Because Princess Elena commanded that it should be so, that is why," giggled Bethany, a petite, blue-eyed blonde. Bethany might be a merchant's daughter—clearly with connections—but she definitely had winning ways and knew how to present herself.

"Otherwise, you would not have the time of day for me, Lady Alexandra," whispered Mirabella, almost under her breath. But not quite.

"I didn't realize that I do," Lady Alexandra murmured. There was a reason Lady Alexandra was in this finishing school before being set loose upon society. Miss de Beauvais admonished the Duke of Glazebury's daughter often, telling her to 'hold her tongue' if she wished to be a lady and to attract a young man. That, of course, was like the hurricane telling the wind to be still.

Princess Elena looked up momentarily from her sewing, a vision in white lace, but said nothing—which was perhaps worse than saying something.

"And because it saves us from ze *ennui*," stated Jacqueline, the daughter of an English earl and a French Mama. Jacqueline was above average height, even more buxom than Mirabella, but otherwise very thin—almost skinny. All in all Jacqueline was quite the show-stopper, though Mirabella didn't think the protected French miss had more than a slight inkling of her inevitable appeal to the masculine gender.

"It is quite unfashionable to be anything but bored," murmured Mirabella. This she had quickly learned in dealing with the upper class.

"We must be the most fashionable girls in all of London then," remarked Bethany, her attention focused on her sewing.

"I am never bored," stated Mirabella. "I don't see how anyone could be with so much to learn."

All four of the young ladies looked at her with something approaching dismay.

Mirabella knew that her ultimate goal was to become a scientist. She had no reason to feel inferior to these ladies, with the exception that she had thus far failed at her job: that of presenting herself as a well-bred lady and being accepted by her companions as such.

To find that she had once again failed at the task given to her was quite depressing, even though she had told Sherlock how it would be and had pleaded with him to send a more competent person!

If it weren't for Princess Elena's acceptance—who was the only princess in the group—Mirabella doubted if anyone would have the time of day for her. In all fairness, Bethany was kinder than the rest. The merchant's daughter could not bear to be uncharitable to even the most irredeemable of unsophisticates.

"Oh, my," Bethany sighed, her concern evident. "You are a sweet girl, Miss Carnegie."

It is hopeless. This is the worst assignment ever to be given to an unrefined, ugly duckling.

"Although this charity project is not as ridiculous as that finger-printing thing-a-majig Miss Carnegie wasted our time showing us." Alexandra smiled condescendingly, her golden brown eyes studying Mirabella's handkerchief with unveiled disdain even as she feigned laughter. "You are so amusing, Miss Carnegie."

That finger-printing thing-a-majig is on the cutting age of science and is the future of criminology.

"I will not apologize for the fact that science fascinates me," Mirabella replied with a shrug, her eyes glued to her needlework. "If it weren't for science, we would not have indoor plumbing, would you like that Lady Alexandra? We would not have steamships to bring your dresses from your Parisian modiste. Nor cameras to take photographs of you in them."

"Humph! Mirabella Carnegie, must you always have the last word?" Lady Alexandra demanded. "It is unladylike. Furthermore, I assure you that I would have the most fashionable dresses with or without steamships!"

"But you could not flush a lavatory without science."

"Hee hee hee hee!" Bethany giggled uncontrollably.

"Mademoiselle Carnegie!" exclaimed Jacqueline, but she was also giggling. "*Vous êtes tellement naughty*! You should not say such things!"

"And chemistry is most useful," Mirabella insisted. "Surely that very beautiful rouge that Lady Jacqueline is wearing was concocted by a chemist."

"*Moi?* Wear paint on my face?" Jacqueline protested. "I would never do so!"

"Pardon me. I forgot that we are never to admit that we paint our faces—although we *all* do," Mirabella murmured.

"You see, Miss Carnegie! Always the last word!" Lady Alexandra interjected.

At least I provide fodder for the slaughter. No doubt the minute my back is turned the gossip runs rampant. At least Lady Alexandra was nasty to her face.

"Oh, *my*, have you seen Hugh Fortescue from Devon? *So* handsome," exclaimed Bethany, distracting Mirabella from her thoughts.

"Hugh is only a viscount!" replied Alexandra. "He wouldn't do at *all*!"

"Viscount Ebrington is in line to inherit an earldom," Bethany countered. Alexandra rolled her eyes.

"Which shall put Fortescue in the House of Lords," murmured Jacqueline. "I think he is divine. My papa says he is quite the sportsman in the hunt."

"Do not become too attached to Hugh," stated Princess Elena quietly, almost in a whisper.

"Oh?" all of the ladies present with the exception of Mirabella turned to the princess with interest.

"He favors his cousin, Emily," Elena replied succinctly, as was her custom.

"What do you think of the viscount, Miss Carnegie?" Alexandra asked.

"I couldn't say." Mirabella looked up from her embroidery to smile sweetly. But not too sweetly. She knew that she often went so far as to entertain the horrible transgression of expressing too much emotion— even delight, on occasion. Worst of all, gossip did not interest her on any level, but particularly about the marriageable young men in high society.

I have already heard enough on that subject to last a lifetime.

Chapter Fourteen

"I see you are properly attired, Miss Belle." It was Sunday, but there was no rest for Mirabella. Her lessons continued.

Mirabella felt anything but proper *or* attired in the wire mask, padded buckskin plastron across her chest, and the buckskin gauntlet, but she had an idea that she was going to need the protection before she left this room. Sherlock Holmes never did anything short of pushing her to her limit.

And usually beyond.

Speaking of the devil, Holmes was similarly dressed except that he wore no mask over his Corinthian features. No doubt the moment she was given a sword he would wear a veritable barricade. The Great Detective might be exceedingly brave, but she had learned that Sherlock Holmes was a man who took his personal protection seriously.

And he was a man who consistently underestimated her abilities—and her aim.

"Miss Mirabella." Holding his mask, Dr. Watson bowed to her, ever respectful and kind.

She could not manage to suppress a giggle.

"What is it, Miss Mirabella?" he asked, returning to an upright position. A strand of blonde hair remained across his forehead, and his blue-turquoise eyes were sparkling despite his unwavering gentlemanly demeanor. "Is something amiss?"

"It's just that . . . well, I . . ."

"Yes?"

"Are you wearing a three-piece suit underneath your fencing garb, Dr. Watson?" she giggled. "I have rarely seen you waver from your formal attire, night or day. I must admit I find it difficult to picture you in anything else."

"You would have it so, Miss Mirabella," he chuckled. "A plaid tweed of a most high quality wool blend."

"Do not lie to me, Dr. Watson!" She smiled, wishing for all the world to straighten the lock of hair on his forehead. He was the dearest, not to mention the handsomest man imaginable. She had sorely missed having someone in her midst who was kind to her.

"I do wish you would call me *John*, Miss Mirabella," he murmured softly, his aqua blue eyes transfixed upon her.

She felt herself blush, smiling up at him. "I should like to call you by your first name, Dr. Watson."

"Then why don't you?" He smiled broadly.

"Hmmm . . ." She studied him. "It just doesn't fit you. John is simply too plain for you. What is your middle name?"

"Hamish," he replied.

"I can't call you that!" she protested.

"I should hope not!" Dr. Watson laughed.

"*Hamish* means 'James' in Scottish Gaelic." She considered. "I should like to call you James. It fits you so much better than John, don't you think?"

"Uh-hmmm." Sherlock cleared his throat, and Mirabella spun around to see that her employer was standing not three feet from her! She had been so absorbed in her conversation with the charming Dr. Watson that she hadn't even known Sherlock was there!

Much like a plague which had not yet expressed itself in symptoms. The difference being that ordinarily *everyone* was aware of the Great Detective's presence from a ten-kilometer distance.

"If we have all been properly introduced and amply amused, do let us get down to business," Sherlock continued, his expression unusually harsh, adding, "Miss Hudson's life could well depend upon it."

"Yes, yes, of course." John's soft gaze which had been like bathing in a turquoise waterfall turned suddenly serious and unrevealing.

"And besides, you are neither 'James' nor 'John,' you are simply Watson!" corrected Sherlock absolutely.

Sigh. Time for work. Although she doubted she would be in any danger whatsoever, Mirabella resolved to do her best, as this was the part of the case which interested her the most. Especially now that she had met all the debutantes.

They had begun a course in rudimentary fencing, and even she was surprised at how quickly she was comprehending the art—particularly in light of the continuous barrage of insults from her ever-impatient employer.

"Keep your eye on your opponent *at all times*, Miss Belle!"

"A strong strike, Miss Hudson; however, it was accomplished by swinging almost your entire body to the point of impact."

"*Faster! Faster!* Never hesitate or you are dead!"

"I am not your employer today—*I am your enemy!*"

Today and every day.

"*Lunge,* Miss Belle! You *must* develop your strength!"

Finally she could endure it no more. "I'll show you just how strong a country girl is, Mr. Holmes, growing up with three obnoxious brothers."

Between the girls at the school who tolerated her at best, and treated her like the dirt underneath their feet at their worst moments, and a demanding employer who never once praised her for her efforts, she had just about had all she could endure!

"I am terrified, I am sure." She could picture Sherlock yawning from behind his mask as he easily deflected her onslaught. "There is some truth in what you say, however. Rather than spending your time corseting yourself and breaking your ribs—you were out slopping the hogs. It bodes well for your strength—but not your waistline."

"If I were you, Mr. Holmes, I would not insult a lady with a sword who is only just learning to control it!" She saw her opening and took it, lunging forward.

"Very true, Holmes," Dr. Watson exclaimed from the sidelines. "Sometimes the most dangerous fighters are the beginners—those who are utterly lacking in control."

"A very good effort, but not good enough," Sherlock pronounced, evading her sword and returning his own. "At this time I am more interested in inflaming her than in controlling her."

"You may live to regret that decision, Mr. Holmes," Mirabella replied, thrusting her sword towards him.

"*Touché,* Miss Belle," Sherlock replied in the instant he was struck by her sword. "And now, you shall take your turn with Dr. Watson."

***

"You have excellent hand-to-eye coordination, Miss Mirabella," Watson remarked, beginning to breathe more rapidly.

"And excellent stamina," added Holmes, hovering nearby as he kept pace with them from a distance of about two meters. "She is not even winded."

"I shall not be able to show my face having lost to a novice—and a woman." Dr. Watson smiled even as sweat began formulating on his face, visible through the mesh of his fencing mask.

"I did not say that you are losing—merely that she has surpassed your stamina, Watson."

"I am accustomed to being run all over London," replied Dr. Watson. "And yet, possibly you work Miss Mirabella even harder than you work me, Holmes."

"Well, let's be certain of that, Watson. Miss Hudson, let us take a short break for a glass of lemonade, then you will fight the both of us."

"At once? I know I have done well for a beginner, but *both . . .* ?"

"Have you? Did I say that? At any rate it is a scenario you may come against."

"Yes, but I am not likely to have a sword with me," she argued as she took off her mask and shook her damp hair. She was excessively tired and uncomfortable, but she would never admit it.

"That is where you are wrong, Miss Belle." Sherlock returned to the sidelines to retrieve a cane of sorts: long, sleek, and white.

"Ever since an unfortunate incident with a large Russian gentleman, Holmes has kept one of these nearby whenever he is on a case," Watson confided in her.

Handing her an elaborate ladies' white walking stick, Holmes added softly, it seemed with almost tenderness in his eyes, "You don't think that we would send you to the wolves ill-prepared, do you, Miss Belle?"

"You already did. I've been there two weeks," she murmured.

"Ah, but you weren't ready then. A weapon in the hand of someone who doesn't know how to use it is more dangerous than no weapon at all."

She studied the polished white walking stick before pulling at the handle, guessing his intent. To be sure a beautifully sharp blade some sixteen inches in length emerged.

But there was more to come.

"You shall have an arsenal of weapons at your disposal. This will fit nicely in your reticule," Sherlock added. As she sat drinking her lemonade, he held up a six-inch metal cylinder, approximately the size of a cigar, with a small brass sphere on one end and an even tinier one on the opposing end.

Crack! Suddenly he snapped his arm straight down to his left side. Even as she jumped, some of her lemonade splashing on her suit, eight inches became eighteen.

"This is a little invention of my own," Holmes continued.

"What is it, Mr. Holmes?" she asked, awestruck and confused at the same time, as she set down her glass and reached for the peculiar object.

"I call it the *telescoping truncheon*. You may call it *life or death*."

"Oh, I see," she murmured, even as she studied the object. "The sections of steel friction-lock together."

"Very good, Miss Hudson."

"But what is its purpose?" she asked, returning her gaze to him.

"To increase one's strength, I should say," considered Dr. Watson. "Similar to the concept of the police baton or the eastern nunchakus— capable of killing a man."

"*Precisely*." Sherlock nodded. "The ball on the end is a force-multiplier. Having a weapon to multiply the force of a strike will do much for ensuring success in a confrontation, particularly for a woman of questionable strength."

"It is a question you might not wish to have answered, Mr. Holmes," she retorted.

"In addition, the small snap-out guard enables one to deflect and possibly even trap a blade," Sherlock added, illustrating the point.

She studied the weapon, entranced, immediately seeing the implement's advantages if dealing with a stronger opponent. "Whatever inspired you to produce this object?"

"On a recent visit to Japan, I was fortunate enough to train in a truncheon martial art called *Jutte-do*, the rudiments of which I shall be teaching you over the coming week."

He handed her the instrument and she instantly felt completely out of her element. But she would not allow him to observe her lack of confidence; she watched him intently while inwardly awaiting his directions with trepidation.

"Step back, Watson." He returned his unrelenting gaze to her. "Raise your striking hand to the height of your shoulder and snap your arm down as hard as you can."

She did as she was directed.

"*Ouch! Oh! My leg!*" The sting was almost unbearable.

Dr. Watson rushed forward to examine her, but Holmes held up his hand. Watson looked at her, and only when she nodded, biting her lip, did he retreat.

"Now, try again, Miss Hudson, and this time strike your *opponent* not *yourself.* It is the *other person* you wish to hurt."

"That conviction is impressed upon my heart with every word you utter, Mr. Holmes."

"Very good. It is a lesson I apparently should not have skipped, presuming it to be intuitive. Let us waste no more time."

He moved the dressmaker's model some six feet in front of her. "Let me show you. *Again.*" He swung his arm slowly, the brass tip of the weapon pointing almost back toward his shoulder from his back bent wrist. He snapped his wrist forward and a deep line appeared in the figurine's padding. "A whip-like wrist motion will deliver a greater speed to force ratio, thus inflicting greater damage at the penultimate zone of attack."

"But who shall receive the damage?" murmured Mirabella. "That is the question."

"And the answer will be found when you try this a few times slowly in the air, teaching our *friend* here a lesson he shall never forget."

She tried again, this time hitting the target rather than herself, but without much impact.

"Now pretend the mannequin is me," Sherlock advised.

"*With pleasure.*"

Rotating her wrist a few times slowly, she accustomed herself to the motion. She then stepped up to the substitute form and struck it as hard as she could with the whipping motion Sherlock had shown her. To her astonishment the blow penetrated the life-size doll to a depth of several inches. She turned to look at Holmes in amazement, in the process observing a proud smile cross Dr. Watson's handsome features.

"Much better. Full extension, and you did not strike yourself in the leg." Holmes pointed to the manikin. "Strike a man in the temple thusly, and you have given the undertaker a new customer. Strike him with the other end in the same way in the outer mid-thigh and he will drop yowling in pain and possibly vomit."

"Precisely where I struck myself?" she asked.

Holmes raised his eyebrows at her. "Missing a meal will not hurt you. Or losing one."

"Oh, *you! Why, I . . .*"

"You are stronger than the average young English miss," Watson remarked with admiration. He offered her a glass of water and his arm. "She needs to rest, Holmes. She's been at this for two hours—and she's been injured."

Once they were all seated and Dr. Watson was assured she had not suffered a permanent injury—while Holmes acted utterly bored with the proceedings—conversation was renewed.

"I must confess I don't understand the purpose of such an instrument," she complained. "Wouldn't a pistol be more effective? And I already know how to shoot a pistol."

"You shall have one. However, a pistol is not allowed in every venue. Here, for example. I won't allow it."

"Because I might shoot you?" she asked coyly.

"Let us say for the purposes of speculation, Miss Hudson, that *you are a lady*—let us use our imaginations here—and your opponent expects nothing from you. You take out what looks like a cigar and wrest his gun from him. Or, let's say you are taken captive. The gun will be taken from you immediately—this weapon hidden somewhere might not be noticed."

"Supposing she has nothing," murmured Watson, a concerned expression on perfect features.

It is so dear how kindness makes a handsome man even more handsome.

Glancing at Sherlock, she was struck by his determination. His jaw so tight and his eyes so intense that she feared his heart might pound out of his chest.

Why was the Great Detective so invested in her? This was a complete turn-around in their relationship. Sherlock Holmes had practically ignored her for most of the time she had worked for him, making her feel invisible, in fact indicating that he wished she were invisible! And now she was the statue of his creation and he Pygmalion!

I don't know which is worse! If the only two options available to her were being ignored or being the focus of Sherlock Holmes' attention, it was a definite toss up.

Mirabella giggled as she recalled the story of Pygmalion. There was no doubt in her mind that Sherlock Holmes would *not* fall in love with this creation!

"Do you find this amusing, Miss Hudson?" Sherlock demanded, the veins in his neck protruding slightly.

"Perhaps a little," she admitted.

"You shall not find it as amusing if you end up in the morgue as a result of your inattention, I assure you." His expression was one of utter conviction, so much so that she took a step back and gasped.

"She is giving her all, Holmes," Dr. Watson cajoled. "There is no reason to become angry simply because Miss Mirabella finds some enjoyment in the process. I know military men who would find your regimen insupportable."

"Then they should find themselves in the morgue as well." Holmes turned towards her in one swift movement, even as she was patting her face with her handkerchief.

"Let us begin again," Dr. Watson advised, ever the voice of reason. "Supposing Miss Hudson has no weapon. What then?"

"Yes, what would I do?" Mirabella asked, genuinely interested.

Holmes eyes were riveted on her. "When I am through with you, my girl, you will be able to defeat an opponent with *nothing but your enemy's strength.*"

Her hand paused in mid-air. "Whatever do you mean, Mr. Holmes? That is quite impossible!"

"What he means," Dr. Watson interjected, "is that your enemy's strength is your asset."

"Precisely! Now you have it!" Sherlock punched his fist into the air, the unruly dark curls on his head flying everywhere as he did so.

"But that makes no sense." She looked down as she moved closer to her chair, her gaze taking in the worn wooden floors.

"There are certain situations in which it will be necessary for you to defeat the enemy—but to make it look as if you had no hand in it at all," Sherlock replied.

"But how would I?" She was utterly and thoroughly confused.

"Perhaps you are at the opera and would find it detrimental to your social standing to engage in fisticuffs." Sherlock shrugged, as if the answer were obvious, as he always did. "Hence, *Jiu-Jitsu.*"

"You're going to teach *judo* to Miss Mirabella?" Watson asked incredulously.

"Of course. It has been five weeks since we began her instruction. Three more weeks should be enough time for her learn fencing, *Jiu-Jitsu,* and the rudiments of Chinese boxing. The deportment we shall leave to Miss de Beauvais: that I have less confidence about. I do not envy the poor woman."

"Eight weeks total to become both a master warrior and a lady of distinction who fools everyone about my true station in life." Mirabella sunk into her chair. "Why not finish a day early and invent a time machine?"

"When the case is completed. Let us not attempt too much at one time," considered Sherlock.

"Learn self-defense, teach the princess how to speak and win the heart of her prince, and stop the criminal element from killing her," commanded Sherlock.

"That is enough for a young lady just out of the schoolroom on her first trip to London." John Watson chuckled, holding his fist to his mouth.

She sighed heavily.   "I still call it the epitome of underachievement."

Chapter Fifteen

"You are a wretchedly lazy girl, but with my genius we should be able to make something of you," mused Sherlock.

"I don't like it," remarked Watson with so much emphasis that both turned to stare at him. "An endeavor in which a young woman must be trained in the lethal arts to survive is possibly the height of irresponsibility."

"Fortune favors the bold," she muttered. "I would be seriously concerned if Mr. Holmes weren't asking me to risk my life in his employ."

"It would be disturbingly lenient of him," Watson muttered.

Sherlock considered her words before staring pointedly at her. "I assure you, Miss Hudson, I wish no harm to come to you and am taking every precaution to protect you. Please *do pay attention!*"

"He must have a soft spot for you, Miss Mirabella," Dr. Watson winked, chuckling. "I've rarely seen him show a care about anyone."

"To the contrary, I have no 'soft spot' for anyone, Watson," Sherlock replied with a raised eyebrow.

"Hmmm, let's see, someone comes to mind, *who was it*?" Watson brushed his moustache, pretending to recollect. "No, not her . . . Oh, *now* I recall. There was a Miss Irene Adler. Do you recall her, Holmes?"

"Miss Irene Adler?" Mirabella asked, suddenly very interested indeed. "Is it true, Dr. Watson? Who is she?"

"Only a world class deceiver and manipulator." Watson chuckled.

"Are you quite serious, Dr. Watson?" Mirabella asked, utterly astonished. What on earth would Sherlock see in such a person?

"Yes it is very true, Miss Mirabella. The great Sherlock Holmes was found chained to a . . ." Dr. Watson cleared his throat in obvious embarrassment. "It was in a hotel. Let's just say that our good friend was in a most compromising position."

"*Gasp!*" Mirabella covered her mouth with her hand.

"Let us return to the facts at hand and dismiss idle gossip, if it would not trouble the two of you greatly."

"Oh, I don't think it can be classified as gossip: it's in the police record." Watson's expression was serene.

"And who was the inspector? LeStrade," noted Holmes. "I shall say no more on that subject."

"Toby was on the case—and he is very good," Watson considered, rubbing his chin.

"Yes, yes, I'll give you that. But even Toby—the only one on LeStrade's team with an ounce of sense—did not solve the case."

"Who is Toby?" asked Mirabella, her curiosity escalating. "He must be very shrewd."

"Remarkable talent for tracking," Watson agreed appreciatively.

"Is Mr. Toby as clever as the great Sherlock Holmes?" Mirabella asked, taking every opportunity to tease Sherlock, a pleasure as rare as seeing a comet in the sky and ultimately as satisfying as one's birthday dinner.

"Cleverer," nodded Watson without hesitation. "And much more handsome."

Sherlock shrugged, disinterested. "Toby is a handsome fellow, I'll grant you that."

"*Oh.* I should like to meet Toby," murmured Mirabella.

"I forbid it. He has no personal ethics whatsoever," pronounced Sherlock.

"Are you serious, Mr. Holmes?" Mirabella asked, truly curious now.

"Quite," replied Sherlock. "All you need is a steak bone and Toby's morals go out the door."

Utterly perplexed, she turned to Dr. Watson.

"Toby is a hound," John said.

"A hound. Do you mean Toby is a *dog*?"

"Best of the breed." Sherlock cleared his throat. "Back to the matter at hand: Miss Belle has expressed a strong interest in detective work. Perhaps I should not have paid her the compliment of taking her at her word? Like police work, there is an inherent danger which must be fully understood."

"I do understand, and I remain very interested," insisted Mirabella.

"You are fully committed to the case?"

"Against all better judgment, yes I am."

"And you will do whatever is necessary?" Sherlock pressed, clearly not convinced. And for good reason.

"I will. It is very difficult, however." She sighed. "If I could succeed by force of will, I could manage, but it isn't like that."

"Explain," Sherlock commanded.

"The other girls . . . they don't accept me."

"Ah." Sherlock shook his head in disapproval. "I told you to get the glass lenses, Miss Hudson. It is to be expected."

She tapped her finger on her cheek, appearing to consider his evaluation. "I won't be doing so at this time. However . . . I *am* interested in the chains. Of what were they made? *What were you wearing* at the time, Sherlock?"

"Mr. Holmes, if you please." Sherlock raised a single eyebrow at her. "We return her to the finishing school with not a moment to lose."

"Holmes," Dr. Watson admonished. "I still say this is too dangerous. If anything should happen—"

"Nothing will happen, Watson," Sherlock assured him. "I have thought it through."

"The world does not always follow the structured order of your thoughts, Sherlock."

"Are you ill, Watson?"

"Two words, Sherlock: Irene. Adler."

"Everyone is entitled to one mistake. Now take this situation: there is our man and the king's men. The finishing school is a veritable tomb—no one is allowed in or out. Miss Hudson has been trained by us—the very best—and shows a great deal of natural ability in all the necessary areas: strength, reflexes, courage, and intelligence. No, I can anticipate no problems."

"I suppose it is better to have her under our watchful eyes—than sneaking about behind us."

"John Watson, I would never sneak about!"

Both men turned and looked at her in disbelief, raising their eyebrows in unison.

Chapter Sixteen

"Do you already have a beau, Miss Carnegie?" Bethany asked, suspicion making her eyes twinkle.

"Oh, no!" Mirabella felt herself blush.

"See her color! There is someone, I know it!" exclaimed Jacqueline, leaning forward. "I thought you showed no interest in ze boys!"

"Certainly I am not adverse to handsome young men!" A picture of the exquisite Dr. John Watson entered her mind, placing him here in the parlor before her, the candlelight reflecting off his blonde-streaked hair and sparkling smile.

"Get back to work, Miss Belle!" A picture of Sherlock imposed upon her lovely daydream, splitting it into pieces, with only John's turquoise eyes left on a broken piece of glittering glass, now scattered on the floor. Sherlock flexed his arms, revealing his muscles even as his eyes penetrated her vision.

<Giggle> *How foolish I am!* But even she, in her silly, infatuated state, was *nothing* in foolish obsession compared to the ladies of high society. Too much time on their hands and not enough constructive occupation, in her opinion.

Or perhaps it is because no young man in high society would have me. So naturally such a romance would not engage my imagination as it is not an option for me.

And this was why she did not belong to this social circle nor did she fit in. All the young ladies outside of herself, without exception, had the immediate goal of marriage. This mutual goal was critical to being accepted among the girls. Second, and equally as important, *one must love to gossip.*

Clank! Mirabella heard an odd sound in the garden and moved to the window, carrying her embroidery with her.

"How can you have lived this long and not know anything about society, Miss Carnegie?" Alexandra asked.

"What?" Mirabella asked, her eyes glued to the window, lost in thought. "Oh, I don't know, it's a mystery."

"Miss Mirabella has other interests—and talents," remarked Princess Elena. Her voice was almost a whisper, but her piercing black eyes were fiercely resolute, shockingly exotic against luminescent skin. "She does not need society and frivolous young men."

For herself, Mirabella wasn't even certain Princess Elena liked her—or if the princess merely tolerated her.

No one. She saw no one in the yard. She glanced in the direction of her reticule, which held her small revolver, where she had been sitting. But instead of returning to her seat, she sat by the street side window, glancing out occasionally.

Where are the bodyguards? Somewhere in the interior hallway, no doubt. And Sherlock's man? That fellow was almost invisible, just like her employer.

"Such as?" laughed Alexandra, smiling at Elena. Everyone seemed to like the princess, despite her quiet demeanor and strikingly unusual looks. "I'm sure I've never seen Miss Carnegie do anything but read!"

"Quite so," agreed Mirabella, continuing painstakingly on the cross-stitch. "I do nothing else but read."

Outside of criminal investigation, working in the most advanced laboratory in all of London, volunteering at an orphanage, and trailing the greatest detective the world has ever known.

"You must avez quite ze most boring life imaginer, Miss Carnegie," remarked Jacqueline.

"Indeed I do," Mirabella sighed.

"Reading, it bores me to ze tears."

"And what have you read Lady Jacqueline?" asked Mirabella, genuinely curious.

"What avez I read? Grammar, ze text books—and le *Français*, of course."

"That would bore me to tears as well!" smiled Mirabella, genuinely amused. Her curiosity overcame her as it was wont to do, despite her better judgment. "Don't you enjoy novels of romance and intrigue, Lady Jacqueline?"

"*Romance*?" Jacqueline looked at Mirabella blankly, but with some amount of interest. Though well-born, Lady Jacqueline was not talentless: she was the best seamstress among them, even enjoyed cooking much to her mother's consternation, and had a flair for decorating. This French miss would make some lucky man very happy if she could but expand her world a bit.

"Yes, novels about romance. Why, pray tell, are we all here in this finishing school?" demanded Mirabella, moving forward in her seat and setting her embroidery aside with great pleasure.

"To become ze proper demoiselles *bien sûr*," replied Jacqueline.

"I would expect you to be the last person to ask why we are here, Miss Carnegie," Alexandra stated. "I have seen you attempt to cut your meat without sending your dinner flying."

"Hee! Hee!" Even Bethany could not help giggling at Alexandria's remark—which, of course, was all true. "Do forgive my laughter, Miss Carnegie, but the book almost smashed Princess Elena's toe when it fell off your head—"

The person I am here to protect! As for the meat, that was unfair: if the cook had been better at his job, it would not have happened. She herself could cook a far more tender filet. But that she could not reveal.

"Neigh! Neigh!" Mirabella looked up to see a carriage stopping outside their front door. There was a groom with the carriage—no one else—and he wore a large hat and a scarf around his neck which hid his face. Very odd. *It's not that cold outside.*

"Why?" insisted Mirabella. "Why do we wish to become proper young ladies? To what end?"

"Why not?" giggled Bethany, always becoming despite her unfashionable liveliness.

"W-why?" repeated Jacqueline. "Parce que c'est la *thing to do*!"

"Because it is our duty to our parents and our country," replied Princess Elena definitively, her expression both dignified and resolute, approaching haughtiness.

Remember that expression, it could prove useful, Mirabella made a mental note.

"You say the most entertaining things, Miss Carnegie!" exclaimed Alexandra, but she looked far from amused. "*Why* do we become proper young ladies? You may lie, but I shall not. *To marry well*, of course."

"Precisely so," nodded Mirabella.

"Knock! Knock!" Miss de Beauvais entered, handing a letter to Elena as she smiled sweetly and curtsied, the seal of the letter briefly visible. "For you, Princess."

"Thank you," Princess Elena murmured.

Miss de Beauvais exited as quickly as she had entered, closing the parlor door behind her. But all the other eyes in the room were now focused on Princess Elena, if they hadn't been before. Still, no one uttered a sound as they all knew it was impolite to inquire—and as they had no desire to discuss anything else.

Alexandra's gaze caressed the letter now in Elena's hand with no small amount of envy, and all other eyes followed, the thoughts unspoken but known to all.

The letter, only just delivered, was sealed with a wax imprint of the royal seal of Italy. The group sat very close together, so it was not difficult to discern, particularly since the Italian seal had, by now, been memorized by everyone in the room. The princess received just such a letter *every day*, taking it to her room to read in private.

Only today there were *two* letters, both with the royal seal, and Princess Elena was now opening this second letter. The silence was almost unbearable.

Suddenly Princess Elena gasped, placing her hand in front of her mouth.

"What is it?" Alexandra asked, the only one of the ladies with the courage—or the absence of manners, as the case may be—to ask. "Pray tell us. We hate to see you dismayed!

We hate to be left in the dark is the truth of the matter, Mirabella reflected. But she, too, was anxious to learn the contents of the letter.

"It is from Vittorio's mother." Elena's eyes were watering, something none of them ever thought to see.

Mirabella asked quietly, "Is it bad news?"

"No," Elena shook her head, tucking the letter into her reticule. "Queen Margherita says she hopes very much that Vittorio will marry me."

"Are you quite serious?" Mirabella exclaimed, adding in a whisper, "I had always assumed she didn't approve."

"Myself as well," Elena replied.

And Queen consort Margherita, Princess of Savoy, had never met Princess Elena. Could it be a ruse? Mirabella glanced at the visibly shaken princess. Clearly Elena didn't think so.

Alexandra sighed. "I would so love to marry a prince."

"If marriage is a subject of interest to you—indeed, your singular reason for existence—why should you not entertain yourself with books of romance?" continued Mirabella. "What do you think, Lady Jacqueline?"

"Je ne sais pas," murmured Jacqueline, sighing wistfully as she eyed the reticule, now holding the royal letter. *I don't know.*

"Lady Jacqueline, have you read *Pride and Prejudice* by Jane Austen?" Mirabella asked. "It is delightful."

"*Lady Audley's Secret* by Mary Elizabeth Braddon is perfectly sinful," added Bethany in her typical theatrical manner as if revealing a great secret. *"I loved it."*

"Personally I love the Gothic novels," agreed Mirabella, "such as *The Mysteries of Udolpho* by Lady Radcliffe."

"Gothic?" Elena looked up.

"Yes, very dark. Lots of mystery. Murder."

"I love murder." Princess Elena's eyes flew wide open, the words escaping from a head-to-toe vision in white lace. Further accenting her dark words were her ebony eyes and glossy raven-black hair.

Everyone gasped and Lady Jacqueline covered her mouth with her hands, giggling most becomingly. Even her giggle was in French.

Mirabella smiled to herself. Although she could not take the credit, this aspect of her job was being accomplished: socially, the princess was making progress. Rather than answering in one to two-word statements, Princess Elena now utilized entire sentences. Rarely more than one, but an entire sentence, nonetheless. This in only three weeks' time.

Reflecting on the daily letters, one thing was clear: the Prince of Italy was *smitten.* And such an infatuation after only a few moments together at a ball with only a few words exchanged.

Mirabella hoped that Prince Victor Emmanuel III felt the same way when he was in Princess Elena's company for more than a few seconds. Or maybe he wouldn't care if his queen generally looked straight ahead with a serene countenance as if she were bored. Mirabella simply could not fathom the match. If Princess Elena married Prince Victor Emmanuel III, the majority of the Elena's time for the rest of her life would be spent socializing: state dinners, receptions, ceremonies and charity events.

The charity events would suit the princess who had grown up in modest means; Elena gave all her pocket money to the poor when they took their chaperoned walks. If she became the Queen of Italy, no doubt she would care for Her people.

"Tell me, Princess Elena, do you *wish* to marry Prince Victor Emmanuel?" Mirabella asked. "Is this what *you* want?"

"Of course that's what she wants!" remonstrated Alexandra scornfully.

All eyes were on the princess.

"Oh, *yes*." Princess Elena nodded, her countenance serene but her determination clear.

"I had thought you lost your mind and now I am sure of it, Miss Carnegie," Alexandra smiled condescendingly. "Who among us would not wish to marry the prince of Italy?"

All I want is to go to university.

"Please don't think me rude, Princess Elena, but I believe there is more to your wishes than the prince's title and royal standing, isn't there?" Bethany asked.

The princess nodded in agreement.

"Such as love at first sight?" Mirabella asked. Something had passed between the prince and princess in the few minutes they had been together. Nothing else to explained the bond between them.

"Yes," Princess Elena managed to utter.

"Oh, *my*," sighed Jacqueline.

"I must say, Princess Elena," Mirabella sighed, "You have the smallest waist I have ever seen. You must be very tightly corseted."

"Pain is good." Elena nodded, unconcerned, while taking a stitch in her needlework. She appeared uninterested in the drama which the other young ladies tended to. "It makes one strong."

"It is time for our walk." Elena's eyes motioned to the clock revealing eleven a.m.

"Do you think it best that we depart at the same time every day, taking the same path?" asked Mirabella. "I think it much safer—I mean, better—if we were to vary our schedule and to proceed along different routes."

"How then would any young gentlemen follow our pattern and be at the right place at the right time?" Bethany giggled, but she shook her head, her expression being one of disappointment in how much of the obvious Mirabella missed.

"What nonsense are you spouting now, Miss Carnegie?" Alexandra asked.

"I simply think we should be cautious—" but Mirabella was cut off as Princess Elena rose to procure her reticule, the other girls following suit. It seemed that Princess Elena cast a spell on everyone; Mirabella didn't know why anyone was concerned that the princess learn to converse, it might spoil the effect.

"I favor action over caution," Princess Elena remarked.

"Did you hear something outside?" Mirabella asked, turning away from the other ladies.

Suddenly all the ladies present turned to see that the window to the alley had been skillfully and quietly removed. Standing before them was a hooded man with eyes cut into the hood. He had appeared quite suddenly in the parlor whilst they were chattering away.

And he was heading directly for Princess Elena, a gun pointed at her heart.

Chapter Seventeen

"Do not make a sound or you are dead! Fall to za ground or you are dead!" In a muffled voice the intruder warned the girls to remain silent. Another man with a silk stocking on his head followed the first, moving to the door to lock the parlor from the inside while waving a long knife at everyone in the room.

"Get behind ze couch!" the second man commanded quietly, coldly, to everyone except Princess Elena.

The gleaming knife was more terrifying to Mirabella than the gun; at least a gunshot might kill one instantly, while the thought of being attacked with a knife made her shake in her slippers.

Bethany, Jacqueline, and Alexandra were herded behind the couch. Mirabella pretended to be frozen in fear—the fear was not pretend, but the immobility was—a method which risked angering the assailant who held the glistening blade.

I have no choice but to insure I am the first person next to the stocking-head man. Since she was the last to be shoved behind the couch, she was the first in line. This allowed her to peer around the settee even though her face was close to the floor.

"Shhh!" Mirabella jabbed Alexandra who was whimpering in terror. Jacqueline had her eyes covered with her hands, and Bethany sat biting her lip, her eyes wide open. All three were out of view, of which Mirabella was relieved.

Again her eyes moved to the knife.

With a knife, their captor could slit someone's throat without making any noise. The gun was to force compliance only, it was not intended to be used. A gunshot would attract attention and bring people running. Still, she wasn't yet prepared to test her theory as someone could be shot in the experiment--namely her.

Catching a glimpse of the featureless man in the silk stocking, she could not even be certain of his skin color because the head covering was dark. He had a moustache, that much she could see.

The knife he carried was nine inches long. He was no doubt an excellent knife thrower. But from this distance the most inexpert of men could probably kill them all.

I am such a fool! I let myself be separated from my reticule and my revolver. I was too busy feeling sorry for myself for being the outcast of the group to notice the activity outside the window. They were so used to gardeners and all the noises that laborers invariably made about the place that she had not been aware of anything but her own reprobate status.

Now Princess Elena may pay for my self-pity with her life.

Think, useless girl! She could not bear to disappoint those who depended on her any more than she could go on living if Princess Elena's death were to be laid at her door.

Sherlock. At this moment which might be her last, she saw her mother's face, then Aunt Martha's, and finally that of Sherlock, which pushed the others away. That's what he would do if he were here, why not in her imagination?

His was the face which came to her mind and would not leave her. Somehow the image both comforted and strengthened her when she most needed to be brave and to think on her feet.

I cannot disappoint him. In that moment she realized the depth of her devotion to Sherlock Holmes—or to his work, she didn't know which.

Her eyes glued to Princess Elena, Mirabella could see the princess fingering something inside the reticule still wrapped around her wrist. They had all seen the letter from Prince Vittorio carefully folded and placed in the princess' reticule, but why would Elena be touching the letter at a time like this? As a romantic, superstitious gesture? Or worse, a last 'good-bye'?

The gun! Mirabella gasped as she remembered that Princess Elena always carried a gun inside her reticule. As did she, but she had been so stupid as to be separated from her weapon.

At least the princess was not stupid! The last thing the kidnapper expected was that Elena was fingering her gun even as he held her within his grip!

And he still has the upper hand: the princess was a good shot, but she was held in a stronghold and she was corseted to the point of immobility. The hooded man had Elena's wrist firmly clasped with one strong hand. The assailant's other arm was wrapped around the princesses' graceful neck, all the while forcefully pulling her to the window.

And then there was the other man with the large knife.

Princess Elena's only advocate was on the floor, her face to the ground.

Jacqueline, Alexandra, and Bethany were huddled together, shaking, their eyes shut. Mirabella was crawling, inching her way, closer and closer to man who was watching them.

Elena was almost to the window. In a moment the princess would be gone to them forever.

Mirabella knew if she made any noise the man in the stocking head might very well throw his knife at her, killing her instantly. She had to trust in Princess Elena's quick response, though she knew nothing of Elena's fighting skills. Although Mirabella's small revolver was in her reticule, she had a knife strapped to her ankle—which she now held firmly in her hand, hidden by layers of ruffles. She had never been so grateful for ornamental fripperies.

It is a terrible risk. But it might be Princess Elena's only chance.

Mirabella had been to the morgue with Sherlock and Dr. Watson, and she had seen terrible, mutilated bodies, victims of human monsters. She couldn't bear to envision Princess Elena's face on one of those bodies, all because she had been too afraid to act.

"Please don't hurt me!" Suddenly Mirabella began crying and whimpering, hysterical, drawing the attention of both assassins, even as the first was pulling Elena through the window, the second close behind as he backed up across the parlor floor, the large knife in front of his body.

"Zatvorena joj do! Zaklati stariju ženu pripadnicu!" *Shut her up! Slit her throat!*

Both men looked at Mirabella, their attention momentarily abandoning Princess Elena. Mirabella had no idea of the literal translation of their words, but she was fairly certain it was not complimentary from the fact that the stocking-head man moved towards her, swinging his knife.

She stood to do battle with her small switchblade, backing up as the stocking-headed man approached. In that moment, Princess Elena shot her captor's leg through the reticule.

Boom! Boom! The bottom of Elena's reticule puffed out towards the man who held her, covering his wounded leg in the hot wax of the seal of the House of Savoy, her letter disintegrated.

"ARGHH!" The hooded man screamed, releasing Elena, who immediately fell to the ground and rolled away. He limped towards her before the realization hit that the noise of the gun—and his own scream—would bring everyone running.

Stomp! Stomp! Clack! Clack! The sound of someone trying to force the door open, screaming all the while, made the injured man snarl in frustration.

Princess Elena's attacker, bleeding, jumped through the window and ran as best he could with an injured leg.

The stocking-headed man did not retreat, however. He raised the blade over his head, but was unable to find Mirabella's location as she had by now moved behind the couch, watching the princess all the while. Then he remembered why he was there and turned toward the princess.

In the meantime, Elena had pulled a bullet from her corset and hurriedly loaded it in her revolver.

Mirabella scurried to the opposite end of the couch, the three debutantes huddled in the corner, throwing her knife at his heart at the same time Elena fired a second shot at the stocking-headed man. Elena's shot went high and hit the man in the throat, while Mirabella's knife landed lower than she expected, the result of too much fear and adrenalin.

Sherlock was right. I need more practice.

"AIIEEEE!" He fell back. Completely still. It was difficult to know which lady had exacted the fatal stroke.

"Is he dead?" Elena whispered, moving towards him.

"I don't know, but he shan't harm us now," Mirabella whispered, glancing at the window. "But if we don't stop the other man, there might be another attempt on your life."

Without additional words, their eyes glued to each other, Elena pulled a bullet from her bosom beneath her corset and loaded the gun again. Mirabella, who was closer to the window, held out her hands, and Elena placed the gun in Mirabella's fingers.

"Cover the body, Princess," Mirabella commanded in a whisper as she ran to the window with Elena's gun, promising herself that her pistol would never be far from her again. She took aim at a black brougham carriage speeding down the street. She aimed, fired, and was sure she saw the driver flinch—had she hit his arm? —but the horse almost hit a pedestrian in its speedy escape, so she thought better of firing into the crowd.

Thud! Thud! Thud! The enormous bodyguards ran down the hall and were now pounding on the door and shouting. "Otvorena vrata! Mi ćemo ubiti ako vam smetati naša Princeza!" "*Open the door! We will kill you if you hurt our Princess!*"

"It is too late for that," Princess Elena murmured.

Mirabella glanced at the man bleeding onto the oriental carpet and her stomach heaved as her hands shook. Elena yanked at the curtain to cover him.

I hope it was not me who killed him.

And yet, what had he intended to do to Princess Elena? *And to me.* The thought was horrid.

Mirabella glanced behind the couch. *Good, they are all still hidden.* If the other ladies saw the dead body, the reality of what had happened would be greater than their appreciation for being saved. As it stood now, she might be able to turn their relief and fear into gratitude, using it to advantage—unless they saw the body. This would no doubt lead to hysteria, the girls would run screaming to their parents, and the school would be closed.

I will have failed.

"They might have killed you!" Elena exclaimed with obvious admiration in her eyes for Mirabella, after she had yanked a thick orange curtain from the window and thrown it on the body. "How brave you were, Miss Mirabella."

"Not as brave as you, Princess Elena! I had no choice but to cause a distraction," Mirabella replied, returning the smoking gun to Elena. "You acted as I hoped you would. I must commend you for your calmness in the face of danger."

Elena shrugged. "It was them or us, and I did not wish it to be us."

The other three young ladies, Bethany, Alexandra, and Jacqueline, were only now emerging from the couch in a stupor, staring at their rescuers with their mouths wide open, appearing to be in a state of shock. They had not yet seen the lump on the rug under the curtain.

Bethany had the presence of mind to open the lock of the door that the body guards might cease breaking it.

Crash! Nonetheless, one side of the door fell heavily to the carpet, torn from its hinges.

"You may enter," stated Princess Elena, but it was a command rather than an option, and only half of the door was left anyway.

Chapter Eighteen

"*Entre´ vous, s'il vous plait* you meant to say," admonished Miss de Beauvais, pushing the remaining door aside, which fell apart as she did so. Miss de Beauvais entered before the bodyguards, stepping over the wood splinters in her typical fearless manner.

"*Entre´ vous, s'il vous plait*, Miss de Beauvais." Princess Elena's gun was unwittingly pointed straight at Miss de Beauvais' heart as Elena had not yet returned the firearm to her reticule, now torn. Even after being attacked and nearly abducted, her wrists and neck still pink from the pressure, the princess looked quite regal indeed. She might be soft-spoken, but there was no fear in that one.

"Princess Elena! You have a *weapon?*" exclaimed Miss de Beauvais, noticeably shaken.

"I always carry it with me," replied Elena without apology, attempting to return her gun to her reticule before she recalled that the bottom had been blown out.

"*Most* unacceptable!"

"Thank goodness Princess Elena had a weapon or she might now be abducted—or worse," Mirabella murmured, motioning to the covered body with her eyes. Miss de Beauvais mouth opened wide for the merest second before she snapped her jaw shut, positioning her body in front of the other three students' view of the carpet.

Stop it! Stop it! Mirabella's hands wouldn't stop shaking and her teeth began chattering. *Heaven help us! I am the most unprofessional operative who ever lived.* She felt her eyes watering as the thought occurred to her that she was not able to perform this job.

"What is wrong, Miss Carnegie? Are you alright?" Bethany put her arm around her. Which was a good development as it temporarily drew the attention of the other two.

And enabled Mirabella to walk forward. But she couldn't stop the tears from rolling down her cheeks.

"Get the hartshorn!" Miss de Beauvais commanded as she herded the girls into the adjoining parlor. "Girls, there is nothing in here for you!"

"Miss Carnegie is crying for all of us," Bethany stated solemnly. "I don't know why I'm not crying."

"I was so afraid—I almost f-f-failed—" Mirabella took advantage of her body's reaction to create a distraction. Though she didn't know if she would be able to stop herself if she wished, she couldn't seem to stop crying. *It might have ended so badly. I was not prepared.*

A picture of Sherlock flashed before her again, but for some reason he was smiling. One of those rare moments when he showed his appreciation of something she said. The twinkle of his eye, the twitching of the corner of his mouth—as if it pained him to smile, which it no doubt did—and his unruly dark curls flying everywhere.

For all the trouble he gave her, Sherlock believed in her. He had to or he wouldn't have given her the job. *He trusted her.* The great Sherlock Holmes trusted *her.* And she had come very close to proving his trust was utterly misplaced.

Elena was on Mirabella's other side as they walked into the adjoining parlor, whispering into her ear. "They spoke in Serbian."

Mirabella turned her head towards the princess suddenly, the importance of the information immediately obvious to her, which also had the effect of diverting her from the trauma of their experience.

That would come later.

"I wanted to inspire them to speak, and that was accomplished," Mirabella whispered back. "But why would a Serb wish to hurt you, Princess Elena? You are of Serbian blood."

"They may have spoken in Serbian, but it was with a *Turkish* accent," Elena murmured to Mirabella so the other girls might not hear. There was a new respect in Princess Elena's eyes for Mirabella. If the princess approved of her, Mirabella's place in society was now secure.

And I only had to kill a man to accomplish it.

"T-they were after Princess Elena!" Bethany managed to utter, as if realization had just hit. She was now holding Mirabella's hand, for whose benefit it was difficult to say. "And Mirabella acted all frightened, but she wasn't really, she—"

"What happened to ze one who held a knife aimed at us?" Jacqueline asked. "I only heard ze one jump out the window."

"There was s-s-something under the curtain, I think," Alexandra murmured, wringing her hands, her eyes open wide.

"No! Are you quite serious?" Bethany demanded, her cornflower blue eyes so wide they overtook her face. "Was it a body?"

"Certainly not!" Miss de Beauvais stated.

"If it was, I am glad!" Alexandra retorted, regaining her composure. "He tried to hurt us, and he had no business doing so!"

Jacqueline turned to Princess Elena and gave her a hug. "*Mon Dieu!* You killed him! *Je vous aimez!* You saved us, *ma belle princesse!*"

"I do not think you were in danger. They wanted me," replied Princess Elena in a murmur. "And it was Miss Carnegie who saved me. I could not have acted with out her."

"Did the one who had Princess Elena get away?" Bethany asked. "Oh, I wish you had shot him, too!" Everyone was hugging everyone else and talking all at once.

"I *did* shoot him. I think I may have hit him in the arm," Mirabella replied. "In which case he may be caught. A horse team is difficult to maneuver with a wounded arm."

"Mon Papa—what will he say?" exclaimed Jacqueline.

"There is no need to tell your parents," Miss de Beauvais assured them, interrupting their chattering. She raised her chin as she looked at Mirabella, as if she didn't believe Mirabella could have had anything to do with the rescue. "You girls were in no danger. They were after the princess. And he is dead. They will catch the other one."

"Tell my parents! I wouldn't dream of it! They would remove me *immediatement!*" replied Jacqueline, beginning to pace the room, and giggling. "Oh mon Dieu! It was so *excitement!*"

"Oh, my goodness! Princess Elena shot him!" exclaimed Bethany. "There were two *big men*—villains with weapons!—and these ladies scared them away! I was never so amazed in my life!"

Mirabella smiled at Princess Elena. She had no doubt that Elena would not wait for a savior to come to her rescue—she would save herself and everyone else within a ten-mile radius.

"They had guns! And knives! They could have killed us!" Alexandra began sniffling and dotting her eyes with her handkerchief, when suddenly her expression became determined, as if she had hit upon a new resolution. "I wish I had a gun and I wish the one would come back. *How dare he!*"

"They won't be back, there is no need to plan a military maneuver. Come, sit, dear," Miss de Beauvais took Alexandra's hand and led her to the settee. She rang for the maid, commanding, "Bring a hartshorn at once!"

Mirabella thought it more advantageous to channel Lady Alexandra's fear into anger rather than placating her. "I wish you might teach them a lesson as well!"

"Will you . . . teach me to shoot, Miss Carnegie?" Alexandra whispered.

"Of course I will," Mirabella replied. Perhaps Alexandra was so mean because, in spite of her prestigious position, she felt powerless—causing her to attempt to bully everyone around her.

"No you will NOT, Miss Carnegie!" Miss de Beauvais pronounced. "HUSH, Alexandra! You are perfectly safe!"

"Do you think we are s-s-safe, Miss Carnegie?" Bethany turned to Mirabella, for the first time since their meeting looking to her for advice.

"Whether or not there will be another attack and whether or not we are safe are two different issues," Mirabella considered. "Certainly we will be more cautious henceforth!"

Miss de Beauvais cleared her throat, glaring at Mirabella. "Of course you are safe! And, after this, I will triple the security! For goodness sake, where were Princess Elena's bodyguards?"

"Outside in front of the building, I presume," Mirabella murmured. "The attackers entered through the alley window."

"Until the villain is caught, how can we know if we are safe or not?" Princess Elena considered.

"We do not know if these men were working alone or if there are others," agreed Mirabella. "We do not know if they will try again or if we have frightened them away."

Mirabella felt a pang of guilt for threatening the school's continued existence, knowing that she owed it to Sherlock to assist in catching the culprits. If the school were closed down, the assassins would simply follow Princess Elena to her new location. But Mirabella would not lie about the danger to these girls, they must each decide for themselves.

"Nonsense!" exclaimed Miss de Beauvais.

"Where were the Italian police, that is what I wish to know," Princess Elena added in a whisper, suddenly frowning. "And where is Prince Vittorio?"

"Girls!" Miss de Beauvais spoke in a commanding tone. "If you mention even *one word* of this to your parents, you will be pulled from the school, and there will be no debutante ball for you."

"No debutante ball?" murmured Alexandra, looking up suddenly from her seat on the couch. From the look on her face, apparently this outcome was worse than being killed by deranged murderers. "It's all I have dreamed of! I've waited all my life for this!"

"No debutante ball," concluded Miss de Beauvais with emphasis. "My school will be closed down, I will be cast into the street penniless, and it will be another year until you are entered into an acceptable school—if indeed you could find entrance given the scandal—*and there will be no presentation to Queen Victoria.*"

"No presentation to the Queen?" repeated Alexandra. "My father would be outraged, and my mother mortified—she might kill me, in fact."

If no one else does, Mirabella reflected somberly.

"Another year," murmured Bethany, as if it were a lifetime.

"Nothing for you this season," repeated Miss de Beauvais. "Perhaps *never*."

"*Never*?" Alexandra, Bethany, and Jacqueline repeated in unison.

Mirabella doubted if all this was true, but the other girls seemed to take it as fact. And if so, it was a fact that Miss de Beauvais would not hesitate to play upon.

"*Not a word to your parents*," Miss de Beauvais commanded.

"But the security must be increased," Mirabella stated.

"Of course!" exclaimed Miss de Beauvais.

"We will need bodyguards in the same room with us henceforth—and even outside our bedrooms."

"In the parlor?" Bethany asked, covering her mouth with her hand.

"How embarrassing," Jacqueline added. "We will have to watch what it is we say."

"It must be done," Princess Elena stated solemnly.

"*Every* precaution will be taken," Miss de Beauvais emphasized.

"Clearly we are safe if Miss Carnegie and Princess Elena are here!" considered Bethany. "They overcame two assassins! And they were taken completely unaware!"

And next time we might not be so lucky.

Bethany moved to hug Mirabella, "I'm so sorry if I was ever unkind to you, Miss Mirabella."

"You have never been unkind, Miss Allen," replied Mirabella, laughing in spite of the terror of the day. Perhaps terror brought people together. Certainly the facades were momentarily down.

"Do call me Bethany, I never cared a fig for society—but it pleases my father, and I so hate to disappoint him."

"I care!" murmured Alexandra, still dazed.

"Moi, aussi!" stated Jacqueline.

"I wish to be married and to have a family, of course, but this is all so *false*," Bethany continued. "I shall never again take my life for granted."

"We must have a dead body in the parlor to be living the real life?" demanded Jacqueline, revealing that there was a brain in that pretty head after all.

"Better his than ours," murmured Princess Elena. "He was a bad man."

Chapter Nineteen

"I don't like it," John Watson exclaimed, pacing the floor. "Miss Hudson might have died, Holmes!"

"But she didn't, Watson, she performed admirably, just as she was trained." Sherlock replied quietly as he studied his hands, attempting to suppress the feelings of fear. He glared at her, anger rising in his chest. "Essentially without a weapon and even though she became separated from her revolver."

"That will never happen again," Mirabella stated with conviction, his fear mirrored in her eyes.

"I should hope not!" Sherlock reprimanded.

"Holmes, this is not the time!" Watson's voice was elevated. "Miss Hudson might have died in your employ—serving *you.*"

"Miss Hudson, I have to ask . . . do you feel obligated to do this in order to remain in my employ?" Sherlock asked, his voice strangely quiet. "If so, let me disavow you of that notion."

"But you said precisely that, Mr. Holmes," she retorted. "That I had no employment without this case."

"Yes, I know that I did, and it is very true that, without you, this case will be lost—and I may very likely lose my reputation, without which I cannot afford to employ you."

As Sherlock watched her, something soft entered his heart which he could not like. *She might have died. She might not be here in this room with him.*

Bloody hell! His life's work was with criminals and dangerous persons, and he could not afford to have feelings for others or his work was compromised. It was bad enough that he had started to feel the first pangs of happiness since Watson moved in, only nine months ago, something he had never expected to feel. He couldn't recall when he had had a true friend before John Watson.

"You must enter into it willingly, Miss Belle, or the danger is too great," Sherlock emphasized. "Do answer my question, girl: Do you wish to be on the case? Do you come to it of your own accord?" He studied her, her full lashes so open to the world, her eyes so curious— and innocent.

She was young and naïve, of course, and she talked too much, but there was a joy and excitement to her character which was contagious. And, of course, she was efficient, and intelligent, which made her of great use to him.

An excellent employee.

"I presume this is to ease a guilty conscience," she teased.

"I have none," Sherlock conveyed with conviction.

"There, at least, is the truth," Watson muttered.

She nodded, in apparent agreement. "I was so terrified of the finishing school, you know, and then so miserable being there, however . . ."

Studying her soft chestnut curls, he started to wonder if he could bear it if something were to happen to her.

"Yes?" Sherlock persisted.

"I do not think I can stay away. I think I must be on the case."

She is of the same cut, just as I suspected. Sherlock nodded with understanding, a slight smile forming on his lips. Just as Watson needed the stimulation to forget the war as badly as he himself needed the occupation—he knew not why.

And didn't care.

"The dead man, who was he?" she whispered, her eyes troubled.

"We haven't been able to conclusively identify him. Perhaps a Serbian anarchist, someone who hated the monarchy."

"Do you think it is finished, Mr. Holmes?" she asked, struggling with the words.

"I do not," replied Sherlock simply.

She wrung her hands in her lap. He watched her, aware for the first time that she had undergone a terrible change—at his bidding.

"Is it your first murder, Miss Belle?"

"Of course it is, Mr. Holmes, don't be daft!" She couldn't help laughing despite her melancholy mood. She added somberly, "Although I can't be certain it was I who killed him."

"Do you wish you had never been on the case, Miss Belle?" he asked.

She shook her head. "If I had not, Princess Elena might now be dead."

"You're quite certain, Miss Hudson?" Looking at the lovely young woman before him, dressed in a pink linen and cream lace, he noted that she seemed to have become a woman overnight. She, too, had her hopes and dreams, and he would hate to see them cut short.

"Yes," she replied softly.

"Holmes," Dr. Watson admonished. "I still say this is too dangerous."

"Life is dangerous, Dr. Watson," Mirabella replied turning to face the doctor.

"Indeed it is," he murmured, smiling at her.

Chapter Twenty

Who will I kill next?

Blood was dripping from her gleaming six-inch blade as she looked about for who to kill, whose life to end, a person she did not know.

How had lives changed because of the murder she had committed? How had the lives of innocents been altered? Who would be hurt in the next generation because of her?

She looked about at the dark faces with features so different from her own.

I don't know anything about the man I killed. His wounds, the torturous existence that made him into who he was.

Did I kill him or did Princess Elena?

It didn't matter, if she stayed with Sherlock Holmes, there would be another.

Sherlock. His face passed before her and he reached out to take the dripping knife from her hand.

No! No! Don't do it! She knew what he intended to do.

He turned it on himself, ready to kill himself.

She grabbed the knife back from him.

Her skin was so white and her eyes so black. Now she and Sherlock were in the morgue, staring at the mutilated body of Princess Elena.

And what of Elena's children and the lives that would now be changed because she had died, perhaps entire countries affected?

Tears rolled down Mirabella's eyes as she stared at the white-blue body of her friend, so pure and brave, her long black hair disheveled all about her.

Mirabella looked up at Sherlock, tears running down her cheek.

"We are the arm of justice," he murmured. *"We have failed."*

Thank God, that in this life, someone cared to protect the innocent.

She sat up from her bed as she awoke from her dream. shivering and sweating at the same time.

Chapter Twenty-one

"Good day, Miss Carnegie." A handsome gentleman with gorgeous turquoise eyes and streaked blonde hair, impeccably dressed, tipped his hat to Mirabella.

"Oh *my*," whispered Bethany under her breath, the other young ladies turning at once to look approvingly at Mirabella, each with a package in hand. They all carried parcels to make it appear they were out performing errands rather than walking for exercise, as Miss de Beauvais had explained was less to be admired.

Miss de Beauvais attended to every detail with an admirable devotion, even in these life-threatening times.

"And who are your lovely friends?" Dr. Watson asked. His sideburns reached a point just below his ears, and his hair was parted at the side.

"Princess Elena, Miss Bethany Allen, and Lady Jacqueline, this is . . . Hamish." A few days after the attack on Princess Elena, the young ladies took their walk as usual, utilizing a different appointed time and a different path as Mirabella suggested. Only Alexandra stayed in her room, the other four walking with a large, armed bodyguard in the front and at the back of their party. Two new bodyguards, as it were, those from the day prior having been replaced.

"Is it *Monsieur* Hamish?" Jacqueline asked, looking exquisite in a red and white striped linen day dress, her brown hair curled atop her head. She looked as if she had not lost a wink of sleep the night after the attack.

"Just Hamish," Watson replied, bowing and tipping his hat to Jacqueline. "But, you, Mademoiselle, may call me whatever you wish."

Giggling ensued, and Mirabella rolled her eyes. Why is it ladies became positively ridiculous whenever a man was about? Glancing at the dreamy John Watson, she was forced to be more understanding.

"At your service. May I walk with you ladies?" Dr. Watson asked, taking Mirabella's arm to the obvious envy of the others.

Princess Elena simply nodded, her eyes still on her bodyguards and their surroundings. The royal wore a large-brimmed hat in an effort to hide her identity, but her height was difficult to conceal. Naturally all of the ladies wore gloves and carried parasols, providing further concealment. Mirabella wondered if it might have been better to leave the bodyguards at *Miss de Beauvais'* as the guards' presence proclaimed their identity.

"And how do you know Hamish, Miss Carnegie?" Bethany asked, twirling her blue silk parasol, suspicion apparent in her matching cornflower blue eyes.

"I am a family friend," Dr. Watson replied.

"It is good to have ze friends," Jacqueline replied demurely, her admiration apparent.

Mirabella was delighted that John Watson required his right hand to hold a cane and his left arm was in hers, leaving no arm free for the beautiful Lady Jacqueline.

"Hamish is a doctor and a military man by trade," Mirabella added, insuring that the ladies knew he would be unacceptable to their parents as a potential match.

Dr. Watson raised his eyebrow at her, understanding her ploy.

Oh, my goodness! The finishing school is having an effect on me. I now have a ploy! Mirabella didn't know if she liked the change in herself or not. Had she become a schemer?

And scheming over a man, no less!

Yes, I am now one of them.

Regardless of her moral decline, in point of fact, all were delighted to have the company and protection of the handsome young doctor, who kept pace despite walking with a slight limp and a cane. Mirabella observed that John's pistol was strapped to his shirt inside his jacket. He might walk with a stiff leg, but he had an athletic build and she had seen him run under the threat of danger: John Watson was still definitely in his prime.

"Hello Miss Mirabella." A well dressed young man in front of the telegram office utilized by Sherlock Holmes and Dr. Watson nodded to Mirabella, causing Bethany and Jacqueline to study their popular companion with some amount of surprise.

To be popular among the ladies was good, but to be popular among the gentlemen was far more important.

"Do you know all the handsome men in London, Miss Mirabella?"

Bethany asked with a giggle.

*I am forever going there to send telegrams on Sherlock Holmes'
behalf.* "I am about town with my charity work, so naturally I will
meet people," Mirabella replied, holding Dr. Watson's arm more tightly.
"Only acquaintances, I assure you. Outside of Hamish, of course."

Jacqueline put her gloved hand on her mouth, stifling her laughter.
"Thus far the only *people* we have seen are ze men, not ze ladies."

"Mademoiselle," Mirabella paused her walking long enough to
curtsy to Jacqueline, joining in their mirth.

It did feel lovely to be one of them, she had to admit. She was
therefore reluctant to point out that the men she knew would not be
considered marriageable by the girls' parents—nor by they themselves,
if the truth be told.

The party walked along Chancery Lane, heading south on Kingsway.
From the road they could see "The Old Curiosity Shop" as immortalized
in Dickens' novel. They had the happy intention of reaching the Strand
when a strange person emerged suddenly from behind a large oak tree
at Lincoln's Inn Fields. Mirabella immediately clutched her reticule,
fingering her number thirty-two Marlin Pocket Revolver from within
her hand purse, the ivory handle smooth, attached as it was to the silver
embellishments on the barrel of the gun.

"Allo! Allo! Lawd above! Can yew spare a tuppins to an old
woman?" A bent over woman came out of the shadows, waddling
towards them and leaning on a cane. The old lady smiled, revealing
missing teeth throughout her mouth.

"Yes, of course," Princess Elena spoke for the first time, reaching
for her reticule. Mirabella had observed that Princess Elena could not
part with her money fast enough for the poor.

"No, Princess Elena," Mirabella whispered. "You must not let
people approach you. This is a weakness for you."

"Allo! Allo! Kind lady, let me tell yaaahr fortune." The old woman
reached for Elena's hand, but Mirabella dropped John Watson's arm and
moved between them.

"But the poor . . ." Princess Elena protested, reaching for the old
woman's hand.

"And she looks so hungry," murmured Bethany. "So *thin*."

"Lor' love a duck! I am 'ungry," the woman stated.

"She has no teeth, what good would food do her?" Mirabella

took the arm of the old woman, leading her aside forcefully and almost knocking her over. "No, we do not know her, I will attend."

"And who is the handsome gent? He looks to have a bit 'o blunt," the old lady asked as Mirabella shoved her to the side.

Gasp! Bethany stared aghast at Mirabella. John Watson stayed behind with the ladies while Mirabella spoke to the old woman. The good doctor was completely in his element now and could no doubt charm the beauties for hours, Mirabella reflected with annoyance.

She glanced in John's direction, sighing, before looking into the bloodshot eyes of the old woman, the smell of her clothes making her stomach do a half-turn.

"Hello, Miss Belle," Sherlock said with a smile.

"You need to shave," she muttered.

"No time. We're working day and night trying to find the group responsible for your attack, Miss Belle."

"What have you discovered, Mr. Holmes? The dead man, who was he?" she asked anxiously without further ado, pretending to look in her reticule for change.

"We only know that he appears to have been from one of the Balkan states. We haven't been able to identify him as Serbian, but that doesn't mean he isn't either," Sherlock stated. "These telegrams back and forth are not as fast as we would wish. We're still trying to discover if he was a Serbian anarchist who hated the monarchy."

"I don't understand," she murmured, looking up. "An Italian anarchist who hates the *Italian* monarchy would make sense—but Serbian? Princess Elena has Serbian blood in her."

"It is the same principle, Miss Belle," he replied. "These two groups one might lump together. An Italian anarchist despises the monarchy, but most of all the Italian monarchy. He believes the monarchy to be harming his own people, an enemy of the people, if you will. The same for a Serbian anarchist: he hates the Serbian monarchy."

"Don't you remember that the first attackers spoke Italian? Could they be working together?" she asked.

"Doubtful. Anarchists have a dislike of organizations and hierarchy. By definition, they cannot work within a group—even a group which hates groups. There is always a great deal of internal fighting among those with extreme views—which means that the individuals within often work alone though they might share ideologies with others.

Her head was throbbing. She didn't really care who was responsible as much as she cared about the answer to another question.

"Do you think there will be another attack, Mr. Holmes?" she asked, glancing to the gated pathway shaded by the large oak from which he had emerged. She knew that Lincoln's Inn Fields had been here since the twelfth century and that it was once a popular location for duelists. Somehow the violence enacted in the location did not fit the tranquility of the setting.

It was a reminder to her not to become complacent.

"I do," replied Sherlock. "Whatever their motive, now they may wish revenge in addition to their original motive."

"Oh, my! This is terrible." She shivered in her fashionable leather boots, seeing the face of her attacker holding a glistening knife in her mind's eye again.

"The Italian police have increased their efforts, naturally. They have caught the other man as well. He was *wounded*." Sherlock turned his back to the girls, pretending to put Mirabella's coin in his pocket in a fumbling manner. He glanced sideways to look into her eyes. Somberly he added, "Someone shot him."

She shook her head, even as her eyes scanned the park and adjoining square. She had never been calm since the attack. There were so many bushes and so much vegetation that it would be an easy thing to conceal oneself. "I never thought when I took a domestic job cleaning laboratory jars I might be required to murder someone."

Sherlock studied her, as if he were reading her mind.

She had really come to hate that.

"Are you afraid to murder someone else, Miss Belle, should the situation arise?"

"Naturally I would not wish to do so!" She bit her lip, hoping to keep a tear from falling down her cheek. Since that didn't work she feigned laughter and looked away. "But I would to save myself or another innocent."

Everyone turned to look at her laughing. Sherlock patted her on the back as an old woman might regard her benefactor.

"Excellent job, Miss Belle, it had to be done." He eyed her with approval, an expression she rarely beheld from the great Sherlock Holmes.

Ordinarily she would jump through hoops for that expression on

Sherlock's chiseled, dark face. Somehow murdering someone to earn it was . . . well . . . disturbing.

"Otherwise, I have every reason to think that Princess Elena would now be dead—perhaps after being tortured," Sherlock added.

"I know," she nodded. "It was very clear these people meant to harm the princess!"

"When they entered the parlor of a ladies' finishing school with a gun, there was not a lot of room for interpretation," Sherlock stated somberly.

"A gun and a knife," she murmured.

"All Princess Elena wants to do is to marry her love," Mirabella felt her indignation rising, turning quickly into an anger she found difficult to control. And which frightened her at the same time. "Why on earth would someone wish to kill that dear, generous girl?"

"That is the mystery to be solved, is it not, Miss Belle?" Sherlock asked.

"I hope you solve it quickly, before they kill her—and me!"

"It is all in your capable hands, Miss Belle," he murmured. "Never wait for someone else to save your skin."

"*Me*? What can I do?"

"You are with Princess Elena all day. How are you spending your time? What have you learned?"

"I am simply baffled, Sherlock! It has gone round and round in my head. The men were speaking Serbian," she exclaimed, keeping her voice as low as possible. "If it were the Italian anarchists, it would make more sense to me. They hate the monarchy—and everything associated with it. But in addition, they may hate the color of the princess' skin, her race, her language, and her religion as well."

"And what is her religion, Miss Belle?" Sherlock asked, although she knew he knew the answer and was only testing her. "Do you recall?"

"She is Serbian Orthodox, it is a Christian religion." Mirabella glanced at the Serbian beauty, the only one of the party who was not entranced by Dr. John Watson.

"Some Catholics may not think so," he smiled, his eyes suddenly soft.

"How lovely. We have yet one more faction who doesn't wish Elena and Vittorio to wed. Compared to these two, Romeo and Juliet look like an arranged marriage sanctioned by the Montagues and the Capulets."

"And what else have you learned, Miss Belle?" Sherlock asked.

"Oh, I almost forgot. I know what has been bothering me all along: Princess Elena said the men spoke Serbian—but with a Turkish accent."

"Great scott, Miss Belle, why didn't you say so! Don't you know the Serbs and the Turks are enemies?" Sherlock exclaimed, all eyes turning towards them. He immediately lowered his voice, turning towards her.

"I have been so distraught over killing a man that I rather forgot."

"The Balkan states have been under Ottoman—which is to say, Turkish—rule. Now we have something to go on!"

"What? I don't see that we have anything to go on," she protested. "And, even if we did, I don't see how all this academic investigation is going to stop them from killing us."

"Please focus, Miss Belle. Tell me what you know about the Ottoman Empire."

She sighed heavily. "Montenegro is one of the Balkan states, until quite recently part of the Ottoman Empire."

"Very good, Miss Belle. Most assuredly, Montenegro borders Serbia, Turkey, and Bosnia. To the east is Roumania and Bulgaria, to the south is Greece," murmured Sherlock, stroking his chin as an old woman might do in negotiating a good price for the day-old turnips in her bag.

"And they were all on the same side in the recent war with the Ottoman Empire," she added.

"Indeed." Sherlock nodded. "Serbia, Montenegro, Romania, and Bulgaria declared their independence from the Ottoman Empire in the Russo-Turkish War of eighteen hundred seventy-eight."

"So the Ottoman Empire lost a great deal of territory," she murmured, adding, "My head is spinning. There are so many groups who wish Princess Elena ill that I don't know where we are headed. But this seems rather unimportant. The war is over. The Ottomans have already lost. How is killing Princess Elena going to help them?"

"If the assassins were Turkish, I think there is only one interpretation one can put on that," Sherlock mused.

"Yesterday in the parlor there were no bodyguards and no private detectives in there to help us!" She felt herself becoming angry. "How do you interpret that, Mr. Holmes? I will tell you: We had to save ourselves!"

"You did, and I must say I am far more impressed than I ever expected to be," Sherlock murmured.

She glared at him.

"Do you wish to leave my employ, Miss Belle?" he asked softly.

Never. I am having the time of my life. "Not truly," she replied. "But I don't wish to die, either!"

"They will have to kill me first," he murmured.

"Where were you when they attacked, Mr. Holmes?" she demanded. She hated to be so blunt, but the question needed to be asked.

Whether or not Sherlock Holmes would answer was an entirely different matter altogether.

"We had a man guarding the front door, there were two body guards inside the building. Henceforth, there is a body guard inside the room with you at all times."

"I just wish we knew more and that *someone, anyone*—Scotland Yard, the Italian police, Slavic bodyguards—would capture these men!"

"Never fear! We are on the case." His eyes were alight with excitement. Rather like a madman.

"We don't even know who is responsible! How are we going to find them?"

"We will find them, Miss Belle."

"I am much reassured," she muttered.

"Take care, Miss Belle," he stated.

"I will. Thank you Mr. Holmes." She looked inside her purse. "Oh, and I need another knife." *I lost mine in the chest of an assassin.*

"THANK YOU, DEARY," he exclaimed, patting the tuppins in his pocket.

Mirabella returned to the group, and they continued their walk.

"You certainly spoke with that old lady for a long time," Bethany observed.

"She is definitely the type I try to avoid," muttered Mirabella.

"Oh, and what type is that?" asked Dr. Watson.

"Very needy. Demanding. Talkative. The type who believes to know everything but does nothing to help one." Mirabella frowned.

"It is better to humor that type," Dr. Watson agreed.

"And escape at the earliest possible moment," Mirabella added.

"It was a good deed you did," Princess Elena stated. "We should not judge those less fortunate who mean no harm."

"That fortune teller means a great deal of harm, I assure you," Mirabela muttered under her breath.

"G'day, miss," a young door man in front of the *Charing Cross Hotel* nodded to Mirabella after they resumed their walk.

"It seems you have quite a lot of suitors, Miss Carnegie," Dr. Watson interjected with a smile, and it was apparent from their expressions that he was voicing the thoughts of the young ladies.

"It seems that way, doesn't it?" *Although I begin to think nothing is what it seems.*

Mirabella smiled, enjoying John's dancing eyes. *Definitely the best part of my day.*

"Aha! Here we are, the Bank of England, where I shall take my leave. But wait, a carriage. Let me hail it for you and return you to *Miss de Beauvais'.*"

Chapter Twenty-two

"Was it love at first sight for you and Prince Victor Emmanuel?" Mirabella asked that evening when they were situated in the parlor after dinner. All had exhausted talking of the dreadful events which occurred earlier in the week, with Alexandra the only one among them who appeared to appreciate the danger they had been in. And something had changed: *Mirabella was now one of them.* They didn't all roll their eyes every time she asked a question.

Princess Elena glanced at the bodyguard now stationed inside the parlor at the door.

"Yes," nodded Elena, leaning forward to whisper to the girls. "For both of us."

"Why are you here, Princess Elena?" Mirabella asked.

"*Here?* In the parlor? Where should I be?"

"What is the point in being here, in a finishing school? To entice your prince to like you? He already is deliriously smitten, that is quite obvious. To inspire other people to like you? It is beyond your control: people will like you or they won't, and often as not it has more to do with them than with you."

"For shame, Miss Carnegie!" Bethany covered her mouth with her hands, but her eyes sparkled. The evening was when the ladies let their hair down, so to speak. They might be fully dressed and corseted in their daywear—Mirabella was the only one of the girls who wore a wrapper—but the evening allowed them spontaneity of speech. Even with the bodyguard present, they managed to keep their voices subdued.

Miss de Beauvais spent much of the daylight hours with the girls, drilling them mercilessly on deportment, manners, and proper conversation—dinner was exceedingly disagreeable—but the headmistress kept to her rooms in the evening.

"I am here to learn to be charming," Elena answered without the slightest tonality in her voice, patting her pistol inside her reticule. "So I will be acceptable to Prince Vittorio."

"Why aren't you with Prince Victor Emmanuel rather than here, finding out if he likes you—and more importantly, *if you like him*?"

Princess Elena raised her chin. "I wish to learn to be a lady first. Once I have learned to eat and drink, to dance, and to giggle—then we shall find if we are suited."

My goodness, two sentences. Prince Vittorio is obviously a topic of great usefulness in developing language skills.

"Once you have erected the social façade, then you shall strip it away to reveal what was there to begin with, is that it, your highness?" demanded Mirabella, returning to be seated at the couch. Jacqueline and Alexandra peered out the window.

"Yes," replied Princess Elena.

"The façade is needed to attract, *naturellement*," agreed Jacqueline.

CLIP-CLOP! CLIP-CLOP! CREAK!

"I don't see anyone out there," muttered Lady Alexandra, the cuirasse bustle of her maroon silk gown in full view as she gazed at a particularly ornate carriage driving by, her golden brown hair gleaming in the candlelight.

"Of course you see someone. The gas lights are on and this is Regent Street; there is always activity in this most fashionable part of London," argued Bethany, sitting up momentarily.

"I mean no one *suspicious*," exclaimed Alexandra defiantly, placing her hands on her hips, but her gaze remained glued to the window as she moved to sit down beside it.

Bethany was seated near the piano on a beige velvet fainting couch, looking quite lovely in a lavender silk gown, offsetting her platinum blonde hair and blue eyes. Bethany was short and bouncy. Her features were not exceptional, but she was so full of joy that she was instantly made beautiful. Mirabella thought Bethany might well be the one to make the catch of the season.

There had to be one.

"Princess Elena," pressed Mirabella, ignoring Alexandra. "Only but consider. It seems to me that your quiet demeanor has been working for you quite effectively and what is more important is to find out how you and your prince feel about each other. I certainly know how to talk, and people don't like me as often as not."

"Maybe she's afraid her prince won't like her if he learns she cannot sparkle at social events," suggested Alexandra coyly, turning momentarily from her post with the best view of the outside.

"She will simply shoot him then," considered Bethany, shaking her blonde curls as she studied her needlework.

"I would not, Miss Bethany!" Elena giggled for the first time in their presence, quickly mastering that lesson. "However, the prince would have to make a gift of a fine stallion for my trouble."

All the girls laughed, though Mirabella could see the princess was serious on this point.

Mirabella glanced at the bodyguard. He was so quiet that the girls quite forgot he was there. Was she mistaken, or did he look . . . Italian?

She hoped he would be there if danger were to arise.

"Princess Elena she is quite stunning and can *sparkle* without ze speech," added Jacqueline, looking up from her work, the candlelight a glow on her pale skin and dark eyes.

"And she is *genuine,*" added Bethany, glaring at Alexandra. "Quite rare."

"If Prince Victor Emmanuel should not like you, then what will you do, Princess Elena?" demanded Alexandra.

"Return home and look for a true prince," replied Princess Elena, nonplussed.

"A warrior prince," suggested Mirabella, seated next to Elena on the couch opposite the fireplace, as she loved to watch the flickering lights and feel the warmth on her skin. Somehow these evenings with strangers in the gaudiest of surroundings she had come to find very relaxing.

Elena nodded, her expression once again serious. "Like my father. He was a warrior before he was king."

"A true warrior king," Mirabella murmured.

"I fear we will never finish the gifts for these orphan girls we don't even know," Alexandra admonished, returning to her seat.

"Je ne sais pas pour quoi you complain, Alexandra, when I am making ze truly gift difficile: la dress de velours bleu," Jacqueline remarked.

"I wish to play the piano!" exclaimed Bethany, throwing her embroidery down. "Much more fun than sewing! Shall I play now and allow you to practice your dancing?"

"Fifteen minutes more, and then we shall play to our heart's content," proclaimed Mirabella.

All the girls groaned.

"Doing some form of charity works makes one much more appealing to prospective suitors," advised Mirabella.

"My mother says that piano, dance, needlework, and French is all that is needed to catch a husband," pronounced Alexandra. "If one has the right pedigree."

"Or plenty of money," added Bethany, raising her chin and smiling sweetly.

"I suppose you have a considerable amount of money, Miss Allen," Alexandra retorted.

"I am very rich, Alexi," Bethany replied, giggling. "Much richer than you, I expect."

"Then we shall be friends forever," Princess Elena replied without hesitation.

All the girls burst into giggles and laughter.

Jacqueline smiled to herself, not looking up from her sewing.

"I do not hold to excelling at nothing and doing only that which is required," suggested Mirabella. "And having marriage as the only goal."

"One is either married or one isn't," replied Alexandra. "I don't see what else should matter."

"Lady Alexandra . . . what interests you? What do you enjoy doing?" asked Mirabella.

"I'm sure I never thought about it." Alexandra seated herself next to the bay window where she liked to keep watch, but generally during the daylight hours only. The disturbance had brought out her worst side, she was obviously frightened.

"I expect Alexi would enjoy being married to the catch of the season!" smiled Bethany, her ill humor not lasting very long.

"*Doubtful*," murmured Mirabella.

"Have you lost your mind?" demanded Alexandra, looking away from the window momentarily.

"If you never enjoy anything now, what makes you think you would then?" asked Mirabella.

"Spoken like an old maid," chuckled Alexandra, smiling for the first time in days.

Chapter Twenty-three

"I'm sure there are other important goals in life besides marriage," remarked Mirabella, even as one of the maids brought in the evening tea service. "Such as . . . *discovery*, that moment when the mind explodes with enlightenment and understanding." Mirabella hugged herself though she sat on the satin wing-backed day couch next to Lady Jacqueline and Princess Elena.

"Or adventure. Running like the wind on a horse," Princess Elena mused. "Or sword fighting."

"I love so much the sewing," Jacqueline murmured with a sigh. "I wish it did not disturb my mama."

"Why should sewing disturb your mama, Lady Jacqueline?" Bethany asked as she played Beethoven's Moonlight Sonata softly, seemingly more focused on the music than the conversation.

"Because it is a servant's job, of course," Alexandra replied. She was seated on the chair beside the window, facing the other three huddled together doing their needlework on the parlor couch.

"We do nothing but embroidery all day, is that not sewing?" Princess Elena asked without looking up, covered from head to toe in white lace.

"Jacqueline is speaking of making entire gowns!" Alexandra exclaimed. "The clothing one wears must be made by a modiste naturally. A *French* modiste."

"I am Français," replied Jacqueline.

"Do not let someone else take away your joy," advised Mirabella. "Even your mama. Do what you love, Lady Jacqueline. Why are we doing all this if it doesn't bring us happiness?"

"You are an artist very accomplished, Lady Jacqueline," Princess Elena stated softly. "Why do you not draw some dress designs for us? It would save us from much boredom."

Jacqueline's face lit up at this. "I might even paint the gowns with the water colors."

"Whatever you may say about the joys of personal ambition," Bethany shook her head in disapproval, "marriage and children is yet a worthy goal—and can yield much happiness."

"You have found the activity which you love to do and which ignites your passion, Bethany," Mirabella stated softly. "You should encourage the other girls to find theirs as well."

"Ignites her passion?" Jacqueline giggled. "I know my mama would not care for that!"

Bethany continued the sonata, her expression resolute. "With the possible exception of music, I do not think anything can be more satisfying than love—and having a family of one's own."

In point of fact, nothing could have displayed a prettier picture of that which was both heavenly and meaningful in life than the blonde Bethany at the piano in a cornflower blue silk and lace gown, Mirabella reflected. Possibly the addition of a miniature Bethany beside the older version. Miss de Beauvais' oil painting behind Bethany's head was somewhat frightening, but, to her credit, Bethany was able to make even that busy splash of color look as if it were a backdrop to her pure simplicity.

"I agree, children are so enriching to one's life," Jacqueline stated. She sighed, adding, "And having a home of one's own."

Mirabella poured tea from the ceramic teapot painted with purple and yellow pansies. She paused for a moment, staring at the teapot as an idea came to her. "Very true! In fact, we should invite the girls from the orphanage to *Miss de Beauvais'* for a tea party!"

"Orphan girls come *here,*" exclaimed Alexandra. "Are they quite *clean?*"

"Quite," replied Mirabella indignantly, fingering the gold cross around her neck. She had initially conceived the idea as a way to take the ladies' minds off the attack; it was absolutely essential that the fear not be allowed to fester and control them, or she had no doubt there would be dire consequences.

Particularly from Alexandra, who liked to stir up trouble—and was bored. Combining boredom with fear and insecurity did not show Lady Alexandra to her best advantage.

Sigh. An attack by maniacal killers had a way of disrupting one's peace of mind.

Mirabella was all too aware that she was not without her nightmares, but the violence seemed to have taken its toll to the greatest degree on Alexandra—which had elevated Mirabella's opinion of Lady

Alexandra's intelligence, who seemed to be the only one of the girls to perceive the danger. Certainly Princess Elena understood, but the princess was so supremely fearless that her level of fear could not be used as an indicator of her perceptivity.

Unfortunately, Lady Alexandra's awareness had created an internal battle, and which was the last thing Alexandra needed! The Duke of Glazebury's daughter was too afraid to stay at the finishing school—and too afraid to leave.

Or too afraid of her parents.

"Don't stare at me so, Miss Carnegie!" Alexandra exclaimed. "I have heard of lice and other nasty things which you certainly would not wish to have!"

"The girls are merely without parents," Mirabella retorted, moving forward in her seat as her arm brushed the white lace of Princess Elena's gown. "They are not living in filthy conditions!"

"We must do what we can to help them," agreed Bethany, now softly playing a Beethoven lullaby. "We have so much. My father says to those who have been given much, much is expected."

"Oh, je ne sais pas. *I don't know.*" Jacqueline sighed heavily, even as her eyes caught Alexandra's. "C'est good to make ze beautiful things for the little girls—but to come *ici*? Est-ce wise?"

Elena looked up over her teacup. "I will protect you, Lady Jacqueline. Do not fear."

"Miss de Beauvais will never agree to it," stated Alexandra.

"And why should Miss de Beauvais have any objection?" Mirabella asked, smoothing her blue and beige striped wrapper.

"Miss de Beauvais has us under lock and key," Bethany considered. "Especially now. I am surprised that she lets us take our morning walks."

"Only when we are accompanied by a full calvary!" exclaimed Bethany, giggling.

"Exactly so," stated Mirabella. "She can have no objection to a charity event within the walls of the finishing school."

"Miss de Beauvais is not heartless," Bethany added.

I wouldn't be so sure.

"*Bon.* Miss de Beauvais she is exceedingly kind," Jacqueline stated, her beautiful wide eyes filled with admiration.

More likely Miss de Beauvais perceived that the girls were safer out amongst society than they were where the criminals know them to be, Mirabella reflected to herself.

"We are allowed short morning walks," agreed Alexandra, her attention suddenly on Mirabella, "with the exception of Miss Carnegie who appears to be able to come and go as she chooses."

"Would you like to come and go, Lady Alexandra?" Princess Elena asked. "I had not observed it. You are mostly in your room now."

"Not necessarily," Alexandra replied with her chin raised. "I simply cannot for the life of me understand why Miss Carnegie has more freedom than the rest of us. *Maybe she knows something.*"

"If you wish to accompany Miss Mirabella to the orphanage, Lady Alexandra, I've no doubt it would be allowed," proposed Princess Elena, adding with a warm smile, "I will help to arrange it."

"I will do no such thing! And a party for the orphans would be a terrible amount of work. Most unnecessary," protested Alexandra while setting her teacup nonchalantly on the table beside her.

"Work for whom?" asked Mirabella picking up her favorite book of poetry by Alfred Lord Tennyson, being in the habit of reading to the ladies in the evening. "Certainly not for us—we never lift a finger around here!"

"Never lift a finger? You have us working 'round the clock, Mirabella Carnegie," admonished Alexandra, adding under her breath, "When we aren't hiding under the beds for our lives."

"That is not fair," Bethany interjected. "Miss Mirabella and Princess Elena saved us. You can't put that at either of their doors, Alexi."

"Thank you, Bethany," Mirabella acknowledged. "As for the tea party, someone else will do all the cooking and setting up. We already have all the tablecloths and decorations. In fact, it is the perfect opportunity for us to practice the social skills we have been striving to develop."

"I would much prefer to practice with young men than with orphan girls," stated Alexandra.

"I agree!" Bethany exclaimed, giggling without taking her eyes off the piano keyboard as she changed the tune to a Strauss waltz.

Alexandra and Jacqueline both giggled.

"I can assure you it would give these girls the greatest joy to be treated so kindly," pleaded Mirabella. "They receive astonishingly little attention in that place—and *no love* except what they give each other."

"What musical instruments do they play?" asked Bethany, looking up from her keys.

"None," replied Mirabella. "Susan has a beautiful voice—but they have no instruments and certainly no encouragement or musical training."

"A world without music would be a world *without magic*," murmured Bethany, shaking her head.

"We might donate some musical instruments, a used piano, or books to begin their library," suggested Mirabella.

"They don't have a piano*?"* repeated Bethany, the lovely waltz coming to an abrupt halt.

"No," replied Mirabella.

"And no books?" asked Princess Elena. "How do they learn?"

"They have a very few arithmetic and grammar books."

The excitement level was rising and Mirabella was much encouraged. Not only was the plan good for the children, but the project was infusing passion and purpose into this single-minded group.

A group she was coming to like more: She could not discount Bethany's kind heart, who was revealing more of her true feelings very day, and Jacqueline had simply been overly sheltered, she was a lovely girl as well. Alexandra—well, she was bitter but intelligent. Her ladyship used unpleasantness to cover up a wound of some type.

Mirabella had a sudden awareness that these ladies beside her were even less free than she was. Although their worries were not financial, they were far more limited in how they could present themselves to the world. There was a price for their fine dresses and jewels.

Mirabella knew in her heart she wished to set her own course—it might be terribly difficult, and society might fight her every step of the way, but she was determined to try.

"But doesn't the organization's trust provide for these gifts and things you are proposing?" asked Alexandra, sighing heavily.

"Apparently not," Mirabella shrugged. "There must not be much money in the trust, and it is very expensive to run such an establishment. Though I sometimes wonder if it is more a condition of those in charge of the orphanage: their hearts do not appear to be in it."

"It must be a place *très triste*," considered Jacqueline, her eyes suddenly sad.

"I still do not see how we will have time," argued Alexandra. "We are so busy with your project that we have no time to devote to the reason we are here. If I do not find a husband, Mirabella Carnegie, I lay that entirely at your feet!"

"Of course you will obtain a husband, Lady Alexandra, if that is what you wish!" stated Mirabella truthfully, making an expression which she hoped was one of complete boredom. "Your father is a duke, you are rich, and you are quite beautiful."

"It might do well to speak less, Lady Alexandra," Elena offered helpfully.

All the young ladies turned and stared at the Princess even as Bethany placed her hand over her mouth in mirth.

"Why do you look at me?" asked Princess Elena. "I am not the first to say this."

"We must finish these gifts and start preparing for the Christmas Ball!" added Alexandra, nonplussed, waving her handkerchief. "Our *first* ball!"

"In what way do we need to prepare?" asked Mirabella pointedly. "We already have our gowns. We take dance classes every day. We walk across the room with books on our heads. We are taught how to hold our silverware and what we can say and what we cannot. What else must we do?"

"It has nothing to do with us, and I am tired of your acting as if you are in charge here, Mirabella Carnegie," proclaimed Alexandra, her lips tightening.

"We will have a tea party for the orphans," Princess Elena pronounced, lowering her head and speaking in a whisper.

"Well, I simply won't agree to it! And I will go to Miss de Beauvais and tell her how much I dislike the idea!" huffed Alexandra.

"You dislike every idea, Alexi," Bethany stated. Mirabella actually pitied Lady Alexandra, she was very cross, and so afraid. Afraid of not marrying well, afraid of another attack, afraid of her parents' disapproval.

Just afraid.

Princess Elena shook her head in disapproval, her black eyes intent upon Alexandra. "I fear you have learned nothing in this school, Lady Alexandra. I am not sure why you came if you did not wish to learn to become a lady. For me, I had to learn to speak my heart. For you, it is the heart you need."

All eyes turned to Princess Elena, with more than a few dropped jaws.

The Princess of Montenegro had found her tongue.

Chapter Twenty-four

"Miss Carnegie," began Miss de Beauvais gently but without an air of compromise. Sherlock recognized that air very well. "It is all very well to wish to do charity work, but these girls are here for a single purpose—and unfortunately, you are interfering with that purpose."

"It is Alexandra, isn't it?" Mirabella asked.

"No, it is the Duke of Glazebury. He is not pleased."

"As I said, it is Alexandra." Mirabella tapped her fingers on the desk. "If Lady Alexandra does not wish to participate, why is she simply indisposed on the day? I'm sure she does precisely what she likes at every other second of every other day. Is there any reason for her to ruin it for the rest of us—and the orphans, who so badly need the mere crumbs from our table?"

Sherlock felt the corner of his lip fighting a smile. He was rarely amused—and never so entertained as when in the company of Miss Mirabella Hudson.

"Very inappropriate to gossip about the other young ladies who are not present," Miss de Beauvais stated with indignity.

"Not nearly as inappropriate as attempting to expel the young ladies one does not personally like," Sherlock drawled. "Without which we would not be here gossiping. My dear niece would never dream of acting with so little Christian charity. I am surprised that you cater to such self-serving ill will, Miss de Beauvais."

His amusement was by now entirely dissipated, even more so because Miss Belle had suddenly assumed a strange behavior.

Sherlock stared at her with consternation. *Strange even for her*.

He raised his eyebrow in disapproval at his ward, who was fidgeting with the contents of her reticule. Why did she pick this inopportune moment to reorganize her belongings?

Uhm-hmmm. He cleared his throat. His eyes pierced hers and he knew his meaning was clear: *the entire case is on the line at this very moment.*

Miss Hudson grew more and more agitated, items slipping from her fingers.

Both Sherlock and Miss de Beauvais turned towards her in perplexity, the older woman frowning with even more force than she had previously displayed. "Miss Carnegie?"

Suddenly a pound note flew out of Miss Belle's purse, landing on Miss de Beauvais desk.

"Miss de Beauvais, would you mind to hand me my note back?" Mirabella asked sweetly.

The older woman snatched the note with a bit more force than was necessary in the emotion of the moment, an emotion which Mirabella had quite purposely escalated, Sherlock was certain. An expression of annoyance crossed the proprietress' face for an instant before it was contained as she stared down the younger woman.

Sherlock could not help but chuckle, appreciating Miss Belle's commentary. Even without the ruse, the clever Miss Belle knew the one thing Miss de Beauvais would be unable to resist touching: currency.

"What is this?" Miss de Beauvais demanded. "There is some type of ink on this!" She threw the note on the table, which Mirabella promptly picked up by the edges even as Miss de Beauvais searched for her handkerchief. His instructions had been to obtain the proprietress' fingerprint upon his suspicions—and Miss Hudson's timing was impeccable.

"I'm afraid Miss Carnegie is just not working out here," purred Miss de Beauvais consolingly, turning towards Sherlock as she wiped her hand with her handkerchief. "She is *exceedingly* strongwilled."

"Exceedingly. In the Carnegie family we don't consider that a failing." Sherlock Holmes tapped his fingers on the desk. Taking out his pipe he began to fill it with tobacco. "So the other girls don't like my niece?"

"Oh, they quite look up to her, Mr. Carnegie. Otherwise, how could she have any influence one way or the other?"

"So you're saying Miss Carnegie is a bad influence?"

"Precisely."

"Because she wishes to aid orphans?" Sherlock took a slow leisurely puff on his pipe. He had not been so calm with Miss Hudson, accusing her of botching the mission—and rightly so. She was reckless, following her conscience above all things without thought of the consequences.

He might give the girl a hard time for her own good—but let this high flying biddy do so, he would not.

"In a manner of speaking," Miss de Beauvais added after a long pause.

"What type of finishing school teaches girls to be selfish? I thought the purpose of such training was to produce worthy young ladies."

"No," she replied definitively. "The purpose is to produce *marriageable* young ladies."

"And what type of young man does a selfish, conniving young woman attract? Here I have brought you a jewel and you have attempted to taint her finish."

"Miss Carnegie has an excellent character without question. She is simply not *a good fit*. I think it would be best for all concerned if you found other accommodations for her." As greedy as she was, Miss de Beauvais did have to care about her reputation; apparently a duke pushing his weight around trumped a wealthy merchant.

"One would have thought that the proprietress would have felt an enormous gratitude toward one who had saved the life of her prize pupil. And a good thing it is that Miss Carnegie exercised her 'strong will' as you put it," Sherlock stated. Why would Miss de Beauvais wish such an asset removed from her midst?

"Oh, you know about that, do you, Mr. Carnegie?" Miss de Beauvais blushed, something Sherlock would have never thought to see.

"Did you think that by removing Miss Carnegie, all this unpleasant business would simply go away? It is quite the opposite, in fact."

"I did think Miss Carnegie to be the only one of the girls brave enough to spill the beans, so to speak. And it appears I was right." Miss de Beauvais attempted to hide her dislike of Mirabella, but the eyes never lied.

"Or is it that you don't wish Princess Elena to be safe?" Sherlock pressed.

"How can you say such a thing, Mr. Carnegie!" she exclaimed, having lost all composure.

"You need to repay your friends, not kick them out the door," Sherlock mused, taking a puff on his pipe. "What am I to think?"

Miss de Beauvais cleared her throat in an agitated fashion. "I did not wish to bring it up—quite inappropriate—but there is the matter of the . . . the . . . *unmentionables*."

Sherlock raised his eyebrow, glancing at Mirabella.

"She means the corset," Mirabella remarked.

Miss de Beauvais closed her eyes momentarily, apparently quite distressed. "Do you see what I mean? Most inappropriate conversation!"

"You brought it to our attention, Miss de Beauvais. My niece did not. Since your accusation regarding the matter is your justification for dismissing Miss Carnegie, what choice does she have but to explain the matter? If she says nothing, you dismiss her; if she vindicates herself, you dismiss her on the grounds that it was inappropriate conversation!"

Miss de Beauvais shook her head, appearing most discomfited.

"You see, Uncle Lochlan, the school requirement is to utilize the corset to reduce the waist one inch per month until Miss de Beauvais determines the waist is small enough. We have heard rumor that one girl left this school with a fourteen inch waist."

"It is no rumor, it is true," replied Miss de Beauvais with obvious pride. "These type of results set our school apart."

"No doubt they do," Sherlock agreed.

"Some of the girls are fainting, none can eat much, some have headaches," Mirabella continued. She added under her breath, "It is no wonder that Alexandra is a bit ill-tempered."

"And some experience a sort of euphoria . . ." added Miss de Beauvais. "None have complained to me."

"Oh, I think they quite like the competition, and the results," Mirabella continued. "The girls are required to wear the corsets even when they sleep. Being allowed to remove them for bathing, perhaps a few hours a week."

"And you refused to be subjected to this regimen, Mirabella?" Sherlock asked sternly.

"I did," Mirabella replied.

"Good," pronounced Sherlock. "Thus far, Miss de Beauvais, all you have done is point out that my niece is more intelligent than the other girls and not swayed by the admonitions of either you or the group, indicative of an independence which the Carnegies value."

"Independence is well and good among the male population," Miss de Beauvais replied. "But not the female."

"I beg to differ—independent thought has kept my niece alive, and possibly the other girls as well. Moreover, I must note that Princess Elena is extremely independent, and she will very likely be the queen of Italy in the future."

Sherlock would have wished to pursue that line of logic when at that moment there was a frantic knock on the door.

"I am sorry, Mr. Carnegie, but my mind is made up," Miss de Beauvais continued, ignoring the interruption. "Our business is concluded. I think it best that Miss Carnegie find another school."

"Then there is the not so little matter of a refund," stated Sherlock, puffing on his pipe and appearing as if he were settled in for the afternoon.

"We never refund, particularly if it is determined the young lady is unsuitable."

Miss de Beauvais frowned at the maid opening the door. "I thought I instructed you—"

"Miss de Beauvais! A representative of—"

A very large dark-skinned man of African-Arabic descent flung the door wide open, strutting in the room. He was wearing a top hat, a maroon silk Ascot cravat, a white pressed shirt, and black tails.

"Mr. Abdul-Majid," she nodded. "Mr. Carnegie and his niece were just leaving."

Momentarily the large man turned and bowed to Sherlock, who, in point of fact, was not leaving, before resuming his ferocious gaze upon Miss de Beauvais.

Sherlock had to admit that Miss de Beauvais had courage; she did not appear ruffled.

"What is this?" Mr. Abdul-Majid demanded, flapping a piece of paper about.

"I'm sure I don't know; I can't see it. But wouldn't you prefer to discuss it in *private?* Mr. Carnegie, I believe our business is concluded."

Sherlock continued pressing the tobacco into his pipe, feigning disinterest.

"I have a telegram from King Nicholas I of Montenegro. "

Sherlock glanced at the paper in Mr. Abdul-Majid's hands with interest. No doubt King Nicholas had received his telegram stating that there were indications that Miss Mirabella was not in good standing with Miss de Beauvais, the same Miss Mirabella who had saved Princess Elena's life.

He reflected with satisfaction that he had surmised correctly when he had first received a summons from Miss de Beauvais. The only possible explanation for such a summons was the removal of Miss Belle from the premises—or the threat of doing so. The tone of Miss de Beauvais' note had not been congratulatory but ominous.

Please come immediately. There is a matter of grave importance to discuss. He did not know the specific transgression committed by Miss Hudson, but she had a way of ruffling feathers, as was often the case with those of a superior intellect. How well he knew that.

Miss de Beauvais' gaze was now fixated upon Mr. Abdul-Majid, who was pacing wildly about the room. With Miss de Beauvais' eyes averted, Mirabella slipped the pound note to Sherlock.

"What is the meaning of this?" demanded Mr. Abdul-Majid.

"The meaning of *what?*" At this point she stood. "If you would kindly step into—"

"King Nicholas is in a great state of fury. He says you are antagonizing his daughter's particular friend. He can hardly believe the report!"

"I wasn't aware the king's daughter had a particular friend," Miss de Beauvais murmured, her face turning ashen grey. She had obviously assumed that Princess Elena had made no mention of the attack to her parents. A reasonably good assumption given the fact that the princess had not been pulled from the school.

Miss de Beauvais glanced at Mirabella who smiled sweetly. Sherlock took a puff on his pipe, gazing attentively at the woman behind the desk.

"Princess Elena said nothing to me. But, n-no, Mr. Abdul-Majid, antagonize? It is not precisely like that! "

"What is it like *precisely* then?" demanded Mr. Abdul-Majid.

"Yes, what is it like precisely, Miss de Beauvais?" asked Sherlock. "When you told Miss Mirabella to leave, what did you mean?"

Mirabella tilted her head, awaiting the answer, all eyes on Miss de Beauvais.

"Some of the other parents felt—"

"Which other parents? Name them—*immediately.*"

"Well, the duke of Glazebury has some objection to Miss Carnegie's outside activities. His lordship feels that his daughter's time could be better spent . . . But surely you don't wish to discuss this with—"

"What outside activities?" demanded Mr. Abdul-Majid, now leaning on the desk towards Miss de Beauvais.

"I believe our esteemed proprietress refers to Miss Carnegie's charitable works with orphans."

"You object to helping orphans?" Mr. Abdul-Majid exclaimed, his eyebrows raised in interest.

"Certainly not!" Miss de Beauvais replied indignantly, seated once again. "But the time involved takes away from the stated purposes of the finishing school—"

"—Princess Elena told me herself that she has time to learn everything required of her with so much time left over that she doesn't know what to do with herself." Mr. Abdul-Majid smiled for a brief instant. "And I must say she expressed herself more forcefully than she has in the past. Which is the only reason King Nicholas has *not yet* pulled her from this wretched place."

"But as you say, if she and the Carnegie girl are friends—"

"Are you saying that Princess Elena would lie?" demanded Mr. Abdul-Majid.

"Is that what you're saying, Miss de Beauvais?" Sherlock asked, puffing on his pipe.

"No! Of course not!"

"Frankly, it's becoming very difficult to follow your train of thought, which is often self-contradictory," Sherlock muttered under his breath.

"Good," pronounced Mr. Abdul-Majid. "Princess Elena might not be as polished as your girls who never give a thought for anything but themselves, but in my country royalty is nothing more than a call to service. It is not an opportunity for one's own glory. I begin to think your school is not the right one for the princess of Montenegro and I should report as such to his royal highness. The Russian czar is visiting, looking for a school for his daughter, and he will be interested in my report as well."

"Oh, no, Mr. Abdul-Majid, *please*, it is nothing more than a misunderstanding. Of course we shall entertain the orphans. I can't think of anything that would be better for the girls."

"Nor I," agreed Sherlock, nodding with complacent acceptance of the outcome.

"And the *Carnegie girl* as you put it?" asked Mr. Abdul-Majid.

"Delightful girl. I can't imagine the motive behind such an obviously false report." Miss de Beauvais picked up her fan and began fanning himself.

"It is difficult to fathom," considered Sherlock, contemplating the unsolvable mystery.

"Good." Mr. Abdul-Majid tilted his hat to her, but his eyes looked as if they were ready to shoot flames. "I hope I do not have to call again. I cannot say that I have enjoyed my visit."

"It is always nice to see you, Mr. Abdul-Majid. I am sure you are always welcome."

Click. The door shut rather forcefully behind him, causing Miss de Beauvais to jerk in her chair.

"It looks like our little tea party is on, Miss Belle . . ." Sherlock smiled, rising from his seat. "And that charity has returned to London."

Sherlock tipped his hat and moved to open the door, which was momentarily stuck from the force of its previous closure. He then strolled through the mahogany door, twirling his cane. "Good day, Miss de Beauvais. A pleasure, as always."

Chapter Twenty-five

"What is it, Princess Elena?" Mirabella asked as Elena opened a letter with the royal seal of Italy.

"It is from Amadeo, Vittorio's uncle. He wants me to meet him in secret."

Very bad idea. "The duke of Aosta? Amadeo would be the king of Italy if Victor Emmanuel were to die without an heir. Amadeo was once the king of Spain until he abdicated the throne and returned to Italy—and some say he has a taste for being king. Why on earth would he wish to see you alone?"

"Because I wrote to him and asked him to arrange a meeting with Vittorio," she replied simply. "As you suggested Miss Mirabella."

"Me? I never wanted you to meet someone in secret who might wish to kill you!"

"I will do it," Princess Elena stated with finality. "I have decided."

"You will do what?" Mirabella demanded.

"Amadeo has arranged a hunt in Northamptonshire with Vittorio and his friends. I am to join them there in disguise—as a boy. I will hunt with them, then I will reveal myself to Vittorio. In this way, I will show him who I am under the society woman."

"I like everything about your plan except the part about putting yourself in the care of one who might wish you and your love dead."

"That is the only part you don't like?" Princess Elena asked, reflecting on the words.

"Yes. Death and heartbreak, that is all."

"Good. It is a good plan."

Chapter Twenty-six

"What have you discovered, Mr. Holmes?" Mirabella whispered to Sherlock. They sat on a wrought-iron bench in Miss de Beauvais' small garden on Regency street. It was early fall and a bit chilly.

"The attacker was Turkish," Sherlock murmured. "We were able to identify him." He moved closer to her, his arm touching hers. It caused her to feel something unfamiliar and warm. She had the sense for an instant that they were equals—or, at least, *partners*—rather than employee and employer.

She never thought to feel that. "But the Russo-Turkish war was over three years ago."

"Ha! Ha! Wars are never over, Miss Hudson."

"I don't see what you mean, Mr. Holmes. I never thought—"

"What did you think, Miss Belle? That everyone would just pick up their toys and go home?"

And the moment was gone. She was the servant girl once again.

"This is just not the way my mind works, Mr. Holmes," Mirabella replied, exasperated. She had only just risked her life—and succeeded against great odds—and now she was being admonished for failing this history test. "I don't think politically but scientifically. I don't understand taking things from others that don't belong to you, and fighting over property."

"As for politics, imperialism and nationalism play a factor to be sure, but it is much bigger than that," Sherlock replied. "You must learn to study anything that affects human behavior, Miss Belle."

She bit her lip and glanced away.

He frowned. "Miss Hudson, of all the things I will not tolerate, intellectual laziness is the most inadmissible," he warned her, his left eyebrow raised.

"Yes," she murmured, somehow finding her tongue. "It is in the top twenty characteristics of mine which you will not tolerate, Mr. Holmes, that is most certain. Your list keeps growing."

"Answer the question, Miss Belle," he replied softly. His words were stern but neither his voice nor his eyes were. "What feelings might the Turkish and the Balkans have towards each other if they had only been in a war over territory some three years ago? And how does that relate to Princess Elena?"

"Naturally the Turkish do not like the Balkans—if they had a war—but why would they wish to hurt Princess Elena?"

"Why indeed? And why now, with the impending wedding?" It was a question directed to her, she knew. Sherlock appeared amused, but he leaned closer to her, his dark grey eyes penetrating hers.

For some reason his proximity discomfited her at the same time it was somewhat pleasant and comforting. She'd had the absolute fright of her life, yet somehow she felt safe around him.

Entirely illogical since he was the one who threw her into harm's way.

"Do you think it was an act of revenge, then?" Mirabella asked, reflecting on her own words.

"Perhaps." He nodded. "Certainly it must be considered."

"If they killed her, it could be either one, for revenge . . ." She paused to reflect.

"Yes, Miss Belle?"

". . . or two, to stop the wedding."

"Aha! Precisely! Excellent, Miss Belle!" His eyes lit up and the left corner of his lip upturned in his characteristic not-smile. "And how did you come to these conclusions?"

"Because, if she were dead, she could not marry crown Prince Vittorio," she replied with a heavy sigh. "Naturally."

Sherlock seemed to consider her words. "I do not think revenge is the motive. It would be too coincidental that her life is in danger now that the crown prince of Italy has taken an interest in her. Why not three years ago?"

"Quite so," she nodded. "But it still does not answer the question as to why the Ottomans do not want Princess Elena to marry Prince Vittorio." Her teeth started chattering. He placed his jacket over her shoulders, which seemed strangely personal to her. Sherlock Holmes was not given to kind gestures.

"Exactly!" he exclaimed. His eyes now alight. "*Why?*"

"I have no idea!" she exclaimed, glaring at him. "And I'm freezing! May I go now, before I catch my death of a cold, saving the Ottoman Empire the bother of killing me?"

"Ah, but the Ottoman Empire has no interest in you, Miss Belle."

"You might have fooled me when that tall, dark man came after me with a nine-inch blade."

"Mere proximity." He took her cold hands in his, possibly the strangest single moment in her life. His top-hat removed, his raven black curls were wildly unruly, and his steel-grey eyes intense as he looked at her, as if he were seeing her, as if he cared that she were cold.

Heavens to Betsy! Even through her thin white gloves she could feel that his hands were warm! She felt herself heating up quite quickly.

"Miss Belle, I am waiting patiently for your assessment. Who is in pursuit of Princess Elena?"

"I must leave something for you to do, Sherlock Holmes! I am not in charge here! I am just your chief bottle washer and hired assassin when a murder is required." She sighed with frustration, but honestly, she wished to cry. She had never had so much demanded of her, and her emotions were running rampant: fear, guilt, self-recrimination, insecurity, indignation. She was a good, God-fearing girl! She knew she had done the right thing, but it had nonetheless taken its toll. "You are the brains behind the operation, Mr. Holmes. Why do you expect so much from me? Must I do *everything* that is required on this case? It isn't fair!"

He looked at her sternly and she immediately felt remorse—though she'd be cast into nether realm before she'd admit it to Sherlock Holmes.

The fact was that her lack of focus had almost cost her life—and Princess Elena's. Perhaps she should have been more focused on the case and left the orphan girls to themselves.

"And what have you discovered, Miss Belle? Have you learned anything interesting?" Sherlock asked, rubbing his fake beard. He looked so completely different with the beard, top hat and ivory cane—sophisticated even.

"Prince Amadeo has contacted Princess Elena. He wants her to meet him in private," she murmured, worry creeping into her tone. "I have advised her not to go. I see no reason to do so."

"What does Amadeo give as the reason?"

"He says it is to allow her the opportunity to spend some time with Prince Vittorio," Mirabella replied.

"And what do you think is his purpose, Miss Hudson?" Sherlock asked.

"He may think to do her harm. Or he may very well think that, once the two star-crossed lovers are together, the romance will die," Mirabella considered. "I wonder at it myself. The anticipation of something can take on a life all its own."

"Certainly. The best way to make a child want something badly is to deny it to the child."

"Hmmm," Mirabella considered. "Do you think Prince Amadeo might have hired the Turks?"

"Anyone might have. It would be the wise thing to do to draw attention away from the actual perpetrator."

"Did the Turkish man who died belong to any political groups?" she asked. She very deliberately avoided saying *the Turkish man I killed*. Although maybe it was Princess Elena who dealt the final blow.

"Ah, I am so glad we finally come to this question," Sherlock stated, a smile forming on his lips.

"And the answer?" She was sounding more and more like him every day.

"We have not, as yet, identified any affiliations. We have taken the next step and are investigating the Turkish groups who might wish the marriage to not take place. And we are delving deeper into the identity of the assailants, as you suggest, Miss Belle. It is possible, as you say, that they were hired by another party in order to diffuse the identity of the true party behind the attack."

She looked away, stifling a sob.

"What is it Miss Belle?" Sherlock asked gently.

She did not answer, afraid that if she spoke she would break into tears. That would never do with Sherlock Holmes.

"If the man had not come after your friend, you never would have hurt him," Sherlock stated, returning her right hand to his. "He chose his path, which determined yours."

"We do not know what he suffered to become so horrible," she managed. "In his mind, he might have been fighting for his country, just as Britain fights for more territory."

"But we can only deal with behaviors, not motivations. There are people out there who will hurt you if they can, Miss Hudson. One is entitled to defend oneself from attack," he added resolutely, tightening his hold on her hand. "And to protect those one loves."

"I hope you can c-catch these men," she muttered, retrieving her hand and collecting her reticule that she might return inside where it was warm, despite not having been dismissed. She turned to look over her shoulder as she walked to the door. "And that this is not just an amusing p-parlor game, Mr. Holmes. I do not wish to be the b-body in the parlor."

"I am never amused, Miss Belle," he replied softly.

But his eyes said otherwise.

Chapter Twenty-seven

The four little girls dressed in their Sunday best walked into the green, orange and maroon parlor as if they were entering the Taj Mahal. Their faces were scrubbed, their hair neatly arranged, and their shoes polished—and their eyes were lit like an electrical storm in July.

"Oh, *look*, Amity, flowers and candles!" whispered Susan to her sister, bending over in her blue gingham church-going dress, now faded from age. "And *curtains* on the windows!"

"Look at the silver dishes!" exclaimed Candice in a serviceable brown plaid dress, her eyes wide, pointing to the silver-tiered tray filled with cookies, bite-size sandwiches, and pastries.

"It's called a *tea service,*" whispered Gloria, smoothing her pink frock self-consciously even though she was the most stylishly dressed of all the little girls—her dress sporting a full ruffle at the hem. She even wore a matching hat and cape!

"Miss Bella, you and the other ladies are so *beautiful!*" sighed Amity, which was met with sighs of agreement from all the little girls.

"Thank you, dear," Mirabella replied, and indeed, she did feel very smart in her pencil-slim silhouette of a wispy, ivory chiffon which suited her hourglass figure. "And doesn't that brown velvet bow look perfect in your beautiful red hair?"

In truth the velvet bow did much to improve the plain brown dress Candice wore.

Miss de Beauvais' wards watched the little girls tenderly, somewhat in mutual awe, offering refreshments to them first as they had been taught since childhood, and engaging in polite conversation. All seated, the older girls began to pour the tea and serve their guests. There was some awkwardness in alighting on topics of conversation as one could not inquire after the little girls' parents, their wardrobes, their travels or excursions, their upcoming country parties, or their marriage prospects.

Kicking their feet suspended above the chairs, the little girls very politely asked for sugar, stirred their tea, and slowly lifted the china floral pattern to their lips, so terrified of breaking something clearly more valuable than themselves.

It was late fall, so a vast selection of fresh fruit was not available. The apples and canned cherries were the most popular of the lavish selection, with the pastries a close second, but the girls attempted not to eat too quickly.

"Please do eat your sandwiches first, girls," suggested Mirabella. "They are quite small and will not deter your appetite for the pastries, I assure you."

"Am I to understand that you are quite a good singer, Miss Susan?" Bethany asked.

"Oh, I do love to sing," replied Susan modestly, her pale blue eyes looking particularly large against her white skin and simple frock. "But I don't know if I am very *good.*"

"Oh, she *is,*" added Gloria, her dimples showing. "The most beautiful thing you ever heard."

"Yes," agreed Amity, placing her hands on her cheeks. "She sounds like a bird."

"Not a rooster or a peacock, though," explained Candice. "Like a . . . a . . ."

". . . *Nightingale,*" added Gloria.

"Oh, *no!*" argued Susan. "That is Jenny Bend."

"I think you mean Jenny *Lind,*" Bethany giggled, her pale blonde hair and bright blue eyes perfectly accented by cream lace and an ice blue princess gown.

"I think the common wren has quite the prettiest sound," considered Susan. "Prettier than the swan or even the nightingale."

"Quite true," added Mirabella. "I have observed that often those who are less showy on the outside often harbor something special on the inside."

"Oh, I know," agreed Amity. "Everyone talks about the dove, but it sounds like *Bow-Coo* to me."

"Pour quoi, that *is* le sound," considered Jacqueline, smiling and covering her mouth.

"And some birds are so high-pitched, they sound shrieking, like *ZZZreeee,*"offered Susan in almost perfect pitch.

"Or *tseep tseep,*" added Candice, her red hair bobbing.

Mirabella cleared her throat.

"Well, they *do* Miss Bella," Susan exclaimed. "I know because I *listen.*"

Alexandra's eyes opened wide as if she were unaccustomed and surprised by the topic, but there was a softness to her expression which Mirabella had not seen before.

"Indeed you do. You are quite the most observant group of students I believe I have ever had."

"After tea, would you like to sing while I play the piano, Miss Susan?" Bethany asked leaning forward, suppressing a giggle.

Susan nodded aggressively.

"Oh, that is the most expert handiwork I have ever seen," Gloria observed, remarking on Alexandra's handkerchief. "Is it imported *from France?*"

"Thank you, oh no," Alexandra replied, her expression of superiority returned. "I designed it myself."

Gloria stared up at her in awe. "You could be a Parisian *modiste*, you are so good!"

"A *modiste?*" Alexandra replied in alarm, her golden brown eyes suddenly aflame at the insult to her station. "Most certainly I could not!"

"Do not be humble, Lady Alexandra, you *could!*" Gloria added.

"Amity can tell your fortunes," Susan suggested.

"Are you quite serious?" asked Mirabella.

"Yes, she's good at it," nodded Gloria. "She predicts things which happen all the time."

There was a general giggle among the entire party. "Oh, why not? That would be fun. What do you need? Veils? Candle-light?"

"Orange juice," replied Amity. "I would love a glass of orange juice."

"You know, I would too," agreed Elena. "I get quite tired of English tea."

"*Moi aussi.* I love a glass of jus d'orange," admitted Jacqueline. "So rafraîchissant.*"

After the staff had been notified and a round of orange juice procured, along with another pot of tea for the older girls, all the ladies arranged themselves in the parlor on the comfortable couches for a concert by Susan and Bethany to be followed by their séance of sorts.

"Who shall we start with?" asked Mirabella, looking about her to see the debutantes as quiet and stiff as befitted their station. "All right then, *I* shall go first."

Mirabella felt surprisingly confident today—probably because she was wearing quite the most beautiful dress she had ever worn in her life: she felt as if she were almost floating in the ivory chiffon, a bustle cascading from her hips to the floor and forming a train. She wore a fitted peach satin vest over the ivory chiffon.

"There are two men sweet on Miss Bella," Amity announced, breaking through her reverie. In a room of youthful beauties, suddenly all eyes were on the mousy little girl with honey-toned hair and large brown eyes.

"*Two* men?" exclaimed the girls in unison.

"I had observed it to be more in the neighborhood of six." Bethany giggled, rolling her eyes.

"Mademoiselle Mirabella she is *very* greedy!" smiled Jacqueline, looking very French indeed as her dark brown eyes danced.

"And sly," admonished Alexandra, smart in a red-trimmed beige silk gown with a square neckline and a profusion of lace at the bodice and sleeves.

"And *wise,* " added Bethany, winking at Mirabella.

"Is it true, Miss Mirabella?" asked Elena, her countenance anything but serene.

"Why, *yes* . . . in a manner of speaking." She smiled, blushing. "But not like *that.*"

"No," Amity disagreed while quietly shaking her head. "It is *like that.* "

"That's enough of that. Let us move forward," Mirabella blushed profusely.

"And Miss Mirabella will imagine something—and it will become real," Amity added. "Something very big."

"Something *real* from the *imagination!* " exclaimed Susan.

My invention. My dream.

Oh, she didn't believe this nonsense; she couldn't even scrape together enough money to go to university, how would she ever invent something as well?

"Who would like to go next?" asked Mirabella.

"I shall go next," stated Princess Elena, sounding much like a royal pronouncement. Indeed she looked very regal covered from head-to-toe in white lace.

"There is a prince who loves her," stated Amity.

The little girls squealed. If a prince was the dream of the well-to-do who had everything, he must certainly mean a great deal more to little girls with no one to protect them and no means of caring for themselves.

"We *all* knew that!" chuckled Alexandra.

Jacqueline, Bethany, Mirabella, and the princess herself turned towards Alexandra simultaneously and frowned.

"*What*? Why do you stare at me? We did know that!" exclaimed Alexandra. "I'm sure all of London does."

"I never told Amity," Mirabella interjected. "Or any of the girls for that matter."

"Will Princess Elena marry Prince Victor Emmanuel?" asked Jacqueline, winking at Amity.

"I don't know." Amity shrugged.

"You see?" laughed Alexandra, her elegant golden brown coiffure bobbing. "She doesn't know. This is *ridiculous*."

"Eh bien go to your room, Alexandra. No personne is making you to stay," retorted Jacqueline.

"Oh, I hope you don't go, Lady Alexandra," begged Gloria.

"Amity, what did you mean, *I don't know*?" asked Mirabella, unable to hide her interest though she had to agree with Alexandra, for once, in thinking this a bit foolish.

"The princess will decide what she wants to do," replied Amity firmly.

"What do you mean?" Alexandra demanded. "I'm sure the prince has more to say to it!"

"No." Amity shook her head. "He doesn't."

"Are you saying, Amity . . ." ventured Mirabella, "that if Princess Elena chooses Prince Vittorio, he will choose her?"

Amity nodded vehemently. "The prince has already chosen her. He wants no one else."

"You cheated, Miss Mirabella," accused Elena, staring at Mirabella. "You *told* the little girl about Prince Vittorio."

"Oh, *no*," murmured Mirabella, dazed, beginning to wonder if Amity did indeed have a gift. Being a scientist, she had never believed in such things. "But how did you know, Amity? I never said a word."

Amity looked at Mirabella incredulously, disappointment in her expression. "You mean you don't remember?"

"Remember *what*?" demanded Mirabella.

"The princess. She is the Sword Princess with the black eyes I told you about!"

"Princess Elena?" Mirabella murmured, trying to keep her hands from shaking.

"The *Sword Princess?*" sighed Jacqueline. "Oh that it is *très beautiful.* Someone should write a novel about her."

"Many people will write books about Princess Elena," added Amity nonchalantly. "If she marries this prince, she will go to meet him in a boat against her mother's will. But—"

"Oh for goodness sake!" uttered Alexandra.

"But *what*, Miss Amity?" asked Princess Elena, leaning forward, and having lost all traces of boredom from her countenance. Indeed, all eyes were on the nondescript little girl who seemed to fill the entire room.

"But right now you are letting everyone else decide for you, your Highness," stated Amity.

"Of course," murmured Princess Elena, fingering her pearl and diamond earrings. "We are taught to obey our parents and to serve our people. What else can I do?"

"Princess Elena, may I ask a question?" asked Gloria, perplexed, her dark brown eyes wide.

"Certainly, child," replied Princess Elena softly.

"Why can't you serve—*and* let your heart choose your prince?"

"If I don't get to choose my own prince, I don't want to be a princess!" remarked Susan. "I want to be the *Queen.* A Badminton Queen!"

"Sukey is quite the best badminton player in Lady Graham's," confided Amity in a whisper.

"In the *world,* " corrected Candice and she motioned wide with her arms.

"I will accept *any* prince who offers for me," muttered Alexandra, her golden brown eyes determined.

"Et qu'en est-il de Mademoiselle Bethany? Whom shall she wed?" asked Jacqueline, the escalating interest in the room reflected in her eyes. Jacqueline was dressed in quite the most ornate of the gowns: a striped rose satin with purple and rust colored bows and ribbons initiating at the hips and continuing down the train.

"Is boys the only thing you ladies care about?" asked Gloria in her typical direct manner.

"I should say that sums it up nicely," nodded Mirabella, covering her hand with her mouth to stifle her chuckling.

"What about you, Miss Gloria?" giggled Bethany. "What do you want to do when you grow up?"

"*I* want to marry a rich Duke. I don't care if he lives with me, but I want his money. And I want to have lots and lots of cats!" admitted Gloria. "And *no dogs.*"

"You want to be *the cat mistress?*" Susan asked, disbelieving.

"The Cat *Duchess* to you!" retorted Gloria, the feisty brunette looking all of her eleven years and very becoming in pink. The large ruffle along the hem of her dress made it quite convincing that she might one day be a duchess.

Alexandra appeared to laugh for the first time that evening. "We shall live next door to each other," she offered.

"And I will be your gardener!" added Candice, her copper-colored eyes bright. "And feed your cats."

"Cats don't like vegetables," replied Gloria, indignant. "And *neither do I.*"

"But you like fruit, Miss Gloria hoighty-toity. You *love* strawberries!"

"And you, Miss Amity? What do you wish? To tell the fortunes of rich, spoiled young ladies?" asked Princess Elena.

"I don't mind," giggled Amity. "I like art and reading and science. And well everything. But what I really like . . . is to tell stories."

"I will sew all of Amity's clothes!" offered Gloria.

"And I will cook her food!" stated Candice.

"And I will win badminton matches!" announced Susan.

"But now may we hear whom Mademoiselle Bethany is to wed, s'il vous plaît?" asked Jacqueline impatiently. "Will she marry?"

"Yes," nodded Amity decisively. "She will marry first, before any of you."

"Marry first?" Alexandra exclaimed amidst her own laughter. "Impossible! She doesn't even have a beau—and, anyway, Princess Elena is practically engaged!"

"I certainly will not!" Bethany laughed along with Alexandra.

"All the girls are more fashionable than I—and more beautiful—and with better connections."

"Except for Miss Carnegie," Alexandra murmured.

"You will marry first, Miss Bethany," pronounced Amity with finality, shaking her head.

"All right then, I shall play along," Bethany giggled. "Whom shall I marry?"

"A man who hangs about with a lot of men with fancy hairdos will ask for your hand. He prefers the company of men most of the time."

All of the girls looked at each other, Jacqueline putting her hand over her mouth.

"Until he meets you, that is, Miss Bethany."

"I see," murmured Bethany, blushing. "How complimentary that is."

"Oh, yes," nodded Amity. "He is *very* handsome."

"*No doubt,*" murmured Alexandra.

"And you will have *hundreds* of children," added Amity.

"That dispenses that theory," Mirabella remarked, releasing her breath. The debutantes responded in an uproarious laughter.

The door to the parlor opened suddenly, causing Mirabella to jump in a way that the laughter did not.

"Girls! You are entirely too noisy!" exclaimed Miss de Beauvais. "It is most disgraceful! I never imagined any girls in my school could behave like this."

"We are so sorry, Miss de Beauvais," Bethany stated, bowing her blonde head. "We were merely laughing."

"Most unacceptable!" stated the proprietress.

"We shall never laugh again," Princess Elena stated solemnly.

"Good. See to it." Miss de Beauvais shut the door behind her.

Shhh!" admonished Mirabella. "If we do not exhibit more ladylike behavior Miss de Beauvais will put an end to our good fortunes!" Glancing sideways at Bethany, she added, "And our questionable ones."

"*How* handsome is my husband-to-be?" pressed Bethany in a whispered tone, fully enjoying herself though her confidence in the prediction was clearly shaky at best.

"The most handsome man in all of England," replied Amity in all seriousness.

"Well, he might just do then," Bethany stated with a shy smile.

"You will be very happy together," added Amity.

"Maybe all my cats will play with all your children," suggested Gloria to Bethany.

"But what about you girls?" asked Bethany to Amity, suddenly somber. "What will happen to *you*?"

"Something will happen soon," replied Amity, her expression distant. "We are all floating madly down the big river."

"The Thames?" Mirabella asked.

"I guess so," Amity replied. "I don't know the name, I just see it in my mind. There is a big bridge. We are on a boat with coal, trying to get out of London. I hope we do not make it, or they will surely kill us."

"Kill us! What are you saying, Amity? You should not scare us so," admonished Mirabella.

"There is an angel coming to the orphanage," Amity continued, but her eyes remained sad.

"An *angel*," murmured Bethany. "Is it Mirabella?"

"No," Amity shook her head while spreading her arms to encompass all of the young ladies at *Miss deBeauvais'*. "But it is one of you."

"I think they are *all* angels," added Susan shyly.

"And a lot of policeman are coming in December."

"The Christmas party," Mirabella confided. "They have it every year."

"And what about Lady Jacqueline?" asked Bethany. "Whom shall she marry?"

"Whoever she wants," replied Amity, shrugging, which brought another cascade of giggles.

"Oh, this is silly," remarked Alexandra.

"You are just angry because you want to know your fortune—and are too proud to ask," stated Princess Elena without emotion.

"Of course not! This is utterly ridiculous. I certainly do not want a husband with a strange hairstyle. I . . ."

"Your father is *mean*," interrupted Amity, staring at Alexandra. "And very important. You try to impress him by acting powerful like he does. Your mother is not very happy."

"Oh, that is *sad*," remarked Susan, all of the orphanage girls turning to look at Alexandra. Though the greatest desire of each of their hearts was to have a family, it was something of a revelation to consider that not every mother and father was worth having.

"Yes, Lady Alexandra is more like us than any of the other ladies here," Amity nodded sadly. "We don't have parents and hers are not nice—sometimes she wishes she didn't have any either."

"More in common with *you! Well, I never.* I'll have you know that my father is a *duke*, my mother a *duchess,* and they are *exceedingly* happy. Bethany's father is only a *merchant* and—"

"Shhh!" murmured Jacqueline forcefully. "And will Mademoiselle Alexandra wed?"

"Yes," replied Amity without hesitation.

"Who? Who?" Alexandra demanded, temporarily ignoring earlier affronts to her person.

"It depends . . ." considered Amity.

"Tell me! Who?" Alexandra took her by the shoulders.

Bethany interfered, taking her hands. "Let her go, Alexi."

"You will only be happy in marriage if you change."

"Change *what?*"

"Change to not be like your father. His voice is in your head and it torments you. Do not listen to the voice and do not impose it upon yourself or others. It is not kind."

There was a knock on the door and Miss de Beauvais entered. Her voice was solemn. "The girls' carriage is here."

Mirabella rushed to the kitchen while the girls did their curtseys and said their 'thank you's, returning with several boxes.

"Here are sandwiches and pastries for later." She bent and they all hugged and kissed her while waving to the other young ladies present who appeared noticeably disappointed to see them go.

Chapter Twenty-eight

Holmes scrutinized the pound note with the very clear fingerprint on it. In an instant his eyes flew open. *"Bloody hell . . ."*

"What is it Holmes?" asked John Watson, looking up from his desk in their shared flat. Something was terribly wrong.

Of the two, John admittedly had the better desk, providing a clear view of Baker Street from the bay window.

John Watson chuckled to himself. As in all things, he preferred the light, and Holmes preferred the dark corners. On the opposite end of the same wall was the Great Detective's desk, a long table for chemical experiments, and bottles of chemicals in a bookcase. On the walls over his flat-mate's desk were scientific charts and Holmes' notes—held in place with a jackknife.

"Damnation! Where are my notes?"

"Pull the knife out of the wall, Holmes," John sighed. *Some things never change.*

Orderliness was an impossibility.

John had his own room on the third floor, but that room was for sleeping—when he could sleep—the difficulty in slumber being the reason why it was so important to keep work and sleep separate. Still, he was utterly and thoroughly grateful: when he had returned from Afghanistan his life was a living hell, and now he was only in hell during the nighttime hours.

"No! No! Not those notes!" Holmes began pulling books out of the bookcase and throwing them on the floor, as if he were in a rage. Or as if there were a million pounds hidden somewhere in the bookcase.

"Calm down, man!" John exclaimed.

"There's not time, Watson!" Sherlock paused in his destruction of the flat momentarily as John stood up from his desk. "Make haste, man!"

"Your fingerprints are all catalogued by name and then typed by the very competent Miss Mirabella—as you are quite aware, Holmes."

Some might call living with Holmes a hell of sorts, certainly a madhouse, but to John Watson, the intensity of living with Sherlock

Holmes was precisely the distraction from his demons that he needed. He had tried to forget with gambling and women, but these were his weaknesses, John knew, and had offered him no lasting help. In point of fact, Sherlock Holmes had saved him.

That Sherlock Holmes was his savior was a peculiar paradox since Sherlock had addiction and melancholy among his own demons. Life was strange that way.

"Yes! Yes! This is what I need!" Holmes grabbed a leather-bound black book from his library and moved to sit at his stool. He began frantically thumbing through the pages, the pound note with the fingerprint positioned just above the open book.

Despite the havoc—or, perhaps, because of it—Watson found that he often preferred to work alongside Holmes in the larger flat, especially now that Miss Mirabella was keeping both the laboratory and the flat dusted and clean.

John smiled. *Miss Mirabella.* There was a woman whom one could easily fall for. Beautiful, intelligent, completely without airs. Pure of heart. She was so much like Holmes, however, stubborn and intensely curious, that she would take unnecessary risks. He chuckled to himself thinking of some of her conversations: Mirabella Hudson could talk for hours on end about a boring chemistry experiment, much as Holmes could.

"Never in a million years . . ." Sherlock murmured, closing his eyes very briefly. "Oh, this is very bad. We must leave immediately, Watson!"

"What is it?" John asked, pulling his service revolver from the top drawer of his desk and throwing on his jacket before he received an answer. In only nine months, he had come to trust Sherlock Holmes completely. It wasn't just gratitude to a man who had inadvertently taken him from the dark aftermath of Afghanistan which had threatened to immerse him in sorrow. Holmes was a peculiar fellow, but he was almost never *wrong*.

And having faced death, John was indifferent about life and death, in much the same way many military men were. Facing death changed a man. Friendship and country were yet more important to him than anything. Certainly he would lay down his life for either.

And perhaps, underneath it all, he wished for death, and the relief it would provide.

"Watson, we have to go!"

John Watson smiled to himself. *In the meantime, life called.*

"I pray to God we're not too late." Sherlock grabbed his coat and headed for the door. Dr. John Watson not far behind.

Chapter Twenty-nine

"I'm glad you decided to ride with us in the carriage, Miss Mirabella," Amity stated, looking down at her shaking hands resting on the worn lace ruffle of her dress which had once been white.

"You should have an adult chaperone, Amity," replied Mirabella.

"They have me," Miss Bickers frowned. She tapped on the window to get the driver's attention, although the volume of her voice was sufficient. "Faster, Sweeney!"

"Yes, of course," Mirabella replied absently, wondering if Amity was cold. It was mid-November, but they were all bundled in their coats—though somewhat worn and most too small—along with their scarves and mittens. She, on the other hand, only had a wrap and was a bit chilled. "Is something wrong, Amity?"

The little girl nodded. "It's happening much sooner than I thought."

"*What* is happening?" asked Mirabella.

"Miss Bickers is stealing something," replied Amity in a low voice. "She is leaving London."

"How did you know?" exclaimed Miss Bickers, grabbing Amity by the arm. "You've been looking in my things! YOU LITTLE RAT!"

"I won't tell anyone," Amity sniffed.

"Leave her alone!" Mirabella exclaimed, indignant, as she took the little girl's other arm. "Whatever are you doing?"

"Miss Bickers has a gun," Amity stated, attempting to place herself in front of Susan.

"What are you talking about?" gasped Mirabella. "I know you have an excellent imagination, Amity, but this is nothing to joke about!"

"It's no joke." Miss Bickers pulled a gun from her pocket and pointed it right at her heart. "Now you have forced my hand, you foolish, foolish girl. Don't you girls try anything, or I will shoot your nosy little teacher. And you know very well I will."

And it did look as if she wouldn't have the slightest compunction in doing so.

"W-what are you doing, Miss Bickers?" Mirabella demanded.

"Have you gone quite mad?"

"We hadn't planned on taking the likes of you, such a nosy little biddy, but it might yet prove to our advantage." The older woman smiled; Mirabella didn't think she had ever seen her look so happy. Apparently the anticipation of killing someone did wonders for her mood. "It will give us insurance if anyone comes after us. No one will fire on a boat of little girls going down the Thames."

"Miss Bickers, this is absurd! One of these children could be hurt! How on earth could this be of any advantage to you?"

"It can't be helped! Once we're out of London, we'll let you go." Miss Bickers laughed with abandon, as if she were enjoying her plan for them.

"Miss Bickers, whatever it is you want, I shall endeavor to get it, just please don't hurt these girls," Mirabella pleaded.

"I don't need help from the likes of you! I have it all well in hand meself!"

Heaven help us! After a short but terrifying ride, the carriage arrived at the Thames where two large men joined them.

"Mr. McVittie! Why are you here?" Sukey exclaimed, staring at one of the men. She pleaded, "We're not hungry. We've already ate."

The cook.

"Shut up!" The one she had called Mr. McVittie raised his hand to strike the child, which Mirabella blocked with her own arm.

"Har! Har!" the other man laughed. "You wuz stopped by a gull!"

"Shut up, Corbie!" McVittie replied, raising his fist against the other men.

Click. Miss Bickers cocked the gun, both turning the attention of the men from each other and showing the captives that she meant business. She was a woman who maintained control at all times, Mirabella reflected, her heart sinking.

"Shhh!" Mirabella admonished Sukey. A young lady in a ridiculously ornate dress and four little girls were no match against Miss Bickers holding a gun and three muscled men, if one counted the coach driver.

Mirabella thought of yelling but was terrified they would harm the girls. There was so much noise and commotion along the docks, and people were so accustomed to turning the other way. Particularly if someone were in danger.

"Stop her! Stop her!" Miss Bickers yelled. With a gun pointed at Mirabella and everyone's eyes on Sukey, the large men ignoring the other children to some degree, Candice slipped away. She made a dash for freedom, her red hair like a streak of sunset across the skyline.

Candice had the courage I was lacking. Mirabella bit her lip, tears filling her eyes.

"You idiots!" Miss Bickers shouted. "You were fighting with each other and weren't keeping your attention where it should be."

Mr. McVittie grabbed the remaining three children with two hands. Corbie set out after Candice who was now out of sight.

He returned shortly without the child. Mirabella sighed a sigh of relief. *At least Candice will live.* Looking at the other little girls with her, she wanted to cry. *Dear Jesus, you may have my life, but please let them live.*

"Never mind! Let's get going!" Miss Bickers commanded. "She was scared to death, I doubt she has any idea what to say or who to say it to."

In that you are mistaken, Mirabella thought. *You clearly don't know your own girls.* Candice was her father's daughter.

"No one would believe her," Miss Bickers added with an evil grin. "And anyway, we have *insurance*."

The small tea party was forced onto a steamboat identical to a dozen other dirty boats on the river Thames. If she had done anything in the coach, Mirabella knew she would have been shot. Now she didn't dare do anything for fear they would hurt the girls.

"Tie them up and put them below. We will gag them if they become too noisy."

"Why are you taking the girls?" demanded Mirabella.

"No one will hurt us as long as we 'ave them. If they are very good, we will release them once we be out of England."

But Mirabella doubted very seriously that they would. Her heart pounded out of her chest as she took in the sight of the children, even as she involuntarily pulled them closer to her. "What do you want, Miss Bickers? Why are you doing this? This is complete and total madness! Please I beg you to let the children go!"

But, instead, they were all forced below deck at gunpoint, even as Mirabella pleaded with her assailants.

There were crates upon crates below deck. Mirabella and the girls were tied up along the side of the boat where it was easy to attach the ropes to metal components. She could look out one of the portholes and see the south bank of the Thames passing by.

Once they had been left alone, Mirabella turned to Amity. "What is in those boxes, Amity?"

"Very pretty pictures," replied Amity.

"Art work? They are confiscating art work?" Mirabella looked around her: so many boxes. And all the same size.

"Yes," nodded Amity. "Miss Bickers did them. I told you she was very good. She has been working on them for years."

"I don't understand. How could that have any value . . . ?"

"Do you think . . . do you think they *will let us go*, Amy?" Susan asked.

Amity shook her head somberly.

"What do you see, Amity?" Mirabella asked as calmly as she could.

"They wish to kill us."

Chapter Thirty

The little girls in her charge began whimpering and crying.

"Hush, girls! No more of that!" commanded Mirabella. "It serves no purpose."

"But Amity said we are going to die!" wailed Gloria.

"She most certainly did not!" replied Mirabella indignantly. "She said they *intend* to kill us. The question is, girls, do we *intend to die?"*

All of the girls looked to Amity, who shook her head in agreement. "Sometimes people can change the future," Amity sniffed.

"If they have a gun," muttered Gloria.

"And there aren't four big, mean men," added Susan.

"Three," corrected Gloria, staring in alarm at the black soot now on her pink dress. "There are only three."

"Oh, it's all my fault," wailed Amity. "I said too much. Maybe if I had kept quiet Miss Bickers would have left us there."

"I have the same problem," murmured Mirabella. "I never know when to keep my mouth shut. As for Miss Bickers, she let her fear take over—and her meanness—when, in actuality, we didn't know enough to stop her." *We still don't.*

"Miss Bickers is *afraid?*" asked Susan.

"Yes," nodded Mirabella, feigning confidence. "We must use it to our advantage. You see, girls? One can always change one's course and thereby change the outcome. It's . . . *elementary,"* forced Mirabella, releasing her breath slowly. *Heavens above! S*he should never have let them tie her up! Now her chances of getting the girls out of this were just about nil! She was a stupid, stupid girl who hadn't learned a thing from her training.

"What are we going to do, Miss Mirabella?" moaned Gloria.

"We must plan our escape and the capture of our captors." She couldn't count on Candice coming to the rescue in time. The boat was moving much more quickly than she had expected.

All three of the little girls, seated on the floor tied to each other and to a long metal bar, turned to stare at her. She herself was seated on a chair with her feet tied and her hands tied—and padlocked—behind her.

"True enough, we are all tied up, but there must be something we can do. There's always *something*. We must not let fear block our thought processes, girls! We are all of us *brilliant scientists!*" Thank goodness she was a fine actress, though it was doubtful if *anything* would make any difference at this point.

There was a small porthole from which she could catch a glimpse of the south bank of the Thames. Only a small amount of the steam engine showed below decks, but from the heat in the room and the speed of the boat, it had to be a powerful engine: they had to be doing fifteen miles per hour or better! They would be out of London in not much over an hour.

Candice would never get anyone to them in time.

Think! Think! You can't give up until it's over.

Unlike herself, the little girls had their hands tied in front of them. She knew she had to think of something soon; she had little doubt that Amity was correct in their eventual fate.

"Alright, girls," she said, showing a confidence she was far from feeling, "Let's put our heads together and formulate a plan to thwart these evil people! What are our assets?"

"W-w-what's an *asset?*" asked Susan, sniffing.

"That's what we have that we can use against them," explained Amity, adding in a confidential whisper. "*Pretend* we're not tied up—that will help you think."

"I have a throwing knife in one of my boots, and a truncheon in the other," Mirabella offered.

"A real one, or a *pretend* one?" asked Gloria.

"A *real* one," replied Mirabella, sighing. *Oh, what had she been thinking?* She was expecting three eight to ten-year-olds to get them out of a mess she herself could not save them from.

"A chrunchun'?" asked Susan.

"It's a metal cigar. Also, I have an amethyst pin in my hair, which, if I could only get into my hands, I could unlock the chains . . ." She felt herself wanting to cry, looking around her. *I mustn't give in to the fear.* "Do you see the decorative stick in my hair? It's filled with a poison dart—if you blow in it and aim it at your enemy, it will put him into a sleep."

"Do you have a gun?" asked Gloria.

"No. I *did*. They found that."

"She couldn't get to it anyway," Gloria wailed, a smudge of soot on her cheek. "Her hands are tied!"

"I thought we were pretending they *weren't* tied," stated Susan, confused.

"We are going *so fast!*" cried Amity.

"Yes, we are," murmured Mirabella.

"This is a *steam* engine, isn't it? With *gears*." Amity's eyebrows drew together in a studious manner. "Why is it going so fast?"

"It must have been modified to go faster with some type of electrical mechanism," Mirabella muttered, her heart falling in her chest.

"No one will ever catch us," moaned Susan.

"What would make the boat *stop*?" asked Amity, thoughtful.

"Something would have to *jam* the gears . . ." replied Mirabella distractedly, without realizing the words had come out of her mouth. But once she heard the utterance with her own ears, the words caught her conscious attention. She pictured the open door into the steam engine where the coal was shoveled. "If something were thrown into the gears so as to jam them . . . but it would require someone with *excellent* aim."

"Sukey is the best badminton player *anywhere*," considered Amity, looking up from her hands, suddenly hopeful. "How big would the jammer-thingy have to be?"

"Oh, it could be as small . . . as small as . . ."

"A cigar?" asked Gloria, squirming under her cuffed hands.

"Yes, a cigar," answered Mirabella dismissively. "But it would have to be heavy and dense—of lead." She almost choked on her own words, hearing them.

"The *crunchin'*!" Susan exclaimed.

"Girls, we have a plan!" exclaimed Mirabella excitedly. "If only our hands weren't tied. "

Bang!

"Heavens! It sounds like someone is shooting at us!" She turned her head and glanced out the little porthole.

"What is it, Miss Mirabella?" demanded Gloria.

"Oh, my goodness!" she barely whispered. "It looks like . . . I think it is . . . Princess Elena! "

"The Sword Princess, " exclaimed Amity.

There, riding along the Thames in the heart of London like a bat out of hell, an Arabian warrior in all her glory, was the princess of Montenegro—carrying a *rifle*. Promenaders dressed by the most elegant French modistes were literally jumping out of her path, waving their parasols in hysteria.

"Yea!!!" the girls yelled in unison. And for the first time Mirabella felt the beginning of hope in the dingy, soot-covered room.

She could hear the men above deck, laughing and guffawing.

"Look at that!" Corbie's harsh voice called out.

"She's chasing us on a *horse*!" McVittie exclaimed. "Is that a hunting rifle she's holding, Minerva? It *is*!"

"I ain't worried," Corbie laughed. "The chance she could actually 'it us, at that disternce, bloody unlikely says I!"

"You fools!" yelled Miss Bickers. "Don' you see? Someone is onto us! If *she knows*, thar' could be others!"

"Wull, that's why we brought the insurance down below," blared out the one called Sweeney.

"*Arggh*!" A second later, a whizzing sound came down the hatch, followed by a loud "*Thop*!" And then McVittie's screams. "I'm hit in me leg! Corbie, get them damn brats up here and line 'em up in front of us! *Hurry*! A' fore I shoot you, too!"

Corbie came down the hatch like a bull for a matador and quickly untied the rope which linked the girls to the floor. Yanking the little girls to their feet, he left their hands tied. "C'mon you lot! Time fer some sightseein'!"

All three girls began screaming at the top of their lungs, rushing towards their teacher and surrounding her, some pretend crying and some crying for real. All within ten seconds Mirabella felt the truncheon leave her left boot and something sharp land into her chained hand: *her amethyst pin!*

Those girls had listened to every word she had uttered! When she had thought they were only whimpering and crying. Once again she was reminded of the difference between street kids and cosseted children. It appeared the previous four minutes had been a gift from God.

She hoped it was enough.

Sweeney came stomping down the stairwell to assist Corbie, yanking Susan so hard that the tiny blonde-haired girl fell to the ground.

But when Susan looked up again there was something in her expression Mirabella hadn't seen before: a flash of anger in her pale blue-grey eyes to rival that of a tiger mama.

"She's just a little girl, you chicken-livered swine!" yelled Mirabella, her country upbringing finding its way into her language as she forgot weeks of debutante training in an instant.

"I'll show you who's chicken-livered, you whore!" Sweeney yelled back, releasing Susan and moving towards her.

"That's right! Release me and fight me like a man—if you dare!" challenged Mirabella, ready to take him on as all her fear washed away with the attack on the little girl.

"Git yer ass over 'ere and let her be!" commanded Corbie, and Sweeney reluctantly turned around.

Blast! It had almost worked!

She calmed her mind as much as she could, and set to the lock with determination. From above, she heard Sweeney shout, "Shoot back at her, dammit!"

"She's at least a hun-derd yards away!" Corbie shouted back, "All I gots is a pistol! We're gonna be a sight better orf wif' these little chits lined up along the edge o' the boat!"

"Look! *Har! Har!*" McVittie gave a loud laugh. "She just ran out of promenade, 'an the police are chasin' *her*! They's not chasin' us but *her.*"

"Shut up, you fool!" exclaimed Miss Bickers.

"What the hell is that contraption?" asked Sweeney. "Some kinda horseless carriage?"

"The police are chasin' *her*! Har! Har!" Corbie laughed.

"Stop laughing and help me tie up me leg!" McVittie commanded. He must be of some importance, Mirabella reflected, as he bossed the other two around as much as Miss Bickers did.

"It's a pair 'o men on bicycles," snarled Miss Bickers. "It's of no consequence."

"Those aren't regular bicycles," considered Sweeney. "They'se movin' awful fast."

Corbie chimed in, laughing, "They ain't movin' near as fast as yer steam engine, McVittie!"

Click. Mirabella heard the padlock fall behind her. Quickly, she set at worming her wrists out of her chains.

"Oh, *shyte*!" she heard McVittie exclaim.

"That's 'im, int it?" Miss Bickers' shrill voice asked rhetorically.

"*Who*? Who is it ont the bicycles?"

"Sherlock *bloody* 'olmes and that doctor o' his!"

Mirabella retrieved the throwing dagger from her right boot. Once her feet were free, she ripped the beautiful chiffon and satin train from her dress. She then started at her knees and tore the pencil-thin dress with her knife, providing some mobility and revealing her petticoats.

She couldn't have cared less.

"Whot the . . . ? " she heard Sweeney exclaim. "Be thar some kinda' motor on them things? I 'kin see 'em peddling—but they be goin' awful fast fer bicycles."

"You idiots! Stop worrying about the bicycles!" Miss Bickers chimed in. "Clearly the peddling charges the engine in some manner— an improvement on the scissor sharpeners. It has nought to do wif us!"

"That rig may be fast," McVittie crowed triumphantly, "but we don' have to dodge th' nobs & gawkers. They're fallin' behind." Mirabella could hear him dragging his leg, so it must have gotten it wrapped up.

"What 'ar they gonna' do on bicycles anyways?" Corbie exclaimed, laughing. "Har Har!"

Mirabella snuck up the hatchway, wiping her sweaty palms on her skirt. It was one thing to play at fighting—but against men with guns this felt entirely different, wondering if she would still be alive in the next two minutes.

I don't think it likely.

But there were children at stake—*her girls*—and she would die trying to save them. Otherwise they were all dead anyway. She was a fool for not seeing that earlier—but she had been so terrified.

She would never forgive herself for that. Even in the grave, which she was no doubt headed for.

Maybe the incident at Miss de Beauvais had drained her of her courage.

The girls were lined up along the gunwale, and as she reached the top of the short stair, Amity looked directly at her. Amity then turned to her sister and nodded very slightly with her chin. Mirabella could see the fear in their eyes mirrored her own.

But these girls had faced fear before—and won. And well they knew it.

Turning ninety degrees to face her captors, Susan raised her tied hands in a passable imitation of a two-handed badminton swing.

"What 'ere ye doin' ye little brat?" McVittie demanded, pointing his gun at her, even as they all gasped.

"Would you like this cigar?" Susan squealed in an amazingly high-pitched voice which momentarily stunned everyone. Swinging her arms forward, the child sent the compact metal baton directly into the open gear box of the steam engine.

For a moment, all involved looked apprehensively towards the mechanism.

Pop! Crack! Grrrrrrnd! One of the brass main gears popped off its axle, cracked on one side.

All the girls began screaming and jumping up and down, suddenly elated. There was no sporting event to match it.

"*Noooo*!!" screamed McVittie as the momentum of the vessel began to slacken.

"You little monster!" screamed Corbie. "I'll kill you!" And he raised his pistol at the suddenly terrified child.

God guide my throw! Mirabella prayed, hurling her dagger at the big man. The blade turned a lazy full spin in the air and settled with a satisfying *thunk* in the crook of Corbie's shooting arm. He screamed like a hyena and the revolver clattered once on the gun rail and then added itself to Davy Jones' armory.

"By God, you'll pay for that!" Corbie growled as he pulled the blood-covered blade from his arm. Probably a mistake as much more blood gushed forth from the open wound. He threw the knife back at her with his left hand, sending it high and wide as it bounced on the deck beside her. She turned to grab it but had run out of time. Corbie had already started towards her with arms wide to entrap her.

She stepped into his embrace, pivoted and slammed her hip into his groin causing him to bend slightly, all the while grabbing his lapel. Bending her knees, she pulled and the fulcrum effect of the *Jiu-Jitsu* maneuver sent him over her shoulder, his appearing to fly for a moment. The hulking man landed hard across his shoulder blades on the upraised gunwale, the force of his fall catapulting him into the water.

Mirabella gasped in surprise. *That had a far better outcome than I anticipated.*

Quickly she glanced at the bicyclers' progress, noting that they were turning towards the Fifth Avenue Bridge, some four hundred feet ahead of the drifting boat. Still, the little steamboat was a long way from shore and the bridge was completely unreachable from the boat.

"Girls!" she yelled, "get to the back of the boat, now!" and the children, though still amazed by her feat, rushed as best they could to do as she ordered, all tied together as they were. As she stood there, she heard a metallic *shhiinng* sound and turned to see Sweeney coming down the walkway with her own sword cane in his hand, its gleaming Sheffield steel ready to eviscerate its owner. She looked around frantically and saw where the knife had fallen.

Just in time she snatched it up but soon wondered if it had been worth the trouble.

Predictably, the rat-faced Sweeney hesitated when he saw his prey had a chance of fighting back, but quickly came to the conclusion that the sword was mightier than the jackknife—as did Mirabella. She tensely watched him maneuver around her, and thought to herself how terrifyingly different a real fencing situation was in comparison with a training session.

A real fencing situation without a sword.

Sweeney came towards her, and she realized she was up against the engine with nowhere to go. He pulled his arm back to deliver the final thrust . . .

Whiz! Oh, he was hit! Sticking in his forehead was a . . . a . . . *poison dart!*

Thud! He fell towards her—and that alone might have been her demise if she hadn't moved in the nick of time.

Turning to look behind her, she saw the colorful container in Gloria's lips! Smiling around the dart gun, her dimples had never shown her to greater loveliness.

Mirabella ran to the girls and they all hugged each other.

"I missed," Gloria stated. "I was aiming for his chest."

"That is the best mistake I have ever seen!" Mirabella hugged her.

"Look, Miss Bickers and Mr. McVittie are gettin' away!" Candice yelled. Evidently Miss Bickers and McVittie had decided to flee incarceration and probable hanging, showing more sense than she would have given them credit for. The two of them were in a very long rowboat that had been tethered to the steam launch and they were pulling away under the high bridge towards shore, several of the boxes from the boat with them.

"There you are, you little whore!" Bickers screeched. "Everything we've worked for, gone in flash! Well, you'll pay, miss! You surely will!" To Mirabella's horror, the older woman raised a revolver that was the twin of Corbie's and aimed it directly at her over the intervening twenty-five yards, growling, "SAY 'YER PRAYERS!'"

Bang! Before Mirabella could move she heard the explosion from the gun, expecting to fall to the ground. Instead she stood where she was. In terror, she looked behind her to see if any of the girls had been hit.

It appeared the shot had gone high. Looking back to the boat, she saw Miss Bickers clutching her bleeding hand with no gun in sight. She looked up to see John Watson standing on the bridge and holding a smoking revolver. Sherlock had always said Watson was a capital shot, and he had not understated the matter!

In addition, what appeared to be a large paving stone fell from the bridge and neatly smashed through the rowboat's bottom. The impact knocked McVittie off balance, leaving him splashing in the Thames. Miss Bickers just sat there, watching the boat fill with water as she clutched her hand.

"We have these two, my dear!" Mirabella heard a familiar voice call out, John Watson waving at her, as the police joined him, apparently tired of harassing Princess Elena.

"It's a little invention of mine I like to call *the rock*," Holmes yelled.

Chapter Thirty-one

Something is not right.

Mirabella and the children were now ashore, and Watson was congratulating them on their intrepid handling of the situation as the little girls enthusiastically told him the tale.

"Well, Miss Hudson, it seems my teachings were not wasted."

She sighed heavily, her torn dress revealing almost the entirety of one leg, her long chestnut brown hair having come loose and fallen past her shoulders, and her skin flushed. "I see. You are going to take credit for this, Mr. Holmes?"

"Naturally. Credit where credit is due."

"I thank you both for your most timely intervention, Mr. Holmes and Dr. Watson," she muttered between barred teeth, looking astonishingly bewitching in her disheveled state.

"You are welcome," Sherlock replied, taking his jacket off and putting it around her shoulders, which did nothing to cover that . . . very shapely . . .leg. "Hmm hmm." He cleared his throat. "We must give you some credit as being an apt pupil, Miss Hudson."

"You astonish me, Mr. Holmes. Heavens, is that a compliment?"

"Although your escapade diverted us from the actual case we are working on, bringing our client we are supposed to be protecting into the open."

"*My* escapade? Do you seriously put this at my door, Mr. Holmes?" she demanded, anger effectively replacing the previous glow in her expression. "I have no control over the criminal element in London any more than you do!"

Sherlock looked over her shoulder, his mood moving from approval—although he would never reveal that to Miss Belle—to hawkish intensity in a moment's time.

Mirabella glanced in the same direction to see what he observed: police officers attempting to lead the princess of Montenegro into a 'paddy wagon.'

"Watson," Holmes looked back at his friend, "Is your Webley reloaded?"

"No Holmes, the counterfeiters are caught, so I thought it unnecessary."

"Always be prepared, my good man. Please reload it, and follow me. I do not like the look of these bobbies."

"The princess will have diplomatic immunity. It will no doubt be cleared up at the station," Watson replied, inserting new cartridges into the heavy revolver even as he protested. "Should we directly involve ourselves, Holmes?"

"How strange," Mirabella murmured, peering in the direction of Princess Elena.

"What is it, Miss Belle?" Sherlock asked.

"The bobbies are carrying weapons. British police do not carry weapons."

"Ah, yes," Sherlock replied. "But we do. Watson, the policemen are armed. American Schofield revolvers, if I am not mistaken. I know you see the import of that."

"Imposters!"

"Indeed, let us make haste."

Sherlock and Watson were both now at a running pace. Princess Elena was not one to be manhandled and was resisting the two men attempting to drag her into the horse-drawn barred wagon. One of the policemen drew his pistol in an attempt to persuade her just as Holmes stepped between him and the princess.

The man raised his forearm so that the gun aimed directly at Sherlock's face.

"I'll take that, my good man." No sooner had the gun swung upward than Sherlock had slammed the edge of his left hand into the man's inner elbow while his other hand slapped the weapon out of the imposter's hand.

CLANG! The revolver fell, sliding underneath the paddy wagon.

The man deprived of his weapon pulled back his arm to strike Sherlock, only to be met with a flurry of rapid Chinese boxing strikes to his face and throat. The stranger toppled over backwards, stunned and bleeding.

The other assailant had recovered from his astonishment at the unexpected attack, drawing his own firearm when he felt the cold barrel of Watson's Webley pressed rather aggressively into his ear.

"Go ahead, my friend," Watson stated in tone of encouragement. "I'm having a bit of a peevish day, and removing a vile assassin from the world might cheer me up immensely!"

Chapter Thirty-two

In the darkness Elena met Prince Amadeo, Duke of Aosta and former King of Spain. He was a large man, six foot six.

He looked all about him and pulled out a rifle. She swallowed hard.

"This is for you, your Highness," he stated. He motioned with his head to his manservant, who handed her clothing.

"Thank you," she murmured. "Why are you helping me?"

"For family, of course," he replied. "I do not wish an unhappy marriage for my nephew."

She did not know how to read Prince Amadeo's expression, whether or not he wished her as far from here as Hades. But regardless of his intent, she would take this opportunity and turn it to her advantage.

She did not wish to marry a man who did not love her.

***

"AIEEEE!" She picked up her rifle and fired, racing over the rolling hills surrounding Althorp, the lands belonging to The Honourable Charles Spencer, the fifth Earl Spencer and the Liberal MP.

"I have to say, Uncle Amadeo, this young friend of yours is truly motivated to wring the most out of life, is he not?" Prince Vittorio asked his uncle, chuckling.

"Indeed." Amadeo replied, pursing his lips. "If one likes exuberance."

"One does."

The uneven ground beneath her horse necessitated both an excellent horse and great riding skill—and fortunately Princess Elena Petrović-Njegoš had both. Initially the party had wished to go to Hatfield House in Hertfordshire, the Seat of the Marquis of Salisbury, but Lord Salisbury was an advocate of "splendid isolation" for Great Britain, with no wish to be part of European affairs or shaping European alliances.

And this was an exotic alliance indeed.

"Who is this madman you found, Uncle Amadeo?" Vittorio asked, laughing. "He is insane. He is a wild man!"

"Do you like him?" Amadeo asked.

"Of course! Why shouldn't I? I would like to enlist him into the Italian army. We would be undefeatable."

"Ah, you would like to keep him close rather than far?" Prince Amadeo pressed.

"Naturally."

"You may have your wish," Prince Amadeo muttered.

Elena returned to the party with the hare and the birds. She took the hat off her head and her long black hair fell to her shoulders. In a moment's work she removed the false moustache.

Vittorio stared at her in shock. "Elena! It is you!"

"Do you still wish to marry me, now that you have seen who I am?"

"My love," Vittorio exclaimed, dismounting from his horse. He took her hands in his, looking at her with the true light of love in his eyes. "I didn't think it possible to want you more, but I find I want to marry you more than ever."

Chapter Thirty-three

"Why are we stopping?" Princess Elena asked. She kneeled before the man who stood with her.

The men who were supposed to be feeding the coal into the fire had ceased their activity, their hands on their hearts as they faced the flag. The boat swayed with the waves under the moonlight despite having come to a sudden stop.

"We will finish our business here," the robed man stated. "We are in the middle of the Adriatic Sea between Montenegro and Italy. It is a beautiful symbolism."

I am not afraid of death.

Princess Elena knew very well that she would not be safe until the wedding ceremony was performed. Once she and Vittorio were married there would be no reason to kill her and the Ottoman threat would be no more. The alliance between Italy and Montenegro would be sealed.

Princess Elena Petrović-Njegoš of Montenegro bowed her head, completely dressed in white, luminescent in the moonlight. The Bishop of Naples laid his hands on her, praying for her and asking that she receive the gift of the Holy Spirit, a confirmation ceremony performed for those who expressed their desire to be part of the Roman Catholic Church.

She prayed with him, for her husband, for her new country, and for the deliverance of her soul.

Amidst the solemn ceremony, Princess Elena smiled, remembering the course of events which had led to her choice of a husband. She recalled the ball at St. Petersburg and all the attention she had received— which she had not wanted.

But she had met Vittorio. That had made it all worthwhile.

She remembered her fear at entering *Miss de Beauvais'*—and how it had been the experience which had taught her that she could be queen.

Elena remembered the day Mirabella saved her life. The young woman who would be her friend, carried always in her heart, until she died. Without Mirabella there would be no marriage to Vittorio, no children, no life to live.

That was a bond of friendship forged in blood.

She recalled with trepidation how she had snuck out dressed as a boy and gone hunting with the prince and his party. She had been fairly certain Prince Vittorio would not wish for such a bride.

Her heart had burst with joy when he had pledged his love to her on the spot.

"In the name of the Father, the Son, and Holy Ghost." The Bishop made the sign of the cross in front of her. "*Amen.*"

Her heart still overflowed with happiness.

When Elena stepped foot onto Italian soil for the first time, she would be a Catholic, eligible to marry Prince Victor Emmanuel III, crown prince of Italy and the prince of Naples.

The queen of Montenegro had been so angered by her daughter's decision that she had refused to attend the wedding.

Sigh. It was a shame since they were cut out of the same cloth.

Princess Elena rose, looking up at the moon as it cast its light on the Italian flag—green, white, and red—depicting the royal dynasty of the Savoy. A tear filled her eye when, in her mind's eye she saw the flag of Montenegro, a two-headed golden eagle holding the coat of arms, the lion of Judah, in the center. She thought of her father, the warrior king, and her brother, Danilo, her best friend from birth. She was forever joined to Montenegro, and now she would be joined to Italy.

I will be so happy to see Vittorio. She sighed. She did not look forward to the jewels, the gowns, the palace, the parties, or the royal court.

Only Vittorio.

Chapter Thirty-four

The Christmas Ball
December 1881
Miss de Beauvais Finishing School for Distinguished Young Ladies

"The Emperor Waltz," Mirabella pronounced as Sherlock led her onto the dance floor. "How lovely."

"As is my partner," Sherlock murmured as he positioned her close to him with arms stronger than she expected.

She felt herself blushing as he held her firmly in his grasp. "I can see why some protective Mamas once objected to the waltz."

"Not at all, those days are gone. Everyone does the waltz," Sherlock pronounced, swinging her across the floor but somehow missing all the other pairs of dancers. "And as you know, Miss de Beauvais is an icon of fashion and taste."

"Naturally." Mirabella giggled.

Sherlock's lips curved slightly in amusement.

Despite having a marvelous time, Mirabella wished she were dancing with John Watson instead of with Sherlock. John was highly intelligent—but without all the strangeness that went along with Sherlock.

And John Watson is a notorious flirt. She glanced over to see John surrounded by ladies, casting his lure particularly at Jacqueline. He was standing near to the kissing ball made of mistletoe and ribbons—no doubt on purpose!—and it annoyed her more than it should. Tanned and blonde, tall and athletic, it was ever evident that Dr. Watson had been involved in competitive sporting events prior to his injury in Afghanistan.

Sherlock twirled her once. He was actually a decent dancer. John, on the other hand, with his injured leg which gave him a slight limp, did not dance. Even so, standing there in a full tuxedo, Dr. Watson's most elegant formal dress, she might be able to overlook it.

"Hee hee hee!" Jacqueline giggled, and at that moment Mirabella decided she did not care for that French miss at all, who had been her friend only five minutes ago.

"Are you not enjoying the dance?" Sherlock asked. He frowned as he glanced in the direction of the kissing ball. "What has captured your attention, Miss Belle?"

"Oh, nothing." She sighed, returning her gaze to look into the stern eyes and unrevealing expression of her dancing partner.

She had yet to meet the woman who could turn Sherlock Holmes' head.

That the temptress existed was clear from Sherlock's reaction to Dr. Watson's recounting of the scene in the police report—but she had never met the woman who could cast a spell on the great Sherlock Holmes.

Mirabella's lips quivered, fighting a smile. She could not care for the idea of the female counterpart to Sherlock Holmes.

One is more than enough. There was a dark side to Sherlock. And she didn't mean how hard he pushed her. That she could forgive because he perceived his demanding ways to be for her own good.

And possibly he was right.

No, the dark side of Sherlock Holmes was in how he pushed *himself*.

In point of fact, most of the time Sherlock tortured himself. And then went in for the kill. And if the danger he threw himself into were not enough, he made a point to torture himself where the criminal element left off.

She looked up and saw him smiling down at her. Sherlock Holmes. *Smiling.* At her.

"It's rather like a father-daughter dance, isn't it?" asked Mirabella, as she floated across the floor. They danced past the Christmas tree decorated with apples, gilded nuts, birds' nests, small baskets, and paper decorations which the debutantes themselves had made.

Looking into silvery grey eyes, strangely intent upon her, there was none of the usual torment she saw there. He was almost . . . jolly! She suppressed a giggle. Sherlock Holmes, jolly indeed!

"A father-daughter dance? I hadn't quite thought of it in that manner," Sherlock frowned, his expression dark again. He had shaved for the occasion, his hair was parted on the side and under control, and he was looking particularly handsome in spite of his characteristic sternness.

"How did you think of it then, Mr. Holmes?" she asked as she glided in the muscular arms which held her surprisingly close. His reply had been vague—Sherlock Holmes was nothing if not direct—which ignited her curiosity.

"Rather like dancing with a beautiful young lady," he replied matter-of-factly, turning her once.

She smiled up at him; it was one of the rare times he had complimented her rather than subjecting her to a barrage of criticisms. "You'd better be careful, Mr. Holmes, or I'll expect flattery instead of insults."

"I won't make a habit of it, Miss Belle."

"Of that I am certain. I am accustomed to your calling me fat simply because I do not have a twenty-inch waist." She only pretended to be offended. "It is most unfair!"

"I have never called you fat, Miss Belle." He suddenly distracted her by whisking her through the waltz. Sherlock too wore a tuxedo, white gloves and a white bowtie, but his was a dinner jacket tuxedo with a shawl collar and satin facing as opposed to Dr. Watson's more standard attire. Sherlock Holmes had always to be different.

"But you are certainly not a feather, Miss Belle," he added.

She glared at him.

"You are far too . . . um . . . well-proportioned . . . for that." He cleared his throat. "And your dress, it is . . . most . . . becoming."

"It is wickedly revealing, isn't it?" she giggled.

"It is," he agreed, a smile forming on his lips along with a scintillating glimmer in his eye. "*Most* wicked."

Mirabella sighed. She supposed that was as close to a compliment as she would receive from Sherlock Holmes.

"But, honestly, Mr. Holmes, as much as I like being called 'pretty,' I would prefer that you pronounce me *capable* on just this one occasion. I have risked my life, fooled everyone as to my true identity, exhibited advanced fighting skills, officially become a debutant, overcome a grown man in a fight—several!—and done all this in a corset while subsisting on very little nourishment. And the only compliment I have received is that I am *becoming*—like every other young lady here. The entire ordeal almost killed me—literally! Do I not deserve to be commended?"

"In the first place, Miss Belle, you are far more beautiful than 'becoming'. And, in the second place, the fact that you are competent is a fact so much in evidence that I did not think it needed to be mentioned."

"Certainly you mention it when I do not exhibit competence," she murmured, but she did not know if she was heard over the music.

And yet, I have received all the reward I need. She glanced at the girls huddled in a circle with Bethany, all giggling and admiring each other's gifts. All the presents had been opened amidst squeals of delight. Susan had received her blue velvet dress with white satin ribbon (and a new badminton racket!), a gift from the Duchess of Glazebury. A piano had also been delivered to the orphanage, complete with a large red ribbon, a gift from King Nicholas and Queen Milena of Montenegro. Gloria had received her tuxedo kitten—named *Sherlock*—and enough fabric, wool, and embroidery thread to keep her busy sewing for a while, a gift from Bethany's merchant father. Candice had been given oodles of seeds for her garden from the Earl of Kilburn—enough to feed the orphanage—and a beautiful doll with black button eyes in a red-checkered dress made by Jacqueline. Amity had been given a set of paints and a tablet—and even a microscope from the Great Detective himself. A window into yet another world.

And all had been given big sisters.

"So, they were all *counterfeiters?*" asked Mirabella, barely believing the words herself, as she regained her breath while Sherlock walked her to the punch table.

"Yes," nodded Sherlock, taking her elbow. "The orphanage was merely a front for the scheme."

Mirabella shook her head as a sadness washed over her. "I was so sorry for Miss Bickers' past suffering. She had a terrible life."

"Not a terrible life, a terrible *childhood*," Sherlock corrected. "She was never able to leave that place of suffering and enjoy the good fortune in which she had found herself."

"If my own family had all died, I might be the same—or worse."

"Feeling sorry for the criminal, are we?" Sherlock smirked. Suddenly his expression softened as he looked at her, a strange longing in the depths of his eyes which she had never before beheld. "She would have killed you, Miss Belle. And the children."

"I know," she replied softly.

"The horror of her upbringing did not make her any less dangerous," Sherlock stated sternly, and her employer was back. Just a moment ago she had been dancing with a man. A handsome, grown man, who appeared to enjoy dancing with her.

She sighed. Sherlock Holmes was probably one of the ten most

intelligent men, not in England, but in the *world*. For a moment she had
felt the union of emotion and intellect as he held her, and it had been
exhilarating, though she hated to admit it to herself. But now the feeling
had subsided—unless bossiness was an emotion—and she was, once
again, talking to a giant brain. In the shape of a judge's gavel.

"You must remember this, Miss Hudson. If you hesitate, even an
instant, you will find yourself dead. There are people out there who
would hurt you if they could."

Mirabella glanced at the red-headed girl in the corner hugging her
ragdoll in a checkered dress with black button eyes. Sherlock followed
Mirabella's eyes as she mused, "It is difficult to believe that same little
girl managed to escape killers and run straight to the police station."

"She is one of your students, Miss Belle." Sherlock looked into
Mirabella's eyes, and for the first time that she could recall, she saw
admiration there. He momentarily looked away as she saw another
emotion: embarrassment.

"Candice knew you were floating down the Thames out of the port
of London," Sherlock added matter-of-factly, looking away. "And she
knew what the boat looked like."

"Not to mention that she was fearless," Mirabella whispered,
searching his face.

"Certainly," Sherlock nodded, now expressionless. "She might
have been shot when she attempted escape, and well she knew it."

"But Candice never got word to you, Mr. Holmes, only to Princess
Elena. How did you recognize the pound note as a counterfeit bill?"
She tried to lighten the mood. It was a ball, after all! Her first ball, as
country barn dances didn't count. "I recalled thinking what a beautiful
new pound note it was."

"Ah, there you have it, Miss Mirabella. It was too perfect, you see.
Like your dress."

"Thank you, Mr. Holmes." She smiled up at him. "I like it myself,
although I have no idea where I will have the opportunity to wear it
again." It was a full-skirted pink tulle dotted with dark brown polka-
dots to match the color of her hair and edged with a flounce of scalloped
brown tulle. Bows of brown velvet ribbon accented the hem and the
velvet girdle as well as the shoulders, holding together the sleeveless
brown velvet Spanish jacket.

She wore pale pink gloves of undressed kid, and her coiffure of glossy chestnut brown curls was wrapped with a Greek bandeaux of pink satin lined in dark brown velvet and a high panache of pink ostrich tips. She carried a pink ostrich gauze fan and wore pink slippers. Her jewelry was a simple pearl necklace and pearl drop earrings, on loan from Aunt Martha.

"*Sherlock*. Call me Sherlock if for tonight only." The openness returned to his expression, if only for an instant.

"Certainly, sir . . . I mean . . . Sherlock." She looked away momentarily before pressing him once again. "And how did you know where I was?"

"Watson and I went immediately to Lady Graham's, only to find that the entire crew was gone. One of the children had overheard some of the conversation, and knew they had gone down to the Thames. It was a logical deduction in any case, the only way out of the country is via the waterways." He cleared his throat. "Perhaps I could take you to the opera some evening, Miss Belle. With Watson and Mrs. Hudson of course."

"Perhaps I could take you to the opera some evening, Miss Belle." He cleared his throat. "With Watson and Mrs. Hudson of course."

"Truly? Oh, that would be wonderful!" They had reached the refreshment table and he handed her a glass of punch which she sipped even as he led her to a seat. "Does Dr. Watson like the opera?"

Sherlock cleared his throat and she thought she observed a frown crossing his face. "Watson has different tastes in music, preferring the cabaret, but no doubt he will yet go with us. I would not wish you to be deprived of his company, Miss Belle."

"It is always best to include everyone in the party." She smiled slyly. "Otherwise people have a tendency to gossip about one." Mirabella glanced over to see Lady Alexandra, who was having a lovely time dancing with Lord Worthington, who seemed quite entranced with her. Alexandra was definitely of a softer bent than she had been upon their first meeting.

"And what does your aunt say about me—in private?" Sherlock asked.

"Why should that concern you, Sherlock?" She laughed, never before having heard the Great Detective express any interest in the opinion of others.

"Just curious," he said with a shrug.

"She says that, between your experiments, playing that devil's instrument all hours of the night, the criminal company you keep, and shooting up her walls, you are the worst tenant in all of London. Possibly the world."

"Ah." He swallowed a bit more punch than politeness allowed. "Your aunt was never one to be vague," he murmured.

"And she said Scotland Yard couldn't get along without you." She wrinkled her brow, placing her finger on her delicate cheek.

"Mrs. Hudson is most astute."

"Mr. Holmes, how did you know the pound note came from the orphanage?"

"It either came from the orphanage or it came from me—you have no other source of funds. And it didn't come from me!"

"But the orphans of *police?*" exclaimed Mirabelle. "Right under the noses of the bobbies?"

"Brilliant plan. Who would suspect them? Officers were walking in and out all day."

"How did it work, Mr. Holmes?"

"You shall call me 'Sherlock,' Miss Belle. Let me have that on this one occasion." He frowned, glancing in the direction of Dr. Watson. "Miss Bickers was the artist of merit, and Mr. McVittie made the plates; Sweeney and Corbie kept the place running minimally."

"Very minimally I should say," Mirabella agreed, taking a sip of her punch.

"Miss Bickers was the real brains behind the operation. They took in the funds for the orphanage and balanced the books to the penny; no one could have found any fault with them. Then they deposited the equivalent amount in counterfeit bills, exchanged the real bills for the counterfeit, and stored away the real bills for their eventual escape."

"Yes," murmured Mirabella. "I thought it was very odd that Miss Bickers was supposedly painting all the time—and yet there were no paintings to be seen anywhere. But wouldn't those counterfeit bills be out in circulation?"

"Well, yes, Miss Belle, but it was a very small operation—and expertly done. It wasn't going to bring the Bank of England down. But it was enough, over the course of several years, to provide a comfortable living. And most people do not look closely when their suspicions are not aroused. Even if it were discovered at some point, it would not be traceable in all likelihood."

"How did you guess, Sherlock?"

"I never *guess,* as you put it, Miss Belle." His piercing dark eyes seemed to swallow her whole even as he glanced about the room, seemingly taking everyone else in as well. "Guessing is for the undisciplined of mind."

"How did you *know* unequivocally and brilliantly, Sherlock Holmes?"

"The first clue was simply listening to your descriptions, Miss Belle. No one at the school appeared to know the job they were hired to do. Mr. McVittie was not a cook. Miss Bickers, the primary teacher—who was actually Mr. McVittie's cousin, by the way—was not very learned. Granted, she was very talented—she was the artist who made the bills—but her talents were neither known nor being lavished upon the children. And then there was the little matter of the bill itself."

"The pound note I gave you with Miss de Beauvais' fingerprint?"

"Precisely."

"But, as you say, they had a marvelous set-up despite their lack of ability—no one questioned them as long as the books balanced. Why did they not merely enjoy their good fortune and do their jobs?"

Sherlock laughed. "You speak from the perspective of the non-criminal mind, Miss Belle. The criminal mind is forever working much harder at getting out of work, exerting far more energy than is actually required for honest labor."

"Hmmm. . . .and what about the threats on Princess Elena's life?"

"With the leads I gave them, Prince Vittorio's secret police found the Turkish nationalist groups responsible. Because of our investigation, I did not think it was extremist groups—but rather individuals very central to the Ottoman Empire—behind it all. And of course I was correct."

"How dreadful!" Mirabella exclaimed. "Essentially they were willing to kill for territory?"

"Isn't everyone?" Sherlock asked. "It is the most common reason for wars since the beginning of time. The Ottomans wish to regain their territory. Obviously they harbor hopes of getting their empire back."

"But Montenegro would fight," Mirabella considered.

"Montenegro is a small country with a small army; she only won the war because of her alliance with Russia, who may or may not stand by Montenegro and Serbia a second time. On the other hand, if Elena marries Prince Victor Emmanuel III, Montenegro will have a strong ally. The Ottomans knew that all hope of reuniting the seven Balkan states was lost were Montenegro to form a powerful ally."

"So . . . Once Princess Elena is married, it is over, there is no point in the Ottomans attempting to stop the alliance between Italy and Montenegro?"

"Precisely. What happens when countries marry each other?"

"Political alliances," Mirabella replied. "Hmmm . . . Prince Vittorio's uncle had nothing to do with the assassination attack?"

"Nothing at all. It was not a usurper to the throne of Italy behind the attack—but rather an enemy of Montenegro and a supporter of the Ottoman Empire."

"But what about the Italians who initially attacked Princess Elena in Montenegro?" Mirabella asked.

"Hired by the Turks," Sherlock replied succinctly, surprising her by appearing more interested in the dancing than in the case. "Mercenaries."

"And do Prince Vittorio's parents support Princess Elena's marriage to their son?" Mirabella pressed.

"Indeed. In particular, Queen Marguerite favors the match. The Princess of Savoy does not hold to cousins marrying and favors the strengthening of the bloodline. She welcomes a bride who is not related to her son—and will be the mother of her grandchildren."

"Most progressive. Yes, it is most unexpected," Mirabella agreed. "Everyone expected the Queen of Italy from the grand House of Savoy to look down on the little Serbian nation, and yet it is the Queen of Montenegro who does not wish the union."

"And yet . . . Princess Elena is likely to be the subject of disapproval all her life—particularly if she marries Prince Vittorio," Sherlock remarked with a shrug. "Nothing out of the ordinary."

"Nothing about Princess Elena's life will be ordinary," giggled Mirabella. "I fear she will empty Italy's coffers and give all the money to the poor. I never met a woman with more generosity of spirit."

"Most unfashionable." Holmes shook his head reproachfully, but his eyes revealed that he approved.

"I do hope Princess Elena's unconventional behavior does not reflect poorly on Miss de Beauvais," Mirabella murmured, unable to place conviction in her voice as she glanced at the proprietress. Even decked out in the latest fashions, Miss de Beauvais still looked stiff and matronly. "I would hate to see her finishing school in ruins."

"To the contrary. That an Arabian princess galloped a horse through Sunbury Park to come to the aid of four young orphans and their ward has elevated *Miss de Beauvais'* to the sensational."

"She must be very happy. It is a relief." Mirabella sighed. "It's so strange that we were all attempting to save Princess Elena—and instead, she saved me. If I hadn't been here attempting to protect her, she wouldn't have known me to come to my aid."

"You did protect her, Miss Belle. I expect the attack in the parlor would have succeeded had you not been there. You distracted the assassins." Mirabella looked up to see him raise his eyebrows, but he was considering her words. "And, in turn, Princess Elena distracted the counterfeiters. Her attack may very well have given the children the courage to go on the offensive."

"All along Princess Elena was completely capable of saving herself—and us." Mirabella added softly, "And now she will save Montenegro."

"Yes, Miss Belle," he murmured. "But you helped Princess Elena discover her voice."

"And she, mine," she replied softly. Suddenly forlorn, she looked up into Sherlock's eyes. "Whatever is going to happen to the orphanage?"

"Do not distress yourself, Miss Mirabella. The trustees have hired someone to run the orphanage—a much more learned person than Miss Bickers. And with a tender spot for the children. As it should be."

"Whom did they hire?" she asked eagerly.

"A Miss Bethany Allen."

"*Bethany?* But she is not even twenty!"

"She came highly recommended."

She raised her eyebrows at him. "*Who* recommended her, Mr. Holmes?"

"Well, there was an inconsequential recommendation by the king of Montenegro—but I think the referral to turn the tide in her favor was that offered by the world's first private detective. That is an endorsement impossible to dismiss," he stated in all seriousness.

"Truly?" she asked.

"And it appears our confidence was well founded," he nodded.

"Miss Allen has already received approval from the Board of Trustees for a library. She has a plan to solicit donations of books."

"Bethany has such a winning personality, I have no doubt she will succeed."

"Miss Allen has even convinced Miss de Beauvais to donate an hour of her time every week for instruction to the girls on manners and deportment."

"Miss de Beauvais has a heart of gold, I am sure," remarked Mirabella, glancing at Bethany hugging Susan. "Hmm . . . I believe Bethany found her calling. She really wasn't cut out for the marriage mart."

"Not precisely correct, Miss Belle."

"Excuse me? What do you mean, Mr. Holmes?"

He shrugged, seeming more interested in studying her in return than in recounting the narrative, an experience completely new to her. The friendly and talkative stance he was taking with her made her pulse quicken and her head swim. To have his attention and focus on her was a bit like being in the middle of an electrical storm. "When a lawyer was hired to go through the orphanage's papers—well, it appears that the solicitor took a particular fancy to Bethany."

"Who wouldn't?"

"A very handsome young man," confided Sherlock. "It appears that the attraction was mutual."

"A man of law," she repeated, suddenly covering her cheek with the palm of her hand. "Do lawyers still wear the full white wigs in court?"

"Of course. We British are not savages." He stared at her oddly.

"Many of us are not," she whispered. *And yet, a touch of emotion might be just what the doctor ordered.* She glanced briefly in Dr. John Watson's direction, who had taken this lesson to heart, and was all the better for it, a new man since arriving at 221B Baker Street. It was unfortunate that the lesson Sherlock had imparted to his friend he was unable to assume for himself.

"Shall we dance again—or would you prefer to mingle?" Sherlock followed her eyes with his own, landing on their mutual friend. For some reason, a sudden frown formed on his lips.

"Oh, I should very much love to dance. I'm not much for sitting about gossiping."

"Yes, there are far greater attractions on this occasion." Sherlock smiled down at her, the light returning to his eyes, as he led her to the dance floor.

The music started and he paused where he stood.

"The dance is a mazurka, Miss Belle. Are you up to it?" Sherlock asked, hesitating. "There is no more difficult dance."

She glanced sideways at Sherlock, purposely bestowing upon him her most alluring look. "I assure you the King of Montenegro did not waste his money. I know how to dance the mazurka."

"I should have known, Miss Belle!" Sherlock took her hand and they embarked upon the mazurka with its strong impetuous beat. "The mazurka is, after all a dance of independence, graceful and bold. Much like yourself, Miss Belle."

"I came to London a country bumpkin," Mirabella agreed. "I am proud to be a country girl, but I am now, officially, a *New Woman*." Certainly she had read *Daisy Miller* by Henry James.

"And—the world's first lady detective," Sherlock added. "You have earned the title, Miss Belle. He continued effortlessly through the demanding dance, frequently embellishing upon the steps with the freedom from restraint which was characteristic of the dance—and of Sherlock Holmes. His intensity of energy was somehow both contagious and invigorating when combined with music.

All eyes were on them as they were, without question, the most vivacious of the dancers.

He twirled her about. At just the right moment he fell to his knees, shooting his arm straight up while Mirabella danced about him.

She smiled down at him and saw something new in the expression of Sherlock Holmes.

Pure joy. He was smiling back at her.

Standing up, they both waited for the next dance through an unspoken agreement, both attempting to catch their breath.

"You spoke of a *mutual attraction* between Bethany and her solicitor. How do you define such a term, Mr. Holmes? Have you run any experiments on the phenomena?"

"No." His smile faded somewhat as he looked away. It was unusual that he should back away from anyone, and most certainly her.

"What about . . . *a Miss Irene Adler*? Did you run any experiments *with her?*" Mirabella persisted. She had no idea why she was so curious—or why she longed to hear the answer. A month ago she would have paid hard-earned money *not* to hear the answer.

"No . . . Yes . . . Certainly not! Well, such things are highly overrated. And most unscientific."

Heaven help me, I want to kick him in the shins! Oh, for heaven's sake, I'm at a party dancing, Sherlock is being perfectly polite, and I still think he is the most incorrigible, aggravating man alive! She bit her lip in an effort to be quiet.

"Is something wrong, Miss Belle?" he asked, glancing sideways at her.

"Yes. I suppose sometimes I would like an honest answer from you, Sherlock. *From the heart.*"

"Don't expect miracles, Miss Belle." He took her by the waist and pulled her close, looking down into her eyes, even though the music had not started again.

"This is Christmas, Sherlock. 'Tis the season of miracles."

"Right you are, Miss Belle." And he took her in his arms and spun her around once for good measure. *"Right you are."*

A Case Solved to the Satisfaction of All

Author's Notes

There actually was a Princess Jelena Petrović-Njegoš of Montenegro who actually did marry Crown Prince Victor Emmanuel III. They were never intended for each other and it was a case of love at first sight. Many of the events described in the novel actually did happen: Princess Jelena was a reputed beauty who incited a duel after a ball in St. Petersburg, she did have a shy Madonna-like countenance, she was a master of the hunt raised in tribal conditions, and she did accept Catholicism in a boat in the waters between Italy and Montenegro against her mother's wishes. The only thing in the book which she didn't do was race through London with a rifle, but indications are that she would have had the need arisen.

In actuality, Princess Jelena of Montenegro, Queen of Italy, was born Jan. 8, 1873 (d. Nov 28, 1952), married Prince Victor Emmanuel of Italy Oct. 24, 1896 (at twenty-three years of age), so I am taking a few years liberty: Elena would only have been nine years of age in 1882. I am writing several novels with historical figures, and I thought it most important to be true to Arthur Conan Doyle's representation of Sherlock Holmes and John Watson's ages while insuring that all figures were actually alive during the dates in question. In addition, King Nikola, although he ruled Montenegro from 1860 when his Uncle Danilo was assassinated, was referred to as Prince Nikola during the time of this novel.

January 6, 1854: Sherlock Holmes' birthday.
Mycroft 7 years older
John H. Watson's birthday on July 7, 1852
1.5 years older than Holmes
Mirabella's birthday: Nov. 7, 1863

"Amadeo I (Italian Amedeo, sometimes anglicized as Amadeus) (30 May 1845 – 18 January 1890) was the only King of Spain from the House of Savoy. He was the second son of King Vittorio Emanuele II of Italy and was known for most of his life as the Duke of Aosta, but reigned briefly as King of Spain from 1870 to 1873. Granted the hereditary title Duke of Aosta in the year of his birth, he founded the Aosta branch of Italy's royal House of Savoy, which is junior in agnatic descent to the branch descended from King Umberto I that reigned in Italy until 1900, but senior to the branch of the Dukes of Genoa."
--Wikipedia

The University of London in 1878 was the first university to admit women and University College London laid claim to be the first institution to run co-educational lessons.

http://www.london.ac.uk/history.html
University of London Senate House Malet Street London WC1E 7HU
In 1878 London became the first university in the UK to admit women to its degrees. In 1880, four women passed the BA examination and in 1881 two women obtained a BSc.

In 1900-1, there were 296 women students at Cambridge and 239 at Oxford. Women did not become full members of the university in Oxford until 1919 and in Cambridge until 1948.

More about the remarkable Princess Elena, Queen of Italy:
From a New York Times article at the time:
http://query.nytimes.com/mem/archive-free/pdf?res=FA0E11FC3B5D12738DDD AB0994D0405B808CF1D3

"If the new Queen has seemed sometimes listless and not inexhaustible at ordinary social functions, those who have seen her on the hunting field can testify to her transformation. Her dark eyes then glow with unsuspected enthusiasm. She loves a spirited horse and hard-won quarry. Firm in her saddle, she dashes across country, following the hounds with special ardor when big game is the prize of the day. None are more fearless or more sure of aim. Like her brother Danilo, she inherits a passion for the chase from a long line of hunting ancestors.

The hunting and fighting tastes of the Petrovicz family are directly parallel with those of the Savoyard Dynasty. The Savoy Princes, holding their mountain-guarded domain against powerful neighbors through ages of valiant resistance, suggest a poetic affinity with the unhumbled Montenegrins who have driven back Turkish hordes and baffled Turkish pretension until the Black Mountain Country is accorded a place among the nations.". . Prince Victor Emmanuel's first meeting with Elena at Venice and his immediate determination to make her his wife. They met again in St. Petersburg, and he became more enamored than ever. In a few months the marriage was arranged, and the eager lover had found his way to Cettinje, to see his bride and sign the marriage contract."

http://madmonarchist.blogspot.com/2011/04/consort-profile-elena-of-montenegro. html

"In 1888 the Tsarevich invited her to a ball at St Petersburg and some began to whisper that it might have been her rather than Alix of Hesse who would one day become Tsarina. However, at the ball she was rather too popular on the dance floor and sparked a fight that led to a duel between Prince Arsen of Serbia and Baron Carl Gustav von Mannerheim of Finland (who was wounded). This left a rather bad impression on the Russian court, nonetheless it was at the later coronation of Tsar Nicholas II that she met the Prince of Naples and the two were immediately love struck. The formidable Queen Margherita was more concerned with the diversity of the royal bloodline (fearing too many cousins being married) and so warmly encouraged the match.

The two were married on October 24, 1896 and in 1900, after the assassination of King Umberto I, her husband became King Victor Emmanuel III and she became Queen consort of Italy. The King and Queen had a very happy marriage, the couple were very devoted to each other and the King would bring his wife roses from the garden every morning he collected himself. If there is one word to describe Queen Elena it is charitable. Almost her entire royal allowance, as soon as it was given, would be distributed by her amongst the poor...By nature a practical and frugal man he <the King >remarked once that if he were not so careful about his money the Queen would reduce them to poverty by giving it all away to the poor."

Author Bio

Suzette Hollingsworth grew up in Wyoming and Texas, went to school in Tennessee (Sewanee), lived in Europe two summers, and now resides in beautiful Washington State with her cartoonist/author husband Clint, six cats, and a stubborn dachshund named Tinkerbelle.

She collaborates on an autobiographical web-comic with her husband, Clint Hollingsworth, which has readers in sixty countries, www.startingfromscratchcomic.com. Visit her on facebook or on her website at www.suzettehollingsworth.com. You can contact her at suzetteholl@gmail.com.

Suzette's writing style combines wit with elegance and can be described as "A Jane Austen and Robert Downey Jr. meet on the African Queen type of Historical Romance".

Her goal in writing historical fiction is that you, the reader, will engage in a magical journey and time travel through her books. She is very excited about her current Sherlock Holmes series in which Mrs. Hudson's niece is a potential love interest amidst this Victorian mystery. Sherlock Holmes is a great, fun hero to write because he is liked from the get-go despite being pompous and insufferable (or perhaps because of it!), something which might result in an unsympathetic hero in another narrative. The series draws on the imagery surrounding the beloved Sherlock Holmes and Dr. Watson (in particular, Robert Downey Jr. and Jude Law), incorporates the witty banter into the relationship between Sherlock and Mirabella, and lends itself well to Steam punk, blending the "Age of Invention" with something old-fashioned, elegant, and slower-paced.

Enjoy. *The game is afoot.*

Thank you for reading this novel. An honest review is much appreciated on Amazon, which enables the author to reach a wider audience, and consequently, to continue writing for a living.

:)

Made in the USA
Middletown, DE
30 June 2019